BATTING FOURTH

LINDA FAUSNET

My books contain steamy sex, bad words, and human beings of all sorts, include gay people. If you're not a fan of those things, you may want to stop reading now. If you're cool with that stuff, come take my hand and join me on this journey...

Published by Wannabe Pride 2022

Editing by Linda Hill

Cover Design by Chuck DeKett

FIRST EDITION.

Library of Congress Control Number: 2022923003

❀ Created with Vellum

1

AMANDA

"He's so beautiful," I said with a sigh as I gazed up at the television above the bar. The sports channel showed a closeup of my favorite Baltimore Bay Bird, Rusty Power. Most people loved Brady Keaton the best. He was the superstar of the team, and all of baseball, really. Brady was great, but I adored the redheaded first baseman with the piercing blue eyes.

"Rusty's not bad," my best friend, Wilder, said after a cursory glance at the television. "But I think Brady's hotter."

"Yeah, yeah," I said with a dismissive wave. "You and everybody else. I like Brady and all, but there's something so sweet about Rusty."

Wilder laughed. One of the perks of having a best friend was being able to gush over my celebrity crush knowing she wouldn't judge me.

I wanted to order another drink, but I would wait until Rusty's turn at bat was over. I didn't want to miss a moment of his rippling muscles and sexy, determined jaw as he stared down the pitcher.

Not that I only watched baseball for the eye candy. I was

a hardcore Baltimore Bay Birds fan, loyal to the end no matter how badly they played. Thankfully, they'd improved a lot over the last few years.

Rusty connected with the ball, and I damn near jumped out of my seat. I had to remind myself not to scream as loud as I would have if I was at the ballpark. Fortunately, this bar was filled with Bay Birds fans, and we all yelled when we saw the ball sail out of the park for a two-run homer.

No wonder they typically had Rusty Power batting fourth, or cleanup as they called it. The hope was that one or more of the first three batters would make it on base, and then my favorite player would drive them home.

"Sweet," said a man who took a seat on the stool next to me at the bar in time to see Rusty's triumph. His buddy sat beside him. "Wonder who's pitching."

"For us, Carey Allen. For Chicago, Manny Hernandez," I answered automatically. The guy turned to me and smiled, looking impressed. I felt partly flattered and partly annoyed that he seemed surprised by my knowledge of baseball. Plenty of women were into sports.

"Thanks," the good-looking guy with dark hair and blue eyes said. "I'm Jake."

"Amanda," I said with a smile.

He glanced up at the TV. "I think the Birds got a shot this year. I really do. I mean, maybe not all the way to the World Series just yet."

"Agreed. Like maybe the playoffs? The Wild Card at the very least?"

"I'd drink to that, but I'm not prepared yet," Jake said with a sexy grin. The bartender finally noticed him and came over to take his drink order.

"Damn," Wilder muttered as she watched Matt Jovey ground out to end the inning.

"You a baseball fan too?" Jake asked.

"Yeah. But not near as much as Amanda," she said, tipping her beer bottle my way.

"You been to any games this year?" He seemed to address the question to both of us.

"Nah," Wilder said. "Not yet."

Her phone buzzed with a notification. She started texting somebody, which gave me a chance to talk more with Jake. He seemed like a good guy, and I was cautiously optimistic that he might be interested in me. Though I wasn't actively on a hunt for a boyfriend, I was open to the opportunity should it arise. Having a guy to talk baseball with was definitely high on my list when it came to ideal boyfriend material.

"I've been to a bunch," I said enthusiastically. "Starting with Opening Day, and then a few others. I have a partial season ticket plan, so I go a few times a month. I'm going this Sunday, actually."

"Good deal," Jake said, holding up his beer bottle to clink mine. "I was at Opening Day too. That's it so far, but I want to get to some more games soon."

That was the perfect opening for him to ask me out. He didn't. Instead, he glanced over at Wilder, who was still focused on her phone. I fought the urge to sigh out loud.

Wilder was beautiful. As in, supermodel beautiful. No question about that. With her long blond hair, blue-green eyes, and tall stature, she attracted attention everywhere she went. I wasn't exactly jealous of her, but being near her did make my plain looks all the more ordinary. I was the polar opposite: five foot nothing with brown hair and brown eyes. But Wilder's lifelong dream was to become a singer on Broadway, so she needed the good looks more than I did.

Jake's friend was also staring at her. I tried not to take it personally, but it was tough not to feel invisible when I was out with my best friend. Not only was she far prettier, but she was more outgoing. More talented, more fun, more *everything.*

As I watched Carey Allen take the mound when they came back from the commercial, I considered saying something about his impressive ERA. Then I thought the better of it. I figured Jake had lost interest in me already.

"This guy here's been on fire lately," Jake said as Carey tossed the first pitch of the inning for a strike.

"Yeah, he has. Got an ERA close to 3.00 right now," I said, fresh hope blooming in my heart. Maybe I still had a chance with the guy.

Jake turned to me, looking even more impressed than before.

"Now if we could just find a closer with those kind of numbers, we'd really be in business," I added.

"Right?" Jake exclaimed. "Enough with these nail-biters at the end of the game."

I laughed and nodded. The Bay Birds had had quite a few close calls of late where they'd barely eked out a win, despite their early lead.

Gesturing at my shirt, Jake asked, "You go to the University of Timonium?"

"It's sweet that you think I'm that young," I said with a laugh. "No, I went to Notre Dame University. I work at the University of Timonium."

"Yeah? What do you do there?"

"I work in human resources."

"Cool," he said. Though I really liked my job, I wished I had something more exciting to talk about. Wilder worked as a bartender between theater jobs, so her life was far more interesting.

"What do you do?" I asked.

"I'm a professional baseball player," he said modestly.

"Are you serious?"

Jake chuckled heartily. "No. I'm messing with you. I wish. Played in high school, but it was clear pretty quick I didn't have what it takes to make it to the minors, let alone the big show. Right now I'm working at an accounting firm."

"I see." I gave him a sympathetic smile. His job was boring too, and that made me feel better.

Wilder frowned at her phone as she typed. She wasn't normally one to ignore me while she played on her phone, so I worried something might be wrong.

"Everything okay?" I asked.

"Oh yeah. Sorry. Don't mean to be rude. I'm just texting my sister and coordinating who can take my dad to and from his upcoming doctor visits." She finished up her text message and set the phone down, looking at me apologetically.

"Nothing serious I hope," Jake said with a look of concern. I was starting to like this guy.

"No, it's not a big deal," Wilder responded. "He just had a knee replacement done and has a bunch of follow-ups and physical therapy and all that."

"That's not too bad, I guess," he said. Jake had such warmth in his blue eyes, and it was sweet that he was worried about the welfare of someone he didn't even know.

Jake turned to look directly at me, gracing me with a smile that set my insides to quivering.

"So, Amanda ..." he began.

I drew in a nervous breath as I waited for him to continue.

Please ask me out. Bonus points if you invite me to a Bay Birds game for our first date.

"Do you think it would be okay if I asked your gorgeous friend here on a date?"

I let my breath out slowly, fighting to keep my expression even.

I should have known.

It was not the first time this had happened. And it wasn't the second time, either. The only difference was the guy in question didn't normally spend much time talking to me before passing me over for Wilder. Usually, he'd say a few words to me while staring at my sexy blond friend.

Usually, I saw it coming.

Wilder still stared at her phone, but I heard her let out a barely audible sigh. She knew how degrading this kind of thing was for me, and she took no pleasure in being the so-called winner in this situation. To her credit, she never went out with any guy who had insulted me like this while trying to get to her.

"Well, I'm not her mother," I said sharply. "I don't decide who she dates."

Jake blinked, surprised at my reaction. Clearly, I'd dodged a bullet with him anyway. As painful as it was for me to feel like I was bland and ordinary, I would never waste time with any man who made me feel that way. No guy was worth it. I was better off alone.

That being said, I longed for marriage and a family someday. How would that ever happen if every guy I met ignored me because I wasn't a tall, thin model? Perhaps Jake was a genuinely nice guy. I didn't know him well enough to be sure. All I knew was he and I had at least some stuff in common, and all he knew about Wilder was that she was hot. He'd made his choice, and I was probably better off without him.

Gazing up at the television, I watched Rusty masterfully

turn a tricky double play with the help of shortstop Brady Keaton and second baseman Matt Jovey. My stomach quivered with attraction as Rusty grinned, exchanging a triumphant look with Brady.

My crush on Rusty suddenly seemed even sillier than usual. It was a fantasy, obviously. But after tonight's events, it seemed especially ludicrous to even imagine a man like Rusty would give me a second glance.

I'd zoned out while I watched the game, so I didn't get to hear Wilder give Jake the brushoff. The next thing I knew, Jake was gone and Wilder was sitting in his recently vacated seat.

"I'm sorry," she said quietly.

"Not your fault."

"It still sucks."

"Yeah, it does," I said, still staring at the baseball game on TV. Turning toward my friend, I added, "This time felt different. Like he was actually interested in me."

"I know," Wilder said glumly. "I thought the same thing as I listened to him talking to you. That just makes him an even bigger asshole."

I chuckled. "True."

Rusty Power might not pay much attention to me if we ever met in real life, but I doubt he would pull a dick move like Jake did. Then again, he wouldn't need to. He dated models and famous actresses, from what I'd heard.

"Wanna get out of here?" Wilder asked.

I considered it for a moment, then said, "No. I'm good."

"Cool." She smiled and nodded. I could tell she was proud of me for not letting Jake ruin my night. She signaled the bartender, who, of course, came running because it was her.

"Get me another too, please," I said to her, knowing I'd

better grab another drink while she had the bartender's attention. "Oh good," I said as I looked at the TV. "The Birds are up to bat again."

Once I took a sip of my fresh beer, I felt better.

Another fairly attractive guy sat down on the other side of Wilder. He didn't even try to hide the fact that he was staring at her.

Sighing, I reminded myself not everybody was meant to stand out and be noticed.

The sooner I accepted that, the better off I would be.

2

RUSTY

Some people take a while to get going in the morning, but not me. I practically bounce out of bed as soon as I open my eyes. We were a couple of months into the baseball season, and I was still excited to play ball. I get so antsy during the off-season—I was bored out of my skull during the winter. Now that it was May, the weather was warming up. A great time to play baseball. Not that there was any bad time as far as I was concerned.

I showered quickly and went to my kitchen to get the coffee going. I turned on the television in the living room—it was tuned to ESPN as always. In my open-plan luxury apartment, I could see my big screen TV easily from the kitchen. As the coffee brewed, I wandered over to the vast bank of windows in my corner apartment to take in the view of downtown Baltimore.

Drawing in a deep breath, I wondered once again how the hell I'd gotten so damn lucky. This was my second season with the Baltimore Bay Birds, and I still couldn't quite believe I was really here. During my rookie season, I'd rented a cheap rowhouse downtown. The life of a Major

League ballplayer seemed too good to be true, and for the whole first year it was like I was afraid it would all be taken away from me. It took until my second year before I allowed myself to spend some of the money I'd earned. Didn't take me long to get used to that. I wondered if I should rein myself in a bit, but it was tough. I had millions of dollars now. *Millions.* To play a game I loved more than life itself. My life was positively surreal.

I gazed out at the Inner Harbor and the gentle waves of the Chesapeake Bay. The only thing that would have made the view from my high-rise apartment perfect would have been if I could see the stadium from here. Unfortunately, the skyscrapers downtown got in the way.

The coffeemaker beeped, so I headed back into the kitchen and poured myself a cup. After a few sips, I whipped up an egg and cheese omelet and grilled some sausage patties. Breakfast was pretty much the only meal I knew how to make. The rest of the time I got food delivered. Most of it was fresh and reasonably healthy. Of course, I did indulge in junk food from time to time, but I needed to keep in shape to play ball.

My eyes were glued to *SportsCenter* as I ate breakfast. Watching the highlights from last night's game made me smile. I loved getting to see the replay of my two-run homer. Sometimes I made the "lowlights" reel if I bobbled a play at first base or something. Rewatching that was far less enjoyable. I always kept up with the sports news because it gave me a chance to see what the other teams were up to. I studied *SportsCenter* each day as if there would be a test later.

After breakfast, I headed into my baseball room. Not that there was much distinction between that room and the rest of my apartment—I had tons of baseball memorabilia and autographed sports photos all over the joint. But the baseball room was even more overstuffed with that kind of thing, and it was where I spent time working on the day's plan.

Sitting down at my desk, I looked online for any information I could find on Chicago's starting pitcher. Doing research like that helped my batting performance tremendously. Since this was only my second year in the majors, a lot of the pitchers I faced were ones I hadn't dealt with before. After conducting my research, I played around on the Internet, indulging in some of the gossip pages. It was a guilty pleasure for me.

The weird thing was, sometimes I was *in* the gossip pages. Talk about surreal. Though I had dated a few celebrities, including a famous social media influencer and a cable television actress, I never actively sought out the publicity.

I didn't mind it either. In fact, I loved it. It wasn't just the attention, but any article that mentioned me referred to me as Baltimore Bay Birds' first baseman. My favorite thing in the world was when people stopped me on the street because they recognized me as a professional ballplayer.

Occasionally I saw my name in the entertainment news, but I much preferred being known for my baseball performance. I dreamed of someday achieving Brady Keaton-level fame. That dude raked in tons of money in endorsements alone, on top of his generous baseball salary. I always thought it would be cool to be like him because even people who didn't follow baseball knew who he was. Not that I was fame-hungry, exactly. I just loved the idea of everybody knowing I was Rusty Power, baseball player. The sport meant the world to me. I wanted my gravestone to be in the shape of a baseball.

I'd already signed up to work on a kids' baseball clinic in

the fall. I loved knowing that I could keep playing ball even when the season was over. Not only could I help kids who dreamed of becoming professional ballplayers, but it was another step in my plan to someday be as great as Brady. He always gave back to the community, and I wanted to do the same.

Still scrolling through the gossip rags, I came across an article about myself. It only mentioned baseball in passing: the main focus was my recent breakup with Emily Martindale. She starred in a popular detective show called *L.A. Mysteries*. My eyes landed on the photograph of her in the article. Emily was an astonishingly beautiful woman, with her dark green eyes, blond hair, and supermodel frame. I'd be lying if I said her beauty had nothing to do with why I dated her. Even now, I felt that familiar flicker of attraction to her. No, attraction wasn't right. Lust. I still lusted after her.

But I didn't miss her.

We'd dated for a few months, and she was perfectly nice and all that, I just didn't think a long-distance relationship would work. During the baseball season, I was either in Baltimore or traveling with the team. In the off-season, I used to live in West Virginia, where I was from and where my family still lived, but now I mainly stayed in Baltimore. Emily's show was filmed in Los Angeles. We barely saw each other when we were dating, so we agreed it was best to break up.

I had a feeling she didn't miss me much either. It was fun while it lasted, but I wasn't exactly devastated when it ended.

After killing a little more time on the Internet, I started to get antsy. So I headed to Old Bay Stadium super early, like I usually did. Though I was always eager to get going, my excitement level went haywire on perfect spring days like this. When the sun was shining and the weather was warm, there was no better place than on a baseball field. I even felt slightly dizzy from all the excitement. Chuckling to myself, I realized I needed to calm down a bit.

But since calming down was not in my nature, I pushed myself even harder instead. I put in a strenuous workout, which I didn't usually do right before a game. I'd been on a hot hitting streak lately, and I wanted it to continue.

Batting practice went well, and I launched a few good ones into the stands. Some of the hardcore fans showed up early to watch us practice, and I loved hearing their happy shouts when I connected with the ball. As usual, after I finished batting, I walked off to the side and over to the warning track. Everybody knew this was part of my pre-game routine, and they left me alone. Any other time, I loved talking with players and anybody who worked at the stadium, but I needed a few minutes of quiet to get my mind centered and focused before the game.

Finally, it was 7:05. Game time. The announcer rattled off the Bay Birds lineup; the cheers for my name seemed to get louder every day. Of course, last night's two-run homer had me on the crowd's good side right now.

The first inning was uneventful. Nobody on either side scored, and things were pretty quiet. So it was odd when suddenly, before the start of the second inning, the crowd went wild. I, along with several of the guys on the team, looked up at the Jumbotron to see if they were showing something that had excited the crowd.

Turned out, they were.

The announcer boomed, "Please welcome the newest member of the Baltimore Bay Birds family, William Flynn Ridgerton!"

Up on the Jumbotron was a photograph of our catcher,

Trace Ridgerton, making the rock-and-roll sign with one hand while he held his tiny newborn son in his other arm. The baby sported a motorcycle onesie, clearly taking after his father already. His mother, Trace's girlfriend, Sarah, also worked with the Bay Birds organization. The photo showed her in the hospital bed. Without makeup and looking exhausted but happy, she'd never looked more lovely.

They made a beautiful family. I felt a twinge of longing, but I reminded myself that I had plenty of time to get married and raise a family. Right now, my focus was on baseball.

The crowd was on its feet, still applauding their congratulations.

Brady gazed out at the crowd, a look of deep reverence on his face. He was usually a loud, lovable goofball. This was a rare moment of quiet reflection.

"The best fans in all of baseball," Brady said. "Right here."

"Agreed," I said with a smile. Brady Keaton was born and bred in Baltimore and was deeply passionate about the city. I, too, had grown to love it already in my brief time here.

Filled with even more excitement, I eagerly jogged out to my position at first base.

Time to get to work.

3

AMANDA

I slept until mid-morning on Sunday. When I opened my eyes, I remembered it was a game day. I had a lower-tier season ticket plan, so I could attend around sixteen home games per season. I wished it were more, but that was all I could afford right now. My top priority was saving up for a house, which was why I currently lived in a tiny apartment in Towson. Though I still hoped to get married and have a family someday, that dream was far from a certainty. I needed to be realistic. If I wanted to own a home, I might have to do it all on my own.

That was the hard part about wanting to marry and have children eventually. The uncertainty. Sure, anybody could run out and get married, but if you wanted a *happy* family, you couldn't force it. You either met the right guy or you didn't. And so far, I hadn't. As much as I longed for a family of my own, I wasn't about to settle for just anybody.

I jumped out of bed, eager to get going. Game time wasn't until 3:05, but I always got there super early to watch batting practice. My season ticket plan included two seats per game, and usually a friend or one of my sisters would accompany me. Nobody could make it to today's game, but that was okay. As much as I liked having company, I enjoyed a little time by myself at the stadium. There was nothing more relaxing than a beautiful day at the ballpark, and it was a lovely way to unwind after a long workweek.

On my way to the bathroom, I paused to look at the framed picture of Rusty Power that hung in my bedroom. A gift from one of my sisters, the gorgeous photograph of my favorite redhead was actually signed by him. Penny had found it in one of those sports memorabilia stores, and it had probably been expensive. I loved gazing at it, especially on days like today when I knew I would actually get to *see* Rusty in real life. My seats at Old Bay Stadium were in a good spot: lower reserve on the first base side. Perfect for me, since Rusty was the first baseman. That was a happy accident. I'd had these tickets for years, long before he joined the team.

I showered and dressed in my beloved Bay Birds jersey and blue jeans, then ate a quick bowl of cereal before heading to the ballpark. I drove my beat-up Toyota to the Light Rail station so I could take the small commuter train downtown. Parking in Baltimore was such a nightmare; it was much easier to take the Light Rail that dropped me off close to Old Bay Stadium.

My stomach quivered with excitement as I gazed out the window as the train zoomed toward downtown Baltimore. There was nothing better than a sunny afternoon at the ballpark. I always felt a kind of camaraderie with fellow riders who were clad in Bay Birds gear. I saw several Brady Keaton jerseys of course. I wished I had a Rusty Power one, but official jerseys were so expensive. For now, I'd stick with my generic Bay Birds jersey. Besides, it would be my luck to drop several hundred dollars on a Rusty baseball jersey only to have him be traded to another team.

At last, the Light Rail arrived at the Old Bay Stadium stop. I practically skipped out of the train and headed toward the ballpark. I drew in a deep breath, relishing that familiar smell of hot dogs and crab cakes.

"Have fun," the ticket-taker man said as he scanned my phone for my admission.

"Thanks," I said with a smile. Everybody was always so kind here at the park. I got the feeling that the people who worked here were genuine Bay Birds fans. Talk about a dream job.

As soon as I plopped down in my seat, I scanned the field for Rusty. I found him quickly. He was off to the side, stretching. Fresh excitement rippled in my stomach. It was always such a thrill to see him in person after seeing him all the time on television.

The home team went first during batting practice. Once the Bay Birds were done, I'd have a chance to wander around the stadium and maybe grab some food. But now, all my attention was on my hometown heroes.

Batting practice was fun to watch because the guys launched a ton of balls into the seats. It was like a home run derby. The pitchers, who were often not official pitchers but coaches instead, frequently tossed the ball straight down the middle. They made everybody look like a bona fide home run hitter. There weren't a lot of fans here yet, but the ones in attendance still cheered as much as they would during a game.

Matt Jovey stepped up to the plate and hit a few dingers. Then Brady Keaton stepped up, and the crowd went wild. I giggled and shook my head. The guy hadn't even done anything yet. But he was wildly popular, and everything he did got attention.

As usual, my eyes wandered over to Rusty while all other eyes were on Brady. I watched as Rusty jogged around the warning track, hearing all the typical cheers and whistles for Brady in the background. Rusty slowed, walking the warning track by himself. He did that sometimes. Just went off all alone, like he was gathering his thoughts. That fascinated me, as it gave him an air of mystery. Of course, I'd read everything I could about the man, so there wasn't *that* much mystery.

I let out a soft sigh as my eyes followed him, remembering all the good things I'd read about him. Rusty did lots of charity work for the team. I'd seen pictures of him collecting donations for the needy and visiting kids in the hospital. In fact, he once did a meet-and-greet with Trace Ridgerton where you could say hi and shake his hand if you brought some food for the local food bank. I was still heartbroken that I'd heard about the event *after* it had happened. Ugh, to think I could have actually met the guy!

Still on the warning track, Rusty stopped walking.

When he started moving again, he staggered backward a few steps.

Then he collapsed.

I stared at him, trying to figure out if he was joking. It certainly didn't seem like it. He lay there, utterly motionless.

Whipping my head around the field, I hoped to see somebody—*anybody*—who'd noticed what was going on with Rusty. I expected to see a teammate or perhaps one of the grounds crew running over to check on him.

People started cheering and laughing for Brady, which probably meant he was blowing kisses to the crowd or something to get them even more riled up. That was the problem. All eyes were on Brady, so nobody had seen Rusty collapse.

I was frozen with indecision for a few seconds. My instinct was to start screaming for somebody to help, but what if I was wrong? What if I made a complete fool of myself and Rusty was just kidding around?

Panic gripped my heart when I saw him still lying there. He could very well die while I did nothing.

I jumped up out of my seat and ran down the concrete steps toward the field.

"Hey!" I yelled in the direction of the field. "Hey! Somebody check on Rusty Power!"

A bunch of players and Bay Bird employees on the field turned to look at me instead of Rusty. I saw motion out of the corner of my eye and realized there were several security guards running toward me.

Oh God. Everybody here thinks I'm crazy. Security's gonna tackle me and later they're gonna find Rusty dead on the field.

My heart surged with panic and fear. Rusty still wasn't moving.

Just two weeks ago, they'd done a CPR demonstration at work. I was hardly a medical expert, but I might be Rusty's only chance right now. Nobody seemed to realize I'd been yelling for help. All they saw was a woman in a Bay Birds jersey screaming and running toward the field while Brady was at bat.

In a split-second decision, I jumped over the railing and landed on the field before the security guards could grab me. I ran toward Rusty, and now the guards on the field were running after me.

Panting heavily, I knelt down beside Rusty.

His face was positively *ashen,* and his lips were dark blue. This was no joke. For all I knew, he was already dead.

I leaned down to check on him.

My blood ran cold.

"He's not breathing!" I managed to scream to the security guards who had caught up to me. That stopped them in their tracks.

My head spun as I forced myself to focus, to remember what I'd learned in that brief CPR class.

Check for bleeding and injuries.

I gave him a quick cursory glance, but I knew he hadn't been injured because I'd been watching him.

Oh God. His chest was still. SO. STILL.

I started doing chest compressions. Just as our instructor had warned us, it was harder than it looked on TV. You were supposed to do about 100 compressions a minute, which is *a lot*. While I was pretty petite, Rusty was huge. After the first compression, I felt a sickening crunch beneath my hands. The teacher had said that was normal, and it may or may not mean I had broken a rib.

I did my 100 compressions and then breathed into his mouth. There was no thrill during the bizarre experience of actually pressing my lips to my celebrity crush's. There was only sheer terror because he still wasn't breathing.

My entire body broke into a sweat as I did more compressions. It was hard physical work, but the adrenaline surging through my body helped power me through.

The crowd had gone mostly silent, and I figured all eyes were on me and Rusty.

"Miss? Miss?" came a loud male voice behind me.

I couldn't answer. I was too busy trying to save Rusty's life.

"You're doing great," he said firmly. "I'm one of the trainers. Finish this set of compressions, and we'll step in, okay?"

"Yes," I said in a trembling voice. It wasn't a moment too

soon, because even my adrenaline couldn't help me keep this up much longer.

I counted the compressions in my head, and just before I reached 100, Rusty's eyes flew open.

Relief flooded through me as his chest finally started to rise and fall on its own. We locked eyes for a brief second; those piercing blue eyes were so familiar to me. The same ones I'd stared at on the photograph on my wall, the ones I'd seen on television so many times. This was utterly surreal.

The trainer carefully but firmly pushed me away, and the medical team surrounded Rusty.

I sat down on the field, covering my face while I sobbed. The whole experience had been so terrifying.

"Hey, hey," came a gentle male voice from above me. "It's okay. Everything's okay."

I uncovered my face to find Brady Keaton himself standing over me.

For a second, I truly believed this was all a dream. It was the only way any of this made sense. Everything had happened so fast, and it was all so strange.

Brady held out a hand, and I accepted it. He pulled me into a standing position, put his arm around my back, and led me off the field. I saw him shoot a quick worried glance in Rusty's direction before turning his attention to me. He led me to the dugout and helped me sit down on the bench.

"I'm gonna get you some water, okay?" Brady asked.

I nodded, still in a daze.

Matt Jovey walked into the dugout. "Are you okay?"

"Y—yes. I think so," I managed to say.

I saw a bunch of other Bay Birds standing outside the dugout, watching all the commotion over Rusty. It was incredible to be allowed to sit in the dugout and see the field from this perspective, but what a terrible way to receive that honor.

Drawing in a few deep, cleansing breaths, I reminded myself that Rusty was breathing and awake. At least he had been when I left his side. I knew he could have brain damage from his heart having stopped for so long, but I tried not to think about it.

Brady returned with a paper cup of water, and I accepted it gratefully but with shaky hands. The chill of the water helped clear my head a bit, and my adrenaline rush began to ease.

"A little better?" Brady asked, his eyes filled with concern for me.

Brady's eyes, too, were familiar to me. Warm and brown, they were usually filled with humor and mischief, from what I saw on television.

"Yes. This helps. Thanks so much."

"What's your name?" Brady asked.

"Amanda. Amanda Miller."

"You did a great job out there, Amanda."

"I hope so," I said, my stomach clenching with fresh worry. "I only had one CPR lesson in my life."

"Wow," Brady said. "Then that really *was* amazing."

"Miss? We'd like to ask you a few questions."

I looked up and saw a bunch of reporters and people with cameras coming toward me.

"Oh no you don't," Brady said firmly, jumping up and going into protective mode. He stood tall before them. "Once she's calmed down, she can do an interview if she wants. That's her choice. But I'm not gonna let you ambush her right now."

"Let's get her inside," Matt said. Brady nodded, and the two men ushered me away from the reporters.

Once we got inside the clubhouse, Matt said, "Let's take her to Julia's office."

Julia's office.

Julia was the head groundskeeper for Old Bay Stadium, and she was also Matt's wife.

They led me to an office inside the stadium and sat me down in a chair in front of Julia's desk.

Matt crouched down to talk to me rather than tower over me as he spoke.

"Listen, I'm gonna go get Julia and see if she can sit with you for a few minutes until things calm down. Do you have anybody here with you?"

I shook my head. "No. Usually I do, but today I'm here by myself."

"Oh, okay," Matt said, his blue eyes filled with concern. It was so sweet. "Julia should be right with you, all right?"

"Yeah. Thank you."

He and Brady left me there alone, which gave me a little time to stop shaking.

Julia rushed into her office a few minutes later. I'd caught glimpses of her while watching Bay Bird games on TV, so I recognized her right away. She had warm hazel eyes, and her thick, curly brown hair was tied back in a ponytail.

"Hi, Amanda," she said, holding out her hand. "I'm Julia."

"Nice to meet you," I said. As much as I adored all the Bay Bird players, being here with Julia was less intimidating. I'd never seen a celebrity up close before today, and in the span of a few minutes, I'd encountered a whole bunch of famous baseball players. Talking with Julia was much less nerve-wracking.

"Is Rusty okay?" I asked.

"I'm not sure yet. The ambulance is here, and they're taking him to the hospital. That's all I really know."

Just then, we heard cheering coming from the field. Julia lifted her gaze to right above my head and she smiled.

"Look," she said, pointing toward the monitor mounted on the wall behind me.

I turned around to see Rusty on a gurney. He was awake and waving to the crowd as they took him away.

"Oh, thank God," I said with a deep sigh of relief.

"Yeah," Julia said. "They'll check him out at the hospital, but he looks pretty good right now. Thanks to you."

I shrugged, not sure what to say to that.

"I'd like to take down your information if that's okay," she said. "I'm sure the Bay Birds will want to take care of you somehow. You know, free tickets or memorabilia and things like that. And I'm sure Rusty will want to know about the person who saved his life."

I saved Rusty Power's life.

I still couldn't quite wrap my mind around today's events, and part of me still wondered if this was all a crazy dream.

"Um, okay. Sure."

"The media will want to talk to you, but that's totally your call. I can give them your name and number if you want to answer their questions, but I don't have to if you'd rather I didn't."

"No. It's okay, I guess."

Julia nodded, and I gave her my full name, phone number, and home address.

"Okay," she said as she wrote everything down on some official Bay Birds stationery. "I'll pass on your phone number to the media, but I don't see any reason for them to know where you live. It's good for us to have your address, though, so we can send you some cool stuff."

"Thanks," I said. "That's really sweet."

"Do you have anybody here at the stadium with you?"

I shook my head. "No."

Then I felt the need to explain why I was here alone. I didn't want Julia to think I was some kind of loser with no friends. "I've got two season ticket seats, but nobody else could make it today."

Julia nodded and smiled warmly.

"Gotcha. I can help you find your way to your seat whenever you're ready. It's kind of a maze down here."

"I can't believe I'm actually sitting here," I said, gazing around at her office.

"So you're a big Bay Birds fan, huh?" she asked as she admired my baseball jersey.

"Huge fan. And Rusty's my favorite player."

"Perfect," she said with a laugh. "Do you need anything, Amanda? Water or soda or something?"

"Oh, no. I'm fine. Thanks, though."

Julia got up from her desk, so I stood up as well.

4

AMANDA

Now that it was close to game time, Old Bay Stadium was crowded with fans getting food and heading toward their seats. My eyes took a few seconds to adjust to the bright sunlight after being inside the dark tunnel under the stadium. I was still kind of in a daze, so I was grateful that Julia was kind enough to take me all the way to my seat.

"Here," I said to her when we reached my row. "Thanks so much for all your help."

"Are you kidding?" she said, eyes wide. "Thank *you* for your incredible bravery. God only knows what would have happened to Rusty if it weren't for you."

"Wait," said a guy in a Bay Birds hat from the row just in front of me. "Are you the fan who saved Rusty's life?"

Nodding uncertainly, I said, "Yeah. How did you know—"

"It's all over the news!" the man told me.

"You're famous, Amanda," Julia said with a smile.

I wasn't sure what to think about that. Feeling shaky, I sat down in my seat.

"Are you all right?" Julia asked me, crouching down to look me in the eye.

I felt a bit queasy, but I was pretty sure it was due to coming down from such an adrenaline high. Once the game started, my nerves would probably settle down. Julia likely had a lot of work to do on the field, and the last thing I wanted was to hold her up any longer.

"Oh yeah, I'm fine. Really. Thanks again for everything."

"You're sure you don't need anything?"

"I'm good. Really," I assured her.

"Okay," Julia said, squeezing my shoulder. "You take care of yourself, all right?"

I nodded. Once Julia had left, the fans around me gave me a lot of curious looks. Fortunately, nobody asked me any questions about what had happened. My emotions were pretty raw, and I didn't feel much like talking. I wished Wilder was here to lean on, though. That would have helped.

On shaky legs, I stood for the national anthem and cheered for the start of the game. It felt so strange that Rusty wasn't playing. Instead, Hiroki Hideo, a relatively new player on the team, was stationed at first base.

I found it hard to focus on the game as my thoughts kept drifting back to Rusty. I couldn't stop thinking about that moment when his eyes had suddenly opened.

I wondered if he would remember me.

After all, it was only a split second after he'd regained consciousness that the trainer had stepped in. It was entirely possible that Rusty would have no memory of me whatsoever. I supposed it shouldn't really matter. The most important thing was his health.

It was truly frightening to think how fast everything had gone down, and how different the outcome might have been. Within my circle of family and friends, I've always been the dependable one. The stable, reliable person they came to when they needed help. And for the most part, I liked that role. Being able to help people and be a positive force in such an ugly world brought meaning to my life.

But it was terrifying to think that sometimes there's just nothing you can do, no matter how hard you try. My God, I really didn't know what I was doing with CPR. All I'd done was apply whatever I could remember from the one day at work. If I'd screwed it up, they'd be notifying Rusty's family by now that he hadn't made it.

By the eighth inning, I was still having trouble focusing on the game. It was a pitcher's duel, with the Birds in the lead 2-1. I decided to leave early. That was something I never did, especially when the score was that close. Though the shock of the Rusty incident had mostly worn off, I was emotionally exhausted and wanted to rest.

On the way home, I stared out the window of the Light Rail train. I still wasn't convinced I'd saved Rusty Power's life. For all I knew, it might have only been a matter of a few more seconds before the trainers rushed onto the field with all their lifesaving equipment, even if I hadn't gotten there first.

All I knew for sure was that this was one hell of a close call. I couldn't stop thinking about how precious life was and how it could be taken away from any of us at any time.

Rusty had survived, but barely. Terrible images suddenly filled my head. I imagined them covering his body with a white sheet as they carried him, lifeless, off the field.

My eyes filled with tears at the thought, and not just because it was Rusty Power. Sure, I had a silly crush on the guy, but I think I would have cried even if this had happened to a total stranger. To think of someone—anyone—dying that young was horrible.

I checked my phone for updates as the train pulled up at my stop.

Still nothing.

5

RUSTY

That was fucking scary. And I don't scare easily.

Lying restlessly in my hospital bed, my mind kept going over and over what happened today. I was still reeling from the fact that I'd damn near *died* on the field. At least that was what they told me.

What the hell happened to me out there?

I'd been in the hospital for hours undergoing a bunch of tests to figure it out. Electrocardiograms, ultrasounds, and I swear they took, like, half my blood to test it for God knows what. The damned blood pressure cuff they had strapped to me that went off every five minutes was super annoying. That, and all the wires and whatnot they had stuck to my chest. The weird thing was I felt fine now. A little dizzy maybe, but fine otherwise. Mostly, I was pissed about missing the game. I'd seen the highlights on TV, although lowlights was more like it. Wound up being a rough game there toward the end, and I hated that I wasn't there to help the team.

It was really bizarre hearing the reports on the news about what had happened to me. Thankfully, the whole thing had gone down before the game started, so my collapse wasn't broadcast on TV. There were amateur phone camera videos, of course, but most of them just caught footage of people huddled around me. That, and video of me being carried off the field on a stretcher.

I shuddered just thinking about it. The last thing I remembered was strolling down the warning track. The next thing I knew, I was on the ground with a bunch of people standing over me. Apparently, some fan saw me collapse and rushed down onto the field and started doing CPR. I didn't know how people dealt with being in a coma for several months, because it was strange enough losing a few minutes of your life. Such an unsettling feeling.

Right now, I was all alone at the hospital. My family was on the way from West Virginia, though, which was less than two hours away.

Dear God, my poor mother had heard about my incident on the news. She'd called the hospital while I was getting my tests done. I hadn't been able to talk to her yet. Knowing her, she would need to see that I was alive and breathing before she could relax.

Just as I started dozing off from sheer boredom, the door opened and my mother, her face blotchy and red, rushed over to my bedside.

"Rusty!" she wailed as she threw her arms around my neck and hugged me close. Pain from my two cracked ribs seared through my body, but I managed not to yell out in agony. My mother did not need to know everything. She'd been through enough.

"It's okay, Mom. I'm all right. I promise," I assured her.

She held on to me for a while, her hot tears dripping on me. I felt like a horrible son. In hindsight, I realized I should have called her as soon as humanly possible. I really had meant well, though. I'd been hoping to be able to call her and tell her that the doctors had checked me out and given me the all-clear. That this was just a one-time, random, scary thing, and that there was nothing to worry about. Instead, I'd probably taken years off her life.

When she finally let go of my neck and started tenderly stroking my face, I said, "I'm sorry, Mom. I should have called you right away to let you know I was okay."

"I'm just so glad to see you," she said in a trembling voice that broke my heart all over again. There were deep worry lines under those blue eyes that looked so much like mine, and I was sure I'd added more white streaks to her reddish hair that had recently begun to turn a tad gray. Though I mostly resembled her, Jane Power was tiny. My height I'd gotten from my father.

"Is Dad with you?" I asked.

"He's on his way. He was over at Bud's house working on a car. I couldn't reach him at first, and I didn't want to wait another minute before coming to see you."

"Okay. Cool."

My mother slid a chair over right next to the bed and took my hand in hers. I watched as her eyes roamed over all the scary-looking equipment I was currently hooked up to.

"I'm okay, Ma. Really. All this crap is just to make sure all my parts are working now, but I'm *fine*."

My poor mother had probably tortured herself the whole drive over, imagining the worst.

"What happened, Rusty?" she asked in a sad, worried voice.

"All I know is that I passed out on the field for a few minutes," I said, trying to sound casual.

"They said your heart stopped," Mom said, tearing up again.

"Well, yeah," I said softly. "It did, I guess."

"My God," she whispered, squeezing my hand.

"It was during batting practice, and I was off to the side and nobody was really paying attention to me. From what they tell me, some woman jumped down out of the stands and started doing CPR on me."

"They ought to give her a medal or something," Mom said.

I laughed. "Yeah, I guess they should."

I'd been so overwhelmed by the day's events that I hadn't given much thought to the miracle-worker who had saved my life. Hopefully the Bay Birds would take good care of her. Set her up with season tickets or something. I would figure out some way to reward her myself, too, once I got the hell out of this joint.

"They're keeping me here overnight," I said with annoyance.

"Well, I should hope so. Do they know what's wrong with you yet?"

I shook my head. "They did a million tests, but I haven't heard anything yet."

Mom sighed deeply, leaning back in her chair.

"I hope you didn't freak Dad out too bad," I said. No doubt she'd been crying hysterically by the time she reached him. Being a mother was not easy.

"No. You know him. He's maddeningly calm about everything."

She sounded annoyed, but her eyes betrayed her affection for her husband of thirty-five years.

"I told him to call Olivia and Zoey to let them know what was going on."

"That's good," I said. Though my older sisters were probably calmer than my mother, I still didn't want them to find out about my medical emergency on the news.

"I'm sure they'll get here as soon as they can."

"Oh, they don't have to do that," I said, waving my hand dismissively. "Hopefully I'll be out of here by tomorrow."

My oldest sister, Olivia, had two little boys, and Zoey had a girl. No sense in disrupting both families by dragging everybody all the way out here.

"We'll see," my mom said.

"This is no big deal."

She did not look convinced. The lines underneath her eyes deepened, and a sorrowful look crossed her face.

"There is a lot going on right now. With planning the funeral and all," she said.

For one crazy moment, I thought maybe I actually had died on the field. I flashed back to my favorite Halloween movie, *Beetlejuice,* where the couple slowly realizes they hadn't survived their car crash after all.

They're planning a funeral?

I snapped back to my senses when I realized she was talking about my great-aunt's funeral. Aunt Sophia had just passed away after a long illness. While not unexpected, her death was still really sad, and the timing couldn't have been worse. She and my mother had been close.

"Shit, I can't believe I almost forgot."

"Language, Rusty," Mom reminded me. No matter how old I got, she still made sure I behaved. It was cute.

"Sorry. I hope I can get out of here in time to make it to the funeral."

Today was Sunday, and the funeral was on Tuesday morning. I had a game that night, but I would have time to attend the services first. If they let me out of the damned hospital by then.

"Don't you worry about that, honey," my mom said. "Just focus on getting well."

"I'm fine," I said. "I'm just *borrred*."

I kicked my feet like a petulant child, making her laugh. It was such a relief to see her smile. That made the agony of aggravating my sore ribs worthwhile.

She got up and kissed me on the forehead.

"I love you, baby."

No matter how old I got, I would always be her baby. And that was cool with me.

"I love you too, Mommy."

She laughed again, like I knew she would.

It always tickled her when her six-foot-two son called her Mommy.

6

AMANDA

I got a good night's rest and felt much calmer Monday morning. I kept the news on as I got ready for work. They mentioned the incident with Rusty, and they even mentioned my name in passing, but I doubted anyone would take any notice. I tended to fade into the background in life, and having a boring name like Amanda Miller didn't exactly help me stand out. Not that I really cared all that much. I didn't need any recognition for what I'd done. What I needed was for Rusty to be okay.

"No word on his condition," was all the news anchor lady had to say.

I couldn't decide if that was good or bad. Maybe the doctors just hadn't figured out what was wrong yet. Then again, maybe the news was so bad that Rusty wanted to make sure his family was notified before he released any kind of statement.

I had given a brief phone interview last night to *The Baltimore Bugle*, but I'd declined to do anything on camera. So the television news had simply quoted some information from the online newspaper interview.

Sipping my coffee at my kitchen counter, I decided to stay positive. There might be good news about Rusty any minute now, and he might be perfectly fine. I even allowed myself to indulge in the memory of having my lips on his. Though there had been nothing even remotely sexy about the experience, I still couldn't believe I'd gotten so close to him. That I'd actually *touched* him. Mostly, the experience had been frightening. Except for one part.

When he'd opened his eyes.

I would have known those deep blue eyes anywhere. Rusty had blinked briefly, looking confused but alert. My adrenaline had been pumping hard, and an indescribable sensation of relief had swept over me when he started breathing again.

As much as I tried to revel in the fact that I'd gotten so physically close to Rusty Power, it was still hard to be excited about it. Until he'd opened his eyes, I'd been terrified that he was already dead. Danger like that might seem romantic in the movies, but it was horrific in real life.

Rather than dwell on yesterday's scary event, I fantasized about the future. Unlikely as it might be, it was within the realm of possibility that Rusty Power himself might call to thank me.

I'd spent much of last evening on the phone, but not with the big man himself. I'd called Wilder first so I could tell her everything as soon as I felt ready to talk about it. Talking to her had comforted me. She'd spoken softly to me as I teared up describing the ordeal, and she had squealed with delight upon hearing that Brady Keaton had wrapped his arms around me. Chatting with her was exactly what I'd needed.

Next, I'd spoken to my mom to let her know what happened. She and my dad were casual baseball fans, but they knew how much of a hardcore Bay Birds fan I was. I knew my parents would get a kick out of my story about meeting some of the players, and I knew they would be proud of me for helping Rusty. That conversation, too, had been comforting.

And yet, I still dreamed of getting a call from Rusty.

As I drove to work, I continued to indulge in silly daydreams about hearing from him. His voice would have been as familiar to me as his eyes were, since I'd seen every interview he'd ever given on television. The idea of hearing that deep, sensual voice on my phone made my stomach tingle.

I parked my car in the University of Timonium lot near the administration building where I worked. When I got inside and headed toward the office of human resources, I wondered if anybody at my work had heard about what had happened at the game. I set my purse and keys on my desk and glanced around. We had one of those open office plans, so our desks were separated only by small wall dividers. A few coworkers said hello, but nobody rushed up to ask me for details about my adventure yesterday.

I felt slightly disappointed. Though I wasn't the attention-seeking type, I found myself wanting to talk about the incident. Sometimes I felt like everybody else around here had such exciting lives compared to me. My boss, Denise, always seemed to be partying on the weekends and having a grand old time. She was tight with Bella, our administrative assistant, and they often went out barhopping. Sure, I went out and did things on the weekends too. Wilder and I often went to bars, and I went to ballgames and the movies and such. But nothing really exciting ever happened. Until now.

"How was your weekend?" Bella asked me, providing me with the perfect opening. I was amazed that she actually stopped filing her nails long enough to notice me. Her fingernails and makeup were always *perfect*. Her work ethic, not so much.

"Eventful, that's for sure." I felt a quiver of excitement about sharing my news.

"Yeah?" she asked as she tied her blond hair back in a ponytail.

"I went to the Bay Birds game on Sunday."

"Oh," she said with a polite smile. She seemed bored with me already.

"Did you hear what happened at the game?"

"No. Did they win?"

"No, they didn't. But I'm not talking about the actual game. I showed up early to watch batting practice like I usually do, and one of the players collapsed on the field. His heart stopped."

"Oh my God," Bella said, eyes wide. "Is he okay?"

"As far as I know," I said. "I'm not totally sure. The thing is, when he first fell to the ground, nobody was paying any attention to him. I was the only one who noticed him and started screaming for help."

"Wow, really?"

"Yeah. When I saw that nobody was going over to help him, I ran down to the field and started doing CPR on him."

Denise stuck her head out of her office. "You did CPR on one of the Bay Birds players?"

"Yeah. I did," I said, watching my boss's mouth open wide as I spoke.

By now, everyone sitting at their cubicles had turned around to listen to the conversation.

"It all happened so fast," I said, enjoying my rare moment in the sun. "At first, I didn't know what to do. I thought maybe he was just kidding around and that I'd look like an idiot in front of all those people by running down onto the field. But then when I got to him ..." I choked up as I remembered Rusty's still chest and frightening color. "I could see he had stopped breathing. Denise, if it hadn't been for that CPR day we *just had* at the office ..."

"Oh wow," Denise said. "That's so crazy!"

"Yeah. When I jumped onto the field, security realized I was trying to help him. I managed to stay with him long enough to get his heart going again before the medical team took over."

"Which player was it?" asked Jacquie, our IT expert.

"Rusty Power," I said.

I saw several blank looks from my coworkers, most of whom did not follow baseball. Rusty wasn't the most well-known player on the team, especially considering this was only his second year in the majors. I kind of liked it that way because having Rusty as my favorite player was more unique.

With the girls hanging on my every word, I knew exactly what to say to impress them.

"I was pretty upset afterward, so Brady Keaton came over and put his arm around me to calm me down."

Squeals and gasps erupted from my small crowd of coworkers; a bigger reaction than I'd expected. This might have been the most attention I'd gotten in my life.

"You're kidding. *The* Brady Keaton?" Bella asked. Most people knew who Brady Keaton was, whether they followed baseball or not. Not only was he gorgeous, Brady was quite a character. He'd appeared in all kinds of commercial endorsements in addition to being an MLB All-Star, so his face was everywhere.

"Yeah," I said, liking the attention but feeling a little weird about it at the same time. I felt like I was bragging.

Still, I might never have another exciting story to tell. Might as well enjoy my fifteen minutes of fame while it lasted. "He was incredibly sweet. I was pretty freaked out by the whole experience. At that point, I wasn't sure if Rusty was gonna be okay. But Brady was super nice. He led me over to the dugout and got me a drink of water."

"Aww, he sounds really sweet," Bella said in a dreamy voice. "Is he as hot in person as he is on TV?"

"Hotter," I answered honestly. "And he's so *big*. They all are up close. Especially compared to me."

Denise nodded. "Wow. Just ... that's all I can say is *wow*. Did you know any CPR before you took that class here?"

"Nope."

"Awesome," she said enthusiastically. "We should do something to promote the fact that you saved this guy's life thanks to the training we gave you here at the University of Timonium."

"That's a good idea," I said. I enjoyed working for the university. It was a good school, and I liked the idea of promoting it. If it encouraged other businesses to follow suit and have CPR training in their offices, so much the better. That could save a lot of lives.

It occurred to me that perhaps this publicity would help me get the promotion I had my eye on. Denise had announced she was leaving soon, and her position as human resources manager would be open. Since I was her HR assistant and knew more about her job than anyone, I stood an excellent chance at getting the job. Still, I wanted to grab any advantage I could get since I desperately wanted that promotion.

"Damn, there it is," Bella said, gesturing at her computer. "'Bay Birds fan rushes onto the field and rescues first baseman, Rusty Power.' It even mentions your name!"

"Have they talked about giving you some kind of reward?" Denise asked.

"Well yeah, kinda. I got to meet the head groundskeeper woman and—"

"She's the one who got proposed to on the field, right? By one of the players?" Bella asked excitedly.

I nodded. "Matt Jovey's her husband. I met him, too."

More squeals, which made me laugh.

"Julia is her name. She was super sweet. She took my name and number and said somebody would probably reach out to me."

"That's awesome," Denise said. "I wonder what they'll do for you."

"Honestly, all I really want is to meet Rusty Power. He's always been my favorite," I said. Now my voice was the one that sounded dreamy.

"Says here you gave him mouth-to-mouth," Bella said with a sly grin.

"Well, yeah. I did." I forced a smile at the memory. One of the many reasons I wanted to meet Rusty was to see him when he was awake and healthy. Our first meeting, if you could call it that, was scary and sad. But I didn't want to talk about that part with my fellow workers.

"That would be cool if you got to meet him," Denise said.

Cool would not even begin to describe it.

"I guess I'll have to wait and see if anybody from the team reaches out to me," I said with a shrug, as if my heartbeat hadn't sped up just talking about meeting Rusty.

"Welp, my weekend was pretty boring compared to that," Jacquie said. Several others laughed and expressed their agreement with her statement.

Denise's phone rang and she excused herself to answer

it. And just like that, we all went back to work. That was fine by me. Being the center of attention was fun, but it was rather strange. I was really more comfortable in the background.

The university had recently hired a bunch of new employees, so there were a ton of forms to process. I didn't think I would be able to focus on my work today, but things got so busy that I was somewhat productive.

Until my phone buzzed with a call.

I gasped out loud when I saw the caller ID, making everyone in the small office turn and look at me. Not much was private in an open-plan workplace.

"Oh my God, it's Ramon Reyes. That's Rusty's agent," I said. My heart was hammering in my chest. I needed to calm down before I answered, but if I waited too long, the guy might hang up. Jumping from my seat, I grabbed my phone and rushed out into the hallway. This conversation would be nerve-wracking enough without an audience.

I walked outside as I answered, trying my damnedest not to sound out of breath.

"Hello?" I said as casually as I could. I didn't want Mr. Reyes to know I was obsessed enough with Rusty Power to know his agent's name.

"Hi," the man said in a friendly voice. "Is this Amanda Miller?"

"Yes."

"My name is Ramon Reyes. I'm Rusty Power's sports agent." He had a slight accent, but I was unsure of his nationality.

"Oh, hi." I tried to sound calm as I paced the sidewalk in front of the building.

"I wanted to reach out to you on behalf of Rusty and the entire Bay Birds organization to thank you for your heroic actions yesterday." Ramon's voice was gentle, and that helped my nerves considerably. I got the feeling that even if I said something stupid, he wouldn't make fun of me for it.

"Well, I'm just happy that I was able to help."

I desperately wanted to ask how Rusty was doing, but I figured if they hadn't released any information publicly on his condition, they wouldn't tell me anything.

"The Bay Birds would be happy to send you anything you like. A signed ball or bat or something like that. Are you a big Bay Birds fan?"

"The biggest! I love the Birds," I said.

Ramon laughed. "Wonderful. That's what we like to hear! We'd be happy to set you up with season tickets if you'd like."

"Uh, well, I already have a partial season ticket plan."

"Okay. In that case, I'm sure we can get you more tickets. Or perhaps we can get you an upgrade on your seats."

"That would be amazing. Thanks so much!"

We chatted for a few minutes about the logistics, figuring out what plan I already had and how to improve it. Though I was truly grateful, I couldn't help being disappointed. Hearing from Rusty's sports rep was exciting, but it was nothing compared to hearing from the man himself. I started to feel silly for thinking even for a moment that Rusty might actually call me.

"Okay, so we will get this all set up for you as soon as possible, Amanda," Ramon said, sounding as if he was wrapping up the conversation. But then he said, "And Rusty would like to thank you in person."

I blinked for a second, hardly believing what I'd just heard.

"H—he would?"

"Absolutely. He would really like to meet you, if that's okay."

"Of course it's okay!" I practically yelled. So much for playing it cool.

Ramon laughed, but not unkindly. "That's wonderful. He's still in the hospital, so you can visit him there if that's convenient."

"Sure. Is he ... Is he okay?"

"Oh, yes. He's doing fine. More than anything, he's annoyed that they won't release him yet. He definitely wouldn't mind having another visitor right now. I guess you're at work at the moment?"

"Yes," I said. "I work at the University of Timonium."

"Good deal. That's not too far away. Do you know where Sinai Hospital is?"

"Yeah. I haven't been since I was born there, but yeah."

He proceeded to give me detailed instructions on where to go and what to do. I would go right after work and be sure to bring my ID.

I'm going to see Rusty Power.

The rest of the day went by in a blur. My announcement that I was going to meet Rusty was met with the loudest squeals yet from my coworkers. It warmed my heart that everyone was so excited for me.

Try as I might, I barely got any work done. Once the initial euphoria wore off, I started to think hard about the reality of meeting Rusty Power in person. What if I was so nervous that I made a complete fool out of myself in front of him? That would be so much worse than never meeting him at all. Then I wouldn't even have the fantasy version of him anymore. Instead, I would cringe every time I thought about him.

What if I acted like a complete idiot and he relayed the

story to the other players about how I'd behaved? Dear God, what if he told the media? It might be a cute story to him, but he would have effectively ruined my life.

There was a reason I tended to fade into the background in life. I *liked* it that way. That was where I belonged.

By the end of the day, I was so stressed out that I wasn't even sure I wanted to go through with it after all.

7

AMANDA

Denise, Bella, Jacquie, and what felt like everybody else at the university wished me luck as I headed out at the end of the day. Word had gotten around quickly about my celebrity encounter.

No pressure or anything.

I sat in my car for a moment, fiddling with the navigation app on my phone and setting its course for Sinai Hospital. Having obsessed for several hours over meeting Rusty, now I *really* didn't want to go. I seriously considered canceling even as I drove toward the hospital. I could just lie to everybody and say Rusty wasn't up to having visitors after all.

But I knew I couldn't back out. I owed it to myself to go through with this opportunity that I'd only thought would happen in my wildest fantasy.

I am on my way to meet Rusty Power in person.

There was no doubt in my mind that I would regret it for the rest of my natural life if I chickened out now. And it wasn't like I would be the only stuttering idiot fan Rusty had dealt with as a pro ballplayer. If he was even half as nice as he seemed on TV and in radio interviews, I shouldn't have anything to worry about.

It took a while to find the visitors' parking garage, and that only ramped up my anxiety. I hated how miserable I was making myself. This was supposed to be fun and exciting. Why was I psyching myself out so badly?

Finally, I parked my car and found the correct entrance to where poor Rusty was holed up in the hospital. Maybe he *would* actually be glad to have a new visitor.

I held my breath in the elevator, then shakily made my way toward the nurses' station on Rusty's floor. I waited for a few excruciating minutes while the nurse finished speaking to someone on the phone.

"Hi, can I help you?" the short, gray-haired nurse asked when she hung up the phone. She seemed busy and a little stressed.

"Yes, I'm Amanda Miller. I'm here to see ... I guess I kind of have an appointment to see Rusty Power?"

Those words sounded positively surreal coming out of my mouth.

"Oh, yes. He's expecting you," she said. "I just need your ID."

"Sure." My hand shook as I handed it over.

She smiled at me. "Don't be nervous, honey. He's a real sweetheart."

"Thanks," I said gratefully. There was a deep fondness in her eyes as she spoke, making it clear that Rusty hadn't been acting like a spoiled sports diva during his stay at the hospital. Perhaps he really was as sweet in person as he was on television.

"Rusty's in that room right there," she said, gesturing to a door across from the nurses' station. "Just give a knock before you go in. He's expecting you."

I nodded and drew in a deep breath. Somehow, I managed to walk over, knock on the door, and not faint all at the same time. That was progress.

"Come on in," came that oh-so-familiar deep male voice. *It's really him!*

I walked in and carefully shut the door behind me. Praying that I didn't look as terrified as I felt, I slowly turned around to face my favorite Baltimore Bay Bird.

Those eyes.

Seeing those baby blues up close and personal took my breath away. I couldn't come up with a single word to say.

He picked up the remote control from his bed and muted the TV that was tuned to some sports channel. "You must be Amanda," Rusty said, his voice warm and inviting.

He knew my *name*. I nodded dumbly.

"Come on in. Have a seat," he said, gesturing to the chair near his bedside.

I'd never been so grateful for a seat in my life. Sitting down made it less likely that I would collapse from nervousness.

Rusty eyed me curiously. "Wow, you're so tiny."

It wasn't exactly what I'd hoped to hear from my celebrity crush. Then again, he was used to dating tall, thin actress and model types.

"Um, yeah. I guess."

Rusty chuckled. "I'm sorry. That didn't come out the way I meant. I'm just saying you're so small and I'm so big. It's really amazing that you were able to do what you did."

He seemed quite apologetic as he spoke. It made me want to make *him* feel better.

"No, I know what you mean. You're a lot bigger in real life than I'd expected."

Nervous as I was, I second-guessed every word. I hoped

he didn't think I was saying he was fat in real life. Worse, I worried that referring to his size would sound like some sort of sexual innuendo.

Rusty laughed heartily. "Yeah. I'm sure I look especially huge right now." Glancing down at his body, he said, "I feel like an overgrown Muppet in a doll bed."

That remark genuinely made me laugh, relaxing me a little.

"That really was incredible what you did, Amanda," he said, gazing at me.

Rusty seemed so sweet. I was relieved to find he was a nice person in real life. Given the situation, of course he would be kind to me, but the fond way the nurse had spoken of him told me he was the real deal. He might date models and all that, but he didn't seem stuck up or anything.

"I didn't even really know what I was doing. I'm hardly a medical professional. Was just dumb luck that I'd happened to learn CPR at work recently," I confessed, trying not to babble. "I was afraid I might have broken your rib or something."

Rusty dropped his gaze.

"Wait ... Did I break a rib?"

He hesitated before slowly raising two fingers.

I gasped in horror. "Oh God, I broke two of your ribs? I'm so sorry."

"Amanda!" he exclaimed. "Don't apologize. It's a small price to pay for staying alive. Besides, they only cracked. They're not all the way broken."

Rusty gazed deeply into my eyes and said solemnly, "You really did save my life. You know that, right?"

I shrugged. There had been a whole team of sports trainers there who knew how to do CPR much better than I did. Deep down I figured somebody would have helped him if I hadn't.

"That's what they told me," Rusty said, glancing toward the door where the nurses' station was located. "They still don't know exactly what's wrong with me or what caused it, but my heart stopped. Batting practice was so busy and hectic, and nobody was paying attention to me. If it hadn't been for you, I most likely would have died right there on the warning track."

I sucked in my breath, trying to wrap my head around his words.

"Had I collapsed during the game, people would have seen me right away, but ... Just thank God you were at batting practice."

"Wow," I whispered softly. Flashing back to how gray and still Rusty had been, I said in a shaky voice, "It was ... frightening."

All the machinery Rusty was attached to now was yet another reminder of how serious his condition was.

Rusty reached over and squeezed my hand. "I'm sure it was frightening. I'm really sorry."

"I'm just glad you're okay," I said. The touch of his hand snapped me out of my sorrow and back to reality. A reality where *Rusty Power was holding my hand.*

He looked into my eyes long enough for me to imagine, just for a second, that *I* was one of his supermodel girlfriends, then he let go of my hand and sat back in his bed.

"So are you a big Bay Birds fan?" he asked.

I was glad he kept the conversation going, because I was still struggling to find much to say. Fortunately, baseball was one of my preferred topics.

"Oh, definitely. I love baseball in general, but of course the Bay Birds are my favorite. My parents took me to the occasional baseball game growing up, and I fell in love with the game."

Rusty grinned, pleased at my devotion to the sport.

"Funny how my parents were casual fans, but I took to it right away. I've been a pretty hardcore fan all my life."

"Me too! I grew up in West Virginia."

I had to bite my tongue to keep from saying "I know." There wasn't much I *didn't* know about him, but there was no reason to tell him that.

"There's no MLB team there, so a lot of West Virginians are Bay Birds fans."

"It must be a dream come true to play for Baltimore."

"Oh, it is," Rusty said with deep reverence. "It truly is. So, who's your favorite player?"

"You are," I confessed shyly.

He laughed, a deep and sexy sound. "Aw, come on now. You don't have to say that."

"No, you really are," I insisted. "That's why—"

I managed to stop myself before I said way too much.

"That's why what?" he asked.

"You're really gonna make me say it, aren't you?"

Rusty's eyes opened wide. "Oh, well now you *have* to tell me."

Blushing deeply and avoiding his gaze, I said, "You really are my favorite player. That's why at batting practice when everybody else was watching Brady Keaton, I was watching you."

He didn't say anything. I was afraid to look up at him because if he laughed at me, I would never get over it.

When I finally peered up at him, his expression was somber.

"Wow. Thank God for that, right?"

My face still hot, I nodded. "Yeah. I guess so."

If he noticed my blush, he was too sweet to let on.

"Well, I'm honored to be your favorite. And I'm really glad you came to see me. I like having visitors, especially a pretty girl like you."

"Thanks," I said. Rusty was just being nice, but I appreciated the compliment all the same.

I wondered if his thanks for the visit was his way of wrapping up our time together. The last thing I wanted was to overstay my welcome, but I couldn't bear to leave quite yet.

Gathering my nerve and reminding myself that this was a once-in-a-lifetime opportunity, I forced myself to ask, "Would it be okay if I got a photo with you?"

"Are you kidding? Of course! Anything for you, Amanda."

My body tingled every time he said my name. I grabbed my phone and clicked on the camera icon. That's when I realized I hadn't thought this through. The poor man was in a hospital bed. Who wanted their picture taken when they were laid up in the hospital wearing only a medical gown?

And yet Rusty had already agreed to get a picture with me. Nothing left to do now but go through with it.

Hesitantly, I stood and approached his bed.

"Get on over here," he said with a friendly grin. "Don't be shy."

Rusty had done his best to put me at ease since the moment I'd walked through the door, and I adored him for it. He'd ignored any awkwardness on my part, and I would be eternally grateful for that.

He stretched out his arm and put it around my back so he could pull me in for a selfie. He winced slightly, but quickly recovered.

Dear God, I just asked a man with two cracked ribs to get a photograph with me.

"Come on, girl. Smile pretty for the camera," he said as we posed.

"I'm just trying not to hurt you."

"I'm good." He added in an exaggerated, macho voice, "I can handle the pain."

I flipped the image on the phone so we could see the picture as we took it. I still looked freaked out in the image.

"Smile, Amanda. Don't make me tickle you."

That made me laugh; I snapped the picture before I could start freaking out again.

Rusty chuckled. "There you go."

I released him as quickly as I could. Not that I wanted to.

"Are you okay?" I asked him.

"I'm fine, really."

"I'm so sorry about your ribs."

"And I'm sorry I ruined your ballgame experience by nearly dying on you," Rusty said with a grin.

Could this man be any cuter? Thank God I hadn't chickened out and bailed on meeting him. If I could get through the rest of the visit without doing or saying something stupid, I would have yet another good story to tell my friends.

I sighed and said, "Well, I guess I better go and let you get some re—"

A knock at the door startled me. Before Rusty could even say "Come in," a woman barreled her way into the room.

She glanced at Rusty and then noticed me.

"Oh, I'm sorry, honey. I didn't know you had company."

With her reddish hair streaked with gray and those bright blue eyes, the woman was obviously related to Rusty.

"Mom," Rusty said. His eyes twinkled but his voice was

one of warning. "I don't want you to get … you know, how you *get*."

His mother put her hand over her heart. "Oh no. Why? What happened?"

Rusty chuckled. "Nothing happened. Chill out. Mom, I would like you to meet Amanda."

The older woman turned toward me and blinked for a second. Then she gasped so loudly that it scared me.

"Amanda? Amanda *Miller*?"

One would think I was the celebrity here by the way she reacted to my presence.

Rusty laughed again. "Yes, Mom. Amanda Miller."

"You're the one!" she cried. "You're the one who saved my baby's life."

I liked Mrs. Power immediately. She clearly adored her precious Rusty. No wonder he had grown up to be such a class act.

She tossed her purse aside and rushed over to grab me, pulling me into a tight embrace.

"*Moooom,*" Rusty moaned with embarrassment.

"Amanda, thank you. Thank you so very much!"

Eventually, she let go of me.

"His doctors all said he would be *dead* if it hadn't been for you," she said with tears in her eyes.

That was the moment it finally hit me that I actually had saved his life. If I hadn't noticed his distress, he really would have died.

As I watched his mother wipe tears of relief and gratitude from her eyes, I was suddenly struck with the realization that she could have been weeping over her son's grave in anguish instead.

My legs suddenly felt wobbly.

Thank God in Heaven I'd been watching Rusty yesterday. The line between life and death was so much thinner than any of us knew.

"Stop. You'll make me cry too," I said with a gentle laugh.

It was true, though. I was deeply empathetic, and I wore my emotions on my sleeve. I couldn't watch anything too violent or tragic on television or in the movies because I reacted strongly to it. While other people could watch that stuff and just walk away, I found it unsettling. That kind of thing stayed with me for some reason.

"Amanda, I'd like you to meet Jane Power."

"Sorry, sorry, sorry! I didn't mean to come bursting in like this. It's so nice to meet you, Amanda," she said, reaching out to grasp my hands and squeeze them.

"Very nice to meet you, Mrs. Power."

"Call me Jane, please."

"Of course. Jane," I said with a smile.

She let go of my hands. "Rusty, I hope you're planning to give her a generous reward." She walked over to her son's bedside and then began stroking his forehead.

"*Mom*," he said, sounding embarrassed. "I'm not a baby."

He kicked his feet like a little kid, making both of us laugh. I saw that wince of pain again, but he powered through it in order to calm his mother. What a good son he was.

"And yes, I was just getting to that part when you twirled in like a maternal tornado."

"Sorry, baby," Jane said with a sweet smile.

"I heard the Bay Birds are upgrading your tickets, right?" Rusty asked me.

"Right. I'm all set there."

"Is there something else—anything—that I can do for you?"

"Buy her a car," Jane said, and I didn't think she was kidding.

"That won't be necessary," I said with a laugh.

"I could do that," Rusty said. He wasn't kidding either.

"Really, I don't need anything," I said. And it was true. I wasn't materialistic, and my needs were simple. I had a car that was in pretty good working order—it got me to where I needed to go. I had a roof over my head, as basic as it was. I was saving up to buy a house. What was I going to do, ask him for the down payment?

"There must be something," Jane said. Rusty nodded.

They both seemed so earnest, and I realized it would be a kindness to let them give me a reward. There was something to be said for graciously accepting a gift.

"You know what I would really love?"

They looked so excited that I had to bite my lip to keep from laughing.

"And I'm not just saying this, Rusty. I swear. But I really want an official Rusty Power jersey. They're so expensive that I haven't had the money to buy one."

"Done," Rusty said.

"And if you can autograph it, even better. I would really love that."

"I will be sure to make that happen," he said.

"All right," Jane said. "That's good enough to start. But I'm not done with you."

Jane reached over and gave me another hug. I was so glad Rusty had a devoted mother here to take care of him.

"I better get going so Rusty can get some rest."

"Do I get a hug, too?" he asked in what could only be described as the highlight of my life.

"Of course," I said. "But wait. I don't want to hurt you. You've got two cracked ribs after all."

"You have two cracked ribs?" Jane yelled.

Dammit.

So much for escaping without saying something stupid.

"I'm so sorry," I told Rusty as I blushed deeply.

He laughed. "Ah, don't worry about it. Was only a matter of time before one of my doctors told her. I still want that hug."

"Okay, but don't lift your arms," I said. I leaned down and wrapped my arms around him, squeezing as gently as I could.

The man was *so big.*

"Thank you," I said, seizing one last opportunity to gaze into his eyes. "It's been so good meeting with you and seeing you so healthy. This here ... This is how I want to remember you. Not, you know, like before."

Rusty nodded and smiled. I didn't want to say too much about what had happened for fear of upsetting his mother.

"Thank *you*, Amanda."

"Take care, Rusty," I said with one last look as I walked out the door.

8

RUSTY

Sooo booooored.

I was completely going out of my mind being holed up in this hospital. I'd had ESPN on for most of the day, and I'd spent a lot of time reading sports news on my laptop. Watching the Bay Birds play without me was physically painful. It felt like a piece of me was missing while I couldn't play. Baseball was pretty much my whole life, and I had no idea what to do with myself without it.

My little incident had happened on Sunday, and here it was Tuesday, and I was still here. I'd done my best to be patient, but I was starting to get pissed off. The staff here was great—they all took good care of me, and they were very nice. And yet nobody seemed to have any answers about what was wrong with me. At this point, I hardly cared what was wrong. I just needed to get the hell out of here. Maybe they could admit defeat already. Come right out and say they didn't know what was wrong and let me go. It was probably just a freak thing. A fluke. Some kind of weird cardiac misfire that would never happen again.

The team was hitting the road tomorrow, and if the hospital

didn't release me soon, I would miss the damned trip. Worst-case scenario, I could leave against the doctor's orders. This wasn't prison or the psychiatric ward where they could hold you against your will. They couldn't stop me from walking out.

But my mother would kill me if I did that.

Besides, the Birds wouldn't let me on the field until I was officially released and given the go-ahead to play. I sincerely hoped I wouldn't end up on the injured list. I'd already missed enough game time. Hopefully, I could convince them to let me play even with two cracked ribs.

Not long after they cleared my lunch tray—and good *God*, did I miss real food—I saw a familiar face walk past my open door.

"Amanda?" I called out in surprise.

She froze in the hallway and slowly turned around. Her cheeks reddened as she saw me, as if I'd caught her doing something embarrassing.

"Uh yeah. Hi," she said. She meandered over and stood in the doorway. "I promise I'm not stalking you or anything."

I laughed, willing myself not to react to the pain in my ribs. That girl was so adorably shy.

"I didn't think you were," I said. "But I am surprised to see you."

"They called to tell me I'd left my driver's license here. I had to show it to visit you yesterday, and they forgot to give it back to me."

"Oh, well it's nice to see you again."

"You too," she said, sounding nervous.

"Do you have time to visit for a bit?"

Her brown eyes opened wide.

"Sure," she said, but she didn't move.

"Come on in." I gave her a friendly wave.

Amanda came in and sat down in the chair near my bed. By the end of our visit yesterday, she had warmed up and been less nervous. Today it was like we were starting all over again. That was okay. She was a sweet girl, and I'd enjoyed our time yesterday.

I got the feeling that she hadn't grasped the fact that I owed her my life. As much as I tried to downplay my illness, whatever it was, something bad had happened out there that day. Amanda had looked haunted when we'd talked about it.

"I ... um ... I don't want to bother you," she said.

"Believe me, Amanda. You are no bother. I'm so damn bored, and I didn't think I'd have any visitors today."

"Nobody from your family is here?"

I shook my head. "No. Maybe later on. Unfortunately, they're all at a family funeral."

Amanda's expression softened. "Oh, I'm sorry to hear that."

"Thanks. It's my mother's favorite aunt who died. She was a sweet lady. Kills me that I can't be there for the family."

"That really is too bad," Amanda said gently.

"So, what are you up to today?"

"Nothing much. Just working."

"Oh shit, am I keeping you from work?"

"I'm on my lunch break," she said. "I'll text my boss and let her know I'll be a little late coming back."

"I don't want to get you in trouble."

"It's okay. Pretty sure she'll understand. Especially once I tell her who I'm with. You've been the talk of the office lately," Amanda said with a laugh.

"Where do you work?"

"University of Timonium. I work in human resources. Not the most thrilling job in the world, but I like it."

As I watched her text her boss, I noticed her hands were shaking. I wished I could do something to make her less nervous around me.

"So that's where you learned CPR? You said you learned it at work?"

"Yeah. In fact, my boss suggested we do some promotion or something about it. To like, you know, tell people that it was the university's free one-day CPR course that helped save somebody's life."

Amanda drew in a nervous breath.

"Now that I say it out loud, though, maybe that's like exploiting what happened to you? Maybe it's not a good idea."

"No, I think it's great. It would be good publicity for the school, and it could even inspire other workplaces to have CPR sessions."

"Yeah," she said with a smile of relief.

Somebody knocked on my open door, and I looked up to see one of my many doctors. Due to patient volume and rotating schedules, I had seen a bunch of different physicians. This one, an older man, looked familiar, but I was blanking on his name.

"Okay, Mr. Power. Got some test results to go over with you," he said, approaching my bedside. He had a younger guy with him. An intern or something, I supposed.

Amanda got up from her chair immediately and walked over to the door.

"I'll give you some privacy."

"No, no. It's fine. They do this a hundred times a day. You're fine to stay."

She nodded uncertainly, staying as far back as possible.

The gray-haired doctor scrutinized my chart. "I apologize that it's taken so long to get a definitive diagnosis, but we wanted to run all the necessary tests to be sure."

"Cool, sounds good," I said, trying to hurry him up. At last, I might get some answers and get the hell out of here.

"Mr. Power, the reason you went into cardiac arrest was because you have a very rare condition known as Elreid Syndrome."

"Okay." I suddenly felt nervous. The whole time I'd been in the hospital, I'd been focused on getting out. I'd spent most of the time downplaying my illness, but the words "cardiac arrest" jolted me back to reality. As much as I'd tried to forget it, the truth was my goddamned heart had *stopped*. That did not happen to normal twenty-six-year-olds.

"Since it is so rare, it took us a while to get a diagnosis. It was much easier to rule things out than to figure out what was wrong."

I nodded, my muscles tight with anxiety. Was I going to need heart surgery? Was I going to *die*?

"Though your condition is serious, fortunately it's quite treatable. We will get you on a course of medication immediately and send you home with instructions on how to make sure you never have this kind of severe cardiac event again. Of course, you will need to find a cardiologist and have regular follow-ups to carefully track your condition. Overall, I see no reason you can't otherwise lead a normal life."

"Oh, thank God," I said, the tension easing from my body. "Now will you let me out of here?"

Gray Doc smiled. "Yes, pretty soon. I'll need to get your discharge papers prepared first. I'll get you a list of recommended cardiologists and get your instructions. Mainly, you just need to take your meds regularly, don't overdo it on the physical activity, and you should be fine."

"Wait, what?" I asked.

"What?" the doctor asked, looking confused.

"What was that part you said about physical activity?"

"Oh. Yes. You can exercise regularly, just nothing too strenuous." Shuffling my chart, he said, "It's noted here that you had been running right before your collapse?"

"Yeah, I was jogging around the warning track," I said, my voice rising. The doctor looked startled at my outburst. "Dude, I'm a professional athlete."

Finally, the truth dawned on this dumb ass. Not that he seemed particularly empathetic.

"Oh, right. You're the baseball player."

"Yes. I'm a baseball player."

He nodded, which gave me a glimmer of hope that he might say *Well, in that case we'll do surgery to fix you and you'll be good as new.*

"I'm afraid you won't be able to play ball anymore," he said as casually as if we were talking about the weather.

Amanda gasped from the back of the room. I'd forgotten she was there.

"What do you mean I won't be able to play ball anymore?" I demanded.

Closing my chart, the old bastard had the nerve to act as if I was wasting his precious time.

"Mr. Power, you were lucky to have survived your heart incident. A lot of people don't. In fact, that's the most common way people find out they have this disease. It's uncovered during the autopsy after sudden death. If you overexert yourself, you could die. That's just the way it is."

I didn't care if I could die while playing baseball. To me, the risk was worth it. Maybe if my heart hadn't stopped on the field in front of thousands of witnesses, including the whole Baltimore Bay Birds team, I could have hidden my disease and kept playing.

But I had gone into cardiac arrest at Old Bay Stadium. There wasn't a team on the planet that would sign me now.

And just like that, my baseball career was over.

"Excessive exertion caused your heart to stop. So long as you take your medication and don't push yourself too hard physically, you can live a relatively normal life," he said, still sounding annoyed.

My entire body went numb. I would never live anything close to a "normal life." My mind could not accept this information. I thought this must be what it feels like when a police officer knocks on your door to tell you there's been a terrible accident.

I'm sorry, sir. But your baseball career is dead. It didn't survive the heart attack.

"I'll get your discharge papers ready," said the gray-haired doctor from hell. He rushed out the door, probably eager to ruin somebody else's day.

The young intern had the decency to stay behind long enough to say, "I'm really sorry, Mr. Power. I wish there was more we could do."

All I could do was stare at him for a moment. Then he headed out into the hallway to catch up with the old doc.

I kept staring at the doorway, as if the doctor would come back in and tell me this was all some kind of sick joke. My gaze was broken by Amanda crossing in front of my line of vision.

Wordlessly, she slid the visitor's chair close to my bedside and sat down. She took my hand in hers and sat there in silence for a moment.

When I finally turned to look at her, she asked quietly,

"Is there somebody I can call for you? Your mother maybe?"

I shook my head. "They ... they're all dealing with the funeral. I don't want to burden them any more. My mother said she might come by later tonight, but ... I guess she shouldn't bother making the trip since I'm getting released soon."

Amanda nodded and kept holding my hand.

Even in my current stupor, I noticed that her nervousness had vanished. It was like as soon as I got my horrible diagnosis, she had slipped right into caretaking mode. This girl knew how to handle a crisis, that was for sure.

"I just ... can't believe it," I said.

"I know. Me neither."

"Of all the things I expected him to say, I never even considered ... I mean, I've been so hellbent on getting out of here and getting back to my normal life that I ... I guess I never even thought about ... That I wouldn't be able to ..."

I was at a loss for words. Nothing could express what I was going through.

"Never occurred to me either," Amanda said with a soft sigh. "I was worried about what they might say, but I don't think it dawned on me that your condition would keep you from playing."

She let go of my hand but stayed close by.

I sat there in bed for a few minutes, not saying a word. My mind was reeling from the shock.

"What the hell am I gonna do now?" I asked, suddenly panicked.

"Just take everything one step at a time," Amanda said soothingly. "Right now you must be completely overwhelmed."

"You're damn right, I'm overwhelmed!" I roared.

Amanda flinched. I felt terrible.

"I'm so sorry. I didn't mean to yell at you."

"I know you didn't," she said. "I'm sure you feel like yelling and breaking things right now, but you can't because you're in a damn hospital."

"Yeah," I said with a bitter laugh. "That's exactly how I feel. I still don't know what to do with my life now."

"You have plenty of time to figure that out."

"You don't understand," I said in frustration. How could she? Nobody could possibly understand how I felt. I tried to explain anyway, the words tumbling out of my mouth. "My entire life has revolved around baseball since the moment I went to my first minor league game when I was seven years old. I got so excited by it that my parents took me to a Major League Baseball game as soon as they could, and that happened to be at Old Bay Stadium. From then on, I've played baseball. I went from Little League to high school baseball, college baseball, the minors, and I finally made it to the big show last year. Pretty much every moment of my day is taken up with baseball. That's true even in the off-season, which is just me waiting around for the season to start. I usually take a few weeks off to chill and eat junk food and heal my body from the season, but after that I hardly know what to do with myself until spring training begins."

Amanda sighed softly, then nodded in sympathy.

"This all happened so fast," she said. "I know it's really sad and really scary, but it will get better."

"But I don't know what to do now," I repeated, sounding like a frightened child.

"You don't have to decide anything now. In fact, you really shouldn't. It's like when somebody you love suddenly dies. They tell you not to make any major decisions for at least a few months. By then, you might be thinking more clearly. You need to take time to mourn this loss, Rusty."

Amanda sounded so much wiser than her years.

"Do you have younger siblings?" I asked.

"Uh, yeah," she said, sounding understandably confused by the random question. "Two younger sisters."

"I bet you're the one who takes care of everybody in your family."

Amanda laughed, finally getting why I'd asked. "I'm the one who takes care of *everybody*. Even in high school, my friends called me Mother Goose."

"That's funny."

"Yeah." There was a hint of sadness in her voice.

"What?"

"It's not the sexiest thing in the world to be thought of as a mother figure. Especially at my age."

"Oh. I get that."

"My friends all come to me with their boyfriend troubles. Usually I'm the one without a boyfriend, so I have plenty of time to help them."

"I can't believe nobody's snapped you up yet, Amanda," I said with a smile.

She waved me off. "You don't have to say that."

I wanted her to believe that I'd meant it. I was about to argue, but she wouldn't let me.

"Anyway, back to your issue."

"You don't have to stay with me. Don't you have to get back to work?"

"I'm not leaving until you get discharged or until somebody from your family shows up," she said firmly. "My work will understand."

She took out her phone and started texting.

"Amanda, please don't—"

"I wouldn't dream of telling a soul about what's going on. It's nobody's business but yours."

"Thank you," I said, relieved. The last thing I needed was word getting out before I had time to tell my family and my teammates.

"I just don't know what to do," I muttered. I knew I kept repeating that, but I'd never felt so lost.

"Right now you need to take care of yourself and your health."

"Fuck my health! What good is it if I can't play ball?"

Amanda's frown made me realize how ungrateful I was being. I'd just said "fuck my health" to the woman who had brought me back from the brink of death.

"I'm sorry. That was a shitty thing to say after everything you've done for me."

"It's okay. I won't take it personally. You have every right to lash out."

"Don't tell my mom I said the F word to you."

Amanda laughed. "I won't."

"Thank you for staying with me."

"You're welcome. I'm just glad I happened to be here."

I was incredibly grateful that Amanda was with me; I wouldn't have wanted to be alone. I was also thankful that she hadn't said things like "You're lucky to be alive" or "At least you can live a mostly normal life." That might be true, but it wasn't what I needed to hear at the moment. Perhaps I'd be more grateful for those things later, but right now I needed to be angry and sad. Amanda was right when she said I was mourning this loss.

"I never took a moment for granted, you know?" I said. "I was so lucky to make it to the majors, and I reveled in every second of it. Sometimes it felt too good to be true. It really felt like one day I might wake up and realize it was all just a dream. And that's kind of what happened. I'm in the middle of a nightmare that I can't wake up from."

Nodding thoughtfully, she said, "That's awful."

Then she gazed at me, waiting for me to continue. She seemed to know I had more to say.

"Why am I being punished?" I asked harshly. Being trapped in the hospital was endlessly frustrating. I *did* feel like yelling and breaking things. It was odd for me, because I was usually pretty chill—never the type to get mad easily.

"I know this guy in the majors. Nobody on our team. This jackass cheats on his wife in every damn city he goes to from what I hear. Spends a ton of money on other women and booze and expensive cars and all that. I'm not trying to judge the guy or anything. I'm just saying, that guy cares a lot more about the perks that come with playing baseball than he does about the game itself. Why couldn't this have happened to him?"

I closed my eyes and sighed, hating how angry and bitter I sounded. It was so unlike me.

I opened my eyes and gazed at Amanda, expecting her to be shocked by the awful thing I'd said.

"You must think I'm a terrible person. I didn't mean I actually want something bad to happen to him."

"Don't be so hard on yourself, Rusty," she said. "I know you're not saying you wish somebody else would suffer a life-threatening illness. You just mean if that guy was told his career was over, he'd be upset but not heartbroken the way you are."

"Yes. Exactly! Guys like that don't even care that much about baseball. He could have been a football player or a movie star or an underwear model. As long as he's got the money and the fame, he doesn't care about anything else. So why *me*? Why did this happen to *me*?"

"The short answer is that life isn't fair," Amanda said wearily. "People say that all the time. Such a cliché, but it really is true. Things happen every day that are infuriatingly unfair. Maybe everything happens for a reason. Maybe there is some bigger picture, some cosmic reason why terrible things happen to good people. But I think as long as we're on this Earth, we're not meant to understand."

"Wow. That's deep," I said with a laugh.

Amanda blushed, laughing uncomfortably. I got the feeling she thought I was making fun of her.

"I guess I get what you're saying," I said, though I didn't really.

"The only thing I know for sure is that awful things happen all the time, and it feels like you have no control. I can only watch the news for so long because it feels like the bad guy always wins while the good guys suffer." Amanda shook her head. "Sorry. I know this isn't exactly helping. I tend to be very emotional, and I take everything to heart."

"That's sweet," I said sincerely. Clearly, Amanda was tender-hearted. She had a sense of weariness about her, and I could see that empathy came with a price.

"You can't control much of what happens in the world. All you can control is how you react to it."

"That's just it. I don't know how to react."

"You just found out about this, Rusty. Give yourself a break." She smiled. "Like I said, you have plenty of time to figure out where to go from here."

"Yeah," I said quietly. "Suddenly I've got all the time in the world."

Amanda seemed so sad for me that I could hardly stand it.

"Was it just me, or was that doctor a total asshole?" I blurted out.

She laughed. "Oh, he was the *worst*. I know doctors are

busy, but come on. Does it take any more time out of your day to say something kind instead of being mean?"

"My friend Lyric is studying to be a doctor, and she has a big thing about the right and wrong way to deliver bad news. She always says that as a doctor, you might forget what you said the minute you walk out the door, but the patient will remember for the rest of their lives exactly what you said and how you made them feel. So you better make it count."

"Brady's wife."

"What?" I asked.

"You're talking about Brady Keaton's wife, right?"

"Oh, yeah. You would know that, wouldn't you? Good little Bay Birds fan that you are." I chuckled and swatted her arm playfully. My damned ribs hurt when I did it, but her smile made the pain worthwhile.

"Speaking of doctors, you should probably get a second opinion."

Holy God, why hadn't I thought of that? I was acting like my fate was already sealed.

"That's a great idea," I said, sitting up in bed and sending fresh pain jolting through my chest. "I need to get another opinion. For all I know, maybe—"

"Rusty," Amanda said in a kind yet firm tone. "It's best to get a second opinion just to be sure. But ... it's probably best if you don't get your hopes up. From what you've said, they've been running a lot of tests since you got here, and this is a very reputable hospital. It's just ... Well, it's pretty unlikely that they got your diagnosis wrong."

I could see pure anguish in her eyes as she spoke. She did not enjoy delivering this "tough love" message, but she was worried about me.

"You're probably right," I said, though I secretly held on

to a tiny ray of hope that this guy's medical prowess was as terrible as his bedside manner.

Now I was the one feeling emotionally exhausted. The initial shock was wearing off, and the heartache was starting to set in.

Remembering the smell of the grass, the feel of the dirt under my cleats, and the pure exhilaration I felt every single time I stepped onto a baseball field, my voice cracked as I said, "I really never took one second for granted."

Amanda's eyes filled up with tears. "I know."

I looked up as my favorite nurse with the graying hair knocked on my open door and came in. "Okay, Mr. Power. It's finally time to spring you from this joint." She smiled, but there was a sadness in her eyes.

She knew.

Nurse Karen had been wonderful during my stay, and I knew she'd been hoping for a better outcome for me. Like with Amanda, it helped to know somebody cared.

"Got a bunch of papers for you to sign here. Then you can get dressed and be on your way."

I nodded, taking the papers and pen from her.

Amanda stood up. "Well, I better get going."

Nurse Karen took a step back to allow Amanda to say goodbye to me.

"Take care of yourself, okay?" she said, her brown eyes filled with worry.

"I will. Thank you for staying with me."

She nodded. Just before she left, she told me, "Everything's gonna be okay. One way or another, everything's gonna be okay."

I watched her walk away, deeply thankful for her kindness.

But I didn't believe her.

9

AMANDA

It had been exactly a week since Rusty received the devastating news about his career.

Having just wrapped up a hectic day at work, I walked across the parking lot to my car. My thoughts turned to Rusty as they frequently did when I had a second to breathe. I opened the car door and a blast of heat hit my face. The late spring weather was heating up, and I needed to remember to crack the car window in the morning from now on. I tossed my purse in the front seat, turned the key in the ignition, and opened the windows to let in some fresh air.

As promised, I hadn't told anybody about what the doctor had told Rusty. Since I'd had to explain to my boss about my extended lunch break, I'd simply told her that he had asked me to stay and visit with him. Not exactly the truth, but he hadn't seemed to want me to leave. I couldn't abandon him at a time like that, when he had no family with him. Ever since then, I'd obsessively checked the sports news, hoping against hope that a second opinion had given him a brighter diagnosis. I hadn't heard a thing.

I was about to put the car in gear when my phone buzzed with a notification. I figured I'd better check the message before I started driving. It was a sports update from the Bay Birds. My heart caught in my throat and my stomach clenched with sick anxiety.

Rusty Power Announces His Retirement from Baseball Due to Illness.

I dropped my phone back into my purse. Closing my eyes, I put my head down on the steering wheel as a heavy sadness flooded through my body.

That poor, dear soul.

Deep down, I had expected this. After seeing Rusty's nearly dead form lying motionless on the field, there was no escaping the fact that something was seriously wrong with him. But Rusty had probably clung to the belief that he might still be okay.

I lifted my head from the steering wheel and started driving home. I couldn't bear to read the rest of the article yet. My heart was heavy thinking about what he must be going through.

All I could do was hope somebody had been there with him when he got the second, probably equally serious, diagnosis. It had been dumb luck that I'd been there in the first place.

Or was it?

I wasn't sure if I believed in fate, but it was incredible that I'd been in the right place for him not once, but twice. I'd noticed his distress on the field when nobody else had, then I'd been called back to the hospital to retrieve my ID on the very day he'd gotten the tragic news. The one day when none of Rusty's family were available to be with him, I was there to hold his hand.

Strange.

Call it fate or coincidence, I would always be grateful that I'd been there to help. I'd been everybody's caretaker for as long as I could remember, and it really wasn't the sexiest thing in the world. I didn't mind being the one people came to with their problems, because I genuinely enjoyed helping others. It gave me a sense of purpose. I'd learned long ago that I wasn't meant to be the type to set the world on fire. Unlike Wilder, I'd never been the lead in the high school play. I wasn't a doctor or a firefighter or a movie star. I just never had that kind of drive or passion. I would always be the kind of person who largely went unnoticed. Being able to provide comfort to people at least made me feel like I had something to contribute to the world.

Too bad I was so squeamish, otherwise perhaps I could have been a doctor or nurse. If I were, I'd break tragic news to my patients a hell of a lot better than Rusty's doctor had. I tried not to judge people like him, but I was still mad about that. No doubt people in the medical profession had seen things that the rest of us could only imagine. I understood the need to build up walls to protect yourself from the day-to-day trauma of the doctor life. But Lyric was right— the patient would never forget the words the doctor used when breaking bad news, so it was best to make them count.

"Couldn't he at least have said 'I'm sorry'?" I asked out loud. My eyes filled with angry tears. I hated how that jackass doctor had added to Rusty's pain. Recalling the intern's kind words, however, helped restore a little bit of my faith in humanity.

My apartment was only about ten minutes away from work, so I was home before I knew it. I dumped my keys in the bowl by the door and pulled my phone out of my purse. I dreaded reading the rest of the article about Rusty. For all I knew, the second doctor had told him he was even worse off than he'd thought.

I took out a leftover bacon, chicken, and cheese casserole from the fridge. Cooking was one of my favorite pastimes, and I usually made stuff ahead of time so I'd have a good meal ready for when I got home. With my dinner settled in the microwave, I finally forced myself to read the article.

Turned out it wasn't much more than a brief news alert. One of those "breaking news" and "this story will be updated" kind of deal. I wished I had clicked on it sooner and saved myself a lot of stress over nothing. I also felt guilty, because a small part of me had hoped Rusty might mention me by name. Maybe he would thank me again for saving his life. Better yet, perhaps he might have mentioned how I'd stayed with him at the hospital.

I knew that was silly, though. Our visit had been deeply personal. Not because it was with me, but because it was the lowest spot of his life. Why would he want to talk about that, especially with the media?

The microwave dinged, and I retrieved my dinner. I didn't have the attention span to read a book while I ate dinner like usual, so I took my meal into the living room where I could watch some mindless sitcom and not have to think. Or feel.

With my stomach full and my mind emptier, I finally began to relax a little. Until I switched over to the local news. I gasped out loud when I saw Rusty's face on the screen. It was just so unexpected. His mouth was moving, but the idiot news anchor was talking over him. They were teasing the upcoming segment with him after the break.

The commercial interruption felt like an eternity, and at last the news came back with Rusty. He was in his street clothes, and I realized he couldn't have known on that fateful Sunday that it would be the last time he put on a Bay Birds uniform. The anchor briefly explained Rusty's heart problem and why it meant the end of his career. Then they cut back to Rusty himself.

"It's tough," Rusty said with a sigh on my TV screen. "Retiring is the last thing I wanted to do, but some things in life you don't have any control over."

His eyes had a haunted look that I'd never seen in him before. Rusty Power had always been known for his cheerful, bright personality. The type who was quick with a joke and a smile. It hurt to look at him. The most painful part was the sheer hopelessness on his face. There would be no more second opinions. No chance of waking up from this nightmare.

Rusty said a few more words about how sad he was to leave the Bay Birds organization, but that was all.

So that's that, I guess.

The end of Rusty Power in my life. I wouldn't even have the fantasy version of him anymore. I'd started out with a girlish celebrity crush on him. The kind that made your stomach tingle when you saw the object of your fantasy. In the hospital, he had become real to me. A real person in real pain. Now, he would be gone from my life forever.

It made me sad to think I'd probably never find out what he ended up doing with his life after baseball. Unless he did something in the public eye, he would fade from view. No more news updates on how he was. All I could do from now on was wish him well and keep him and his family in my prayers.

MY FIRST TRIP back to Old Bay Stadium was bittersweet. Since it was a Friday evening game, I went straight from work, so I missed batting practice. That was just as well, I supposed. It might have triggered memories of what happened last time and been upsetting to watch.

At least I had Wilder at the game with me tonight. The Bay Birds had given us quite an upgrade; now our seats were up close to the action on the third base side.

As we stood for the national anthem, a warm breeze gently caressed my face. Drawing in a deep breath, I smelled the hot dogs and popcorn, and I could feel the energy of the people around me. An evening at the ballpark was exactly what I needed right now. This was my happy place. Win or lose, I loved the Baltimore Bay Birds. I loved everything about baseball, and I was glad to be here.

The game got underway, and we settled in with our beers and food.

"These seats are amazing," Wilder said, taking in the view.

"I know," I said excitedly. "I can't believe I get to sit here. Normally I only get this close to the field when I sneak down here toward the end of the game when the ushers don't crack down much on people wandering in from the cheap seats."

"Well, you earned these seats and then some," she said.

"I guess."

By the fourth inning, the Birds were up 4-0 and life was good. They usually featured some cool stuff on the Jumbotron featuring the players between innings. Sometimes they showed the guys out in the community doing things for the Bay Bird Foundation, which was the official charity fund for the team. I loved that, and I also enjoyed the sports bloopers and the funny quotes from the players.

Tonight, they featured a clip from Rusty Power.

My heart caught in my throat when I saw those big blue eyes up on the screen. He still looked sad, but not quite as traumatized as he'd seemed on the news the other night. I stared at the huge screen as I watched Rusty's recorded statement. His official goodbye.

"It has been the honor of a lifetime, not only to make it to the majors, but to play for the Baltimore Bay Birds. As a kid in West Virginia, I grew up watching the team. There's nobody else I'd rather have played for. So I just wanna thank my incredible teammates and all the awesome fans for their support. My run here was way too short, but believe me, I treasured every minute."

I heard the catch in Rusty's voice as he spoke, and it broke my heart.

With that, he signed off the video by tipping his Bay Birds cap and looking directly into the camera and at us, the fans, saying, "Thanks, guys."

Thunderous applause erupted in the stadium, giving Rusty one last cheer. I cried, of course. I often teared up over stories about strangers on the news and even over particularly touching television commercials. But this was different. I knew Rusty. Not that well, but I knew him.

Wilder put her arm around me, wordlessly lending her support.

The Jumbotron showed a brief shot of the players applauding too, solemn expressions on their faces. This must have been hard on them, too. They'd lost a good teammate, and it had to be jarring for them to realize that any one of them could suffer a career-ending event at any time.

Gazing around the ballpark, I saw thousands of well-wishers showing their support for a man that most of them had never met. Baltimore Bay Bird fans had the reputation of being the best fans in all of Major League Baseball, and I was proud to be a part of that.

"You okay?" Wilder asked as we settled back in our seats.

"Yeah," I said, still sniffling. I grabbed a tissue from my pocket and tried to compose myself.

Some guy in a seat right in front of us turned around and shot me a strange look. He must have thought I was some kind of nut, crying over one of the players.

Wilder noticed, and her eyes narrowed.

"Dude," she said harshly, making sure to meet his eye. "She happens to be the one who saved Rusty Power's life."

"No shit?" the guy said, his eyes opening wide.

Then every fan within earshot turned to look at me, making me feel both proud and uncomfortable at the same time. It reminded me of the way the fans had reacted that day Julia had helped me to my seat.

"Yeah," Wilder continued. "She knows him personally; that's why she's so upset."

"Oh. Sorry," the guy mumbled, sounding suitably apologetic.

The game got underway again and thankfully people turned their attention back to the field.

"I wish Rusty could have been here to see all the support he's getting from the fans," I said quietly.

"I'm sure he knows how loved he is by everybody," Wilder said with a smile.

"I hope so," I said. "I really do."

10

RUSTY

I'd been stuck in my apartment ever since my forced retirement from baseball a couple of weeks ago, and I was slowly going out of my mind. I had no idea what to do with myself and with the endless time I now had on my hands. The baseball season was hectic and could be grueling at times, but I never minded. With 162 games per season, there were very few days off. I hadn't had any weekends free in the spring or summer. Fridays, Saturdays, and Sundays always had a game going. Sometimes more than one per day if we had to make up for rainouts.

Even when I was at home, my every minute had been consumed with baseball. Watching sports highlights, studying up for the day's matchup, or just puttering around the apartment until it was finally time to go to the ballpark.

And now, there was nothing.

Only silence in my head and my heart, with absolutely nothing to fill the void.

I tried to be grateful for what I did have. After all, for most people, getting forced out of their jobs could mean losing their home, their car, their very security. That wasn't going to happen to me. I could afford to stay in my nice, fancy apartment. I could keep the blue Corvette I'd recently purchased, having waited to trade in my old Honda Civic until I'd made it to my second year in the majors.

Times like this, I wondered if it would have been better if I'd never made it to the show. If I'd never made it out of the minors, I wouldn't have had my dream cruelly taken from me so suddenly.

I was a washed up has-been in my twenties. Baseball had been the center of my universe for as long as I could remember. It was my identity.

Now I was just a guy who used to play baseball.

I sat on my couch, staring at the television but not really paying attention. I'd tried watching ESPN, but it hurt too damn much. I still checked the Bay Birds scores on a daily basis because I wanted to know how the team was doing, but that was about as much as I could handle.

It was tough not being around my friends every day. Before making my retirement public, I'd met up privately with the guys in the locker room to break the news. Worst conversation of my life. Everybody was incredibly supportive, of course. But I'd never forget the looks on their faces. Shock, pity, horror. What had happened to me was every player's nightmare.

Brady had looked particularly stunned. He was so much like me, the way he ate, drank, and breathed baseball. More than anyone, he understood my pain.

I would never forget the sorrow in his eyes when he said simply, "Dude, I'm so sorry."

Brady texted me all the time, and I always thanked him and told him I was fine. I told everybody I was fine. Especially my family. My mother was worried sick about me, so I was sure to put on my best cheery act when she called me. And she called a *lot*.

My older sisters, Olivia and Zoey, checked on me frequently too. It helped to know my family had my back, but I didn't want to be a burden on them. They both had their hands full raising their children. I'd always loved being cool Uncle Rusty to those kids, and I'd been excited for when they were old enough to brag to their friends about their uncle playing pro baseball.

Just one of so many things that would never happen now. Every day brought fresh realizations of how much I'd lost.

Amanda had been right—I needed time to grieve this loss, because it really did feel like someone had died suddenly. Most days I still woke up thinking things were normal. And then I would remember and grieve all over again.

Sighing bitterly, I jumped up from the couch. I couldn't stand sitting still anymore, but getting up that quickly sent a jolt of searing pain through my cracked ribs. I roared out loud in frustration to no one and stalked over to my huge windows to stare aimlessly at the city below, where people were going about their daily business.

Times like this, I genuinely felt as if I was losing my mind. I was never one who could sit still. Being sick with a simple head cold always drove me crazy because I couldn't be active and do all the things I wanted to do. Hanging around the apartment all the time was killing me. My doctors had said that regular physical activity was fine—beneficial, even—so long as I didn't overdo it. But I couldn't work out until my ribs had healed more. I'd tried soaking in the indoor pool in my apartment complex, but it had felt too weird being down there alone during the day. Everybody else was at work or school or whatever.

The world had gone on without me.

Staring down at the street below, my thoughts turned to Amanda. I thought of her a lot these days. I'd never forget the way she kept me calm that day. She hadn't said anything to minimize my pain; she'd simply listened without judgment and without flipping out.

I needed a friend like her to talk to.

Brady and the other guys had my back, for sure. Their loyalty and friendship hadn't ended with my career, but they were busy. Hell, the team was in New York right now, so I couldn't hang out with them even if I wanted to.

What I wanted was to see Amanda again. I wanted to gaze into her sweet brown eyes and have her tell me that somehow, some way, everything would be okay.

I fished my cell phone out of my pocket and found the phone number for her that my agent had given me.

11

AMANDA

Hey, how's it going?

I rolled my eyes when I saw the text from an unfamiliar number. At best, it was a wrong number. At worst, it was some creep texting rando digits. Since I have all my friends' and family members' names and numbers saved in my phone, I almost didn't reply. Then guilt got the best of me when I considered that if it was a wrong number, the person who texted might think their friend was ignoring their message.

I placed the bookmark in my book in case it accidentally snapped shut and lost my place. I'd just finished eating dinner, and I was reading at my kitchen counter.

Sorry, who is this? I answered, hoping the person would realize their mistake, apologize, and then move on.

It's Rusty.

No way. There was no way in hell it was actually Rusty Power texting me. Was there?

It could be one of my friends playing a joke.

Except that would not be funny, and none of my friends were mean like that.

Staring at my phone, I knew I had to answer back. But I had no idea what to say, especially if I couldn't be sure who I was talking to. My name had been on the news, after all. Maybe some weird Bay Birds fan had gotten ahold of my number.

Is it really you? How can I be sure?

A few seconds later, my phone dinged. He had texted me a selfie of him with a goofy grin on his face, holding up a peace sign.

Holy God, it was really him.

I was glad he was texting instead of calling; I could freak out all I wanted and not sound like an idiot. I had time to think of what to say.

How are you doing?

A boring, safe way to respond. I couldn't imagine why he was getting in touch with me. Maybe he thought I would no longer want the Rusty Power baseball jersey I'd requested, and he wanted to ask what else he could get me as a substitute.

I stared at the phone, breathlessly waiting for a response. Though I thought of him often, always wondering how he was doing, I never dreamed I would hear from him again.

My phone dinged again. *I'm hanging in there, I guess.*

Still holding my breath, I waited for him to continue.

Then he texted *How are you?*

My nerves were on edge; there were a thousand questions I wanted to ask him. I felt as anxious and jittery as I was the first time we had officially met in the hospital.

The hospital.

As my thoughts drifted back to the last time I'd seen him, my nervousness eased a bit. We'd sat and talked for over an hour while I did my best to keep him calm. Just as I had that terrible day, I began to think of him less as an unbelievably hot celebrity and more as a person. A man who was going through a hard time.

I'm doing okay. I was at the game when they showed your message to the fans on the Jumbotron. It was beautiful. It made me cry.

My heart ached remembering it. I couldn't begin to imagine how hard it must have been for him to deliver that short but powerful speech. It was like he'd given a eulogy. A painful goodbye you don't want to ever have to say, but sometimes you have no choice.

That's very sweet, Amanda.

My heart fluttered in my chest when he texted my name. He was still typing.

This sucks.

Sighing, I answered, *I know it does.*

I would love to take you out to dinner. You know, as a thank you.

I gasped.

"Did Rusty Power just ask me out?" I yelled out loud.

Then I panicked, terrified that I'd somehow turned on the text-to-speech feature and it had sent my words directly to Rusty.

It hadn't, thank God.

Inhaling deeply, I knew I had to get a grip on reality. He hadn't asked me out on a date, exactly. He just wanted to take me out to thank me for saving his life.

Right?

Was this a date?

I honestly had no idea what Rusty's intentions were. I wasn't sure how long I spent obsessing over his last message, but after a while he started typing again.

Fresh panic surged through me. I didn't want to give him a chance to take back his offer.

That would be great, I typed back as quickly as I could.

Awesome. Friday night?

I drew in another sharp breath. Friday was definitely a date night. It wasn't as if he'd asked me out for lunch on a Wednesday. My whole body quaked with nervous anticipation.

Works for me.

I can pick you up at your place.

I was about to respond, but then he texted *Unless you're more comfortable meeting in a public place.*

I sighed dreamily. Rusty was so sweet. But I trusted him completely, and I wanted him to pick me up.

No, it's fine to come get me if you don't mind.

I sent him my address and we settled on 6:30pm.

It's really nice of you to take me out.

Oh please. It's LITERALLY the least I can do after all you've done for me! Rusty texted with a smiley face emoji.

Okay, that sounded like this was a thank you dinner, and not a date dinner.

See you Friday! he texted.

After pacing my apartment for five full minutes to make sure Rusty was done texting for now, I picked up the phone and called Wilder.

"You will not *believe* what just happened!" I said the moment she answered my call.

"I CANNOT BELIEVE you have a date with Rusty Power," Wilder said Friday evening as she fluffed up my hair. She'd come over to my place right after work to help me get ready and to keep me calm. I stared at myself in the full-length mirror in my bedroom.

"I'm still not sure if this is a date," I said.

"Read the texts to me again."

"Wilder. We've read the texts a thousand times. There's no hidden messages in there. No clues as to what this really is." I sighed. "There's no way Rusty actually wants to date me."

Naturally, I'd been obsessing over this ever since the moment he'd asked me out to dinner. I'd constantly pinged between euphoric hope and deep despair over what Rusty truly meant by asking me out.

"Amanda," Wilder said firmly. "Why wouldn't he want to date you?"

"Because guys like him don't go for girls like me," I said quietly.

Wilder gazed at me with concern and understanding, the way only a true best friend could. She knew my heart. She knew my insecurities, and she'd seen firsthand how painful it was for me to get passed over time and time again when she was around.

"Of course he could go for a girl like you," she said with confidence, making sure to look me in the eye. "You're incredible, and he obviously knows that. If he just wanted to reward you for saving his life, he would have, you know, had his 'people' do that. But Rusty asked to see you."

"I guess," I said, losing more confidence every minute. I could accept that I was no great beauty, and for the most part, I was okay with being ordinary. But tonight, with Rusty, I wanted to feel better than ordinary.

"Look, I can't tell whether Rusty meant for this to be a romantic thing or what," Wilder said. "But what I do know is that he wanted to see you again, and that's pretty damn cool, right? You don't ask somebody out to dinner if you don't want to spend more time with them."

Wilder had a point. If all you wanted was a quick meeting, you'd ask somebody to just meet for coffee or something. Rusty had asked me out for a whole meal.

"True," I conceded. "If nothing else, maybe he wants to be friends. I could live with that."

"Amanda," Wilder said, looking me up and down. "You look so beautiful. You don't even know."

Her words were so kind and so heartfelt that my eyes welled up. Wilder knew what I needed to hear, and I was so grateful to have a dear friend like her in my life.

"Don't cry," she said with a laugh. "You'll smudge your makeup."

I took another look at myself in the mirror. My makeup did make my brown eyes look prettier, and I felt reasonably attractive in my jeans and delicate white blouse. My brown hair had a soft, natural wave to it. I'd always liked that about my hair. For better or worse, this was me. I tried not to focus on the tall blond bombshell next to me.

"I told him my apartment was a mess and that I would just meet him outside when he got here."

Wilder nodded.

"If Rusty came up here now and saw you, he'd forget all about me."

"That is *not* true," Wilder insisted. "But you don't need a third wheel on your date. Or, you know, whatever this is."

"I'm scared."

"I know you are," she said. "But you're gonna be fine."

My phone buzzed and I gasped. It was Rusty saying he was here.

"You're going to be *fine*," Wilder said with a smile.

I nodded, though I wasn't so sure.

~

Seeing Rusty Power behind the wheel of a dark blue Corvette in front of my humble apartment building was positively surreal.

How was this actually my life right now?

I swallowed hard as I watched him get out of his car. He smiled at me in a way that made his beautiful eyes sparkle. My legs felt weak and my whole body trembled. Why was I so scared? The last time we'd been together, we'd talked for over an hour, and I was hardly nervous at all.

Rusty looked huge standing next to his car.

"I forgot how tall you are," I blurted out like an idiot.

He laughed. "Yeah, well, I think this is the first time you've seen me standing up. At least in person and not on TV."

"You're right."

I stood there, frozen for a moment. Then he nodded his head toward the car, reminding me to move.

Once again, I felt like an idiot. And yet, his gentle expression told me he understood that I was nervous and he didn't judge me for it.

Rusty opened the passenger door for me, and I suppressed a dreamy sigh. Even if this wasn't a real date, nothing could stop me from pretending it was. But for the fantasy to work, I had to stop being such a wreck around him.

He waited until I had my seatbelt secured before starting the engine.

"I was thinking Phillip's by the water. You like seafood?"

"I'm from Baltimore, aren't I?"

Rusty laughed. "Good girl."

We drove in silence for a minute or two. When we stopped at a red light, he turned to look at me.

"Amanda."

"What?" I said, still having a hard time believing any of this was actually happening.

"You don't have to be nervous around me, okay?"

I swallowed. "Sorry."

"Don't be sorry," he said with a grin. Facing front when the light was green, he added, "Besides, it's not like I'm even a famous ballplayer anymore."

The pain in his voice made my chest ache. I wanted to say something, anything to make him feel better.

"Of course you are," I said, my voice no longer timid. "You'll always be known for playing for the Baltimore Bay Birds. You made it all the way to the majors, and nobody can ever take that away from you."

"That's true," he said, sounding slightly less depressed.

As I had in the hospital, I started to relax around him again. Rusty was huge and attractive and somehow larger than life, and yet deep down he was a person like anyone else. It was in my nature to want to help whenever someone was in trouble, and Rusty was struggling.

We arrived in downtown Baltimore after a short drive and parked in a garage near the restaurant.

As we walked along the Harborplace waterfront, Rusty drew in a deep breath of fresh air. "The weather could not be more perfect tonight."

He tried to sound cheerful, but his words were tinged with sadness. I knew exactly what he must be thinking.

"I know you wish you were on the road with the Birds right now," I said softly.

Rusty briefly glanced at me as we walked, and I saw the

surprise on his face. "Yeah. I do." Then he added quickly, "Not that I don't want to be here with you! I mean, you're—"

"No. I understand," I said, laughing. "I just know it's the perfect night for baseball, and it must feel very strange not to be playing right now."

"It sure does," he said wearily.

We arrived at the restaurant to find a line that extended out the door.

"Ah, damn," Rusty said. "I didn't even think to make a reservation. Let me see how long the wait is."

Hungry as I was, I wouldn't have minded a long wait. Anything to draw out this date-that- might-not-actually-be-a-date experience. If it was just a one-off, I wanted it to last as long as possible.

He held the door for me and we made our way over to the hostess stand.

"How many?" the young woman asked.

"Two, please," Rusty said. "How long is the wait, do you think?"

"Let me see," she said, scanning her computer.

"Alexa!" called one of the waiters. He motioned the hostess over to him.

"So sorry, just gimme a quick minute," Alexa said as she went to see what the guy wanted.

Rusty chuckled as he watched the two of them.

"What's so funny?" I asked.

"I have a feeling a table is going to open up soon," he said, shaking his head.

He was right. After waiting just a few minutes, we were seated beside the waterfront.

Rusty grinned at me from across the table. "I guess I am still famous. For now, anyway."

I nodded, not exactly sure what to say to that. "This is

lovely," I said, gazing out at the gorgeous view of the Chesapeake Bay. I couldn't remember the last time I'd been to a nice restaurant with real tablecloths and wineglasses on the table.

Our server arrived in record time to take our drink order. Rusty ordered a beer, and I asked for a white wine.

We took some time to decide on what to order. While waiting for the server to return, Rusty said, "It's really nice to see you again."

"You too." I scrutinized his every move, still unable to figure out what his intentions were for this evening.

"I admit I had kind of an ulterior motive for asking you out tonight," he said.

My body tensed. "You did?" At last, maybe he would shed some light on exactly what we were doing here.

"Don't worry. It's nothing bad," he said with a smile.

"Okay ..." I said, breathlessly waiting for him to continue.

"I've just been going through a really hard time lately. All I know is that talking to you in the hospital made me feel so much better, and I guess I needed somebody to talk to."

Mother Goose strikes again.

Crushed didn't even begin to describe how I felt. Rusty simply needed a friend. Understandable, of course. But it hurt me to the core to know that he only thought of me as a buddy. A pal he could confide in. Worse, he probably thought of me like a sister or something.

If only I was beautiful like Wilder.

"Is that okay?" Rusty asked, looking alarmed. I realized I must have looked every bit as devastated as I felt.

"Of course it is, Rusty," I said softly, gazing intently into his eyes so he knew I was being sincere. And I was, to a degree. It hurt, but I still wanted to help. I hated seeing anyone in pain.

The waiter arrived to take our order, which gave me a moment to get ahold of myself.

This isn't a date. He wants to be friends. I can do that. I can hear him out and be there for him because that's what good friends do. Plenty of time to cry into my pillow later.

We both ordered crab cakes like the good Marylanders that we were. The server, whose name was Chip according to his name tag, clearly recognized Rusty. He paid extra attention to him; it was kind of cute and probably gave Rusty the boost of confidence he needed right now.

Chip walked away, stumbling a bit as he went. Rusty looked at me and sighed heavily.

"You okay?" I asked.

"I feel like an idiot."

Join the club.

"Why?" I gazed at those blue eyes that still affected me deeply, even here in the friend zone.

"Because you deserve to be taken out to a nice dinner—that, and a whole lot more—without me dumping my problems on you. I'm sorry, Amanda. You've done more than enough for me already."

"Rusty," I said, taking a risk and reaching across the table to squeeze his hand. "It's okay. Really. I want to help you if I can."

I let go of his hand and took a sip of my wine. It was impossible to pretend this was a date anymore, even sitting in a restaurant, sipping white wine while seated across from a devastatingly handsome man. We were just friends hanging out. That was all there was to it.

"Tell me what's going on," I said.

Rusty smiled, eyes sparkling, making my stomach quiver

again. My body, not to mention my heart, hadn't yet gotten the message that this was not a romantic thing.

"This is the first time I've been out, you know, since it happened," he began. "I've been going absolutely crazy at home. It was all so sudden."

I nodded, listening intently as he explained again that in his old life, everything he did revolved around baseball. From the time he woke up to when he headed over to the stadium, he was reading about baseball, watching it, or thinking about it. He'd already told me that at the hospital, but he was probably too distraught at the time to remember.

"It must have been so horrible, having the rug yanked out from under you like that," I said. Losing his career was even more painful for him than I could imagine. I'd never been as passionate about anything as he was about baseball.

"Yeah. I just … I never saw it coming. Amanda, I never could have gotten through that day at the hospital without you. For real, I would have completely flipped out."

"I'm glad I could help. I've thought about that a lot. Like maybe I was supposed to be there to help you."

"Really?"

"Yeah. I mean, who really knows? I just wonder sometimes if things happen for a reason. If that nurse hadn't forgotten to give me back my ID, I would have had no reason to be there. And if you hadn't been looking out into the hallway when I walked by …"

"Wow. That really is weird when you think about it," he said, shaking his head. "And my God, Amanda. If you hadn't been at the game that day …"

"I know," I said quickly, not wanting to think about what the outcome might have been.

Chip arrived with our crab cakes, and they smelled divine. He barely looked at me as he put mine on the table.

Though I understood completely that he was starstruck, between Rusty and Wilder, being ignored got old. Maybe I needed friends who were less dynamic and exciting.

On second thought, nah. I enjoyed being around people like them. Being second fiddle was a small price to pay for having wonderful people in my life.

"Oh my God, this is amazing," I said after my first bite. "Been a while since I had a really good crab cake. I always want to get one at Old Bay Stadium, but the lines are always so damn long."

Rusty nodded sadly, and my face flushed.

"I'm sorry. I didn't mean to bring up—"

"No, don't be sorry. You're allowed to talk about it," he said with a rueful laugh. "And it's not like you're reminding me of it. I can't forget it, no matter what I do. I have to accept that it's gonna hurt for a long, long time."

"Do you have any plans? Like for a job or whatever?"

Rusty swallowed a bite of crab cake and then shook his head. "No idea. Problem is, I can't imagine *wanting* to do anything else. As far back as I can remember, there was nothing before baseball. And I can't begin to imagine what comes after."

"It's perfectly fine to take your time to figure out what comes next. I guess you don't really have to worry about money?"

I said that last part carefully because I've always tried to avoid using the words "at least you have ..." Even if it was true. Rusty likely had tons of money and, for the most part, he had his health. Even so, pointing out the bright side was rarely helpful in times of crisis. Sometimes people simply needed to vent, and my job was to commiserate with them.

"Right. That is a huge plus. I'm good on that front, thank

God. But I sure as shit don't want to sit around all day and do nothing."

Glancing up at me from his food, he said, "Sorry. Language."

I laughed. "I'm not your mother. You're allowed to cuss around me."

Rusty laughed too. "Right, right."

"Your mom is adorable, by the way."

He smiled at the mention of his mother, and I wanted to swoon. Was there anything sexier than a hot guy who loved his mom?

"She's a sweetheart, all right. I'm sure I took ten years off her life with all my health struggles. Thank God almighty it didn't happen during a game. She could have watched me collapse on live TV." Rusty grimaced at the thought. "Even if she missed it, the video would have been all over the news."

I shuddered at the thought of my image featured in the news and sports shows everywhere. I might not like being ignored all the time, but I didn't want to be famous either.

"How about the rest of your family? Do you have brothers and sisters?" I already knew the answer, but he did *not* need to know the extent of my fan crush on him. Ever.

Rusty told me about his sisters, and I told him about mine. It felt like a date again and this was the getting-to-know-you portion. I figured I could go back to pretending, but that was the extent of it. I shouldn't get too carried away with a useless fantasy.

The check arrived all too soon. I couldn't bear to have the evening come to an end. Every time I saw Rusty, I'd thought it would be the last time. But who knew? Maybe we would become lifelong friends.

Or maybe he would figure out what to do with his life and he wouldn't need me anymore.

Chip was still a nervous wreck, nearly dropping the dinner check in Rusty's lap.

Rusty chuckled good-naturedly as he managed to grab the big leather check-holder wallet before it landed on his crotch. Chip blushed deeply. He opened his mouth, probably ready to apologize, but Rusty cut him off.

"You're a big baseball fan, aren't you?" Rusty asked with a grin.

Chip nodded vigorously.

"You know who I am, don't you?" Rusty spoke with friendly amusement in his voice. I got the impression that, even during the height of his fame, he never pulled that snooty "do you know who I am?" routine. Good thing, because I would not tolerate anybody who was nice to me but mean to a waiter.

"Y—yes, sir, I do."

I bit my lip to keep from laughing at the idea of anyone calling Rusty "sir." He was too sweet and laid back for such a thing.

"Would you like an autograph?"

"Yes please," he answered immediately.

"No problem," Rusty said with a warm smile. "You got a pen and napkin, or ..."

"Actually, I got a Bay Birds cap in the back. Would you mind terribly if I ran real quick and got it?" Chip asked, the words tumbling out of his mouth.

"Sure thing. I'm in no rush here. Take your time."

Please take your time. Go out and buy a cap for all I care. Just don't hurry back.

Watching Chip walk away, Rusty said, "I'll miss that. Not that I care so much about being famous, but I love being known for baseball, you know? I love that so much and it's such a part of who I am. Soon people will forget. I'll just be a guy who used to play baseball once upon a time."

All I could say was, "I'm sorry."

He gazed into my eyes.

In that moment, it didn't feel like he was looking at me like a sister.

Maybe it was my fantasy gone too far, but it felt like he was finally seeing me as a woman.

"Do you want to take a walk around the harbor a bit?" he asked. "Or do you need to get home, or ..."

"That sounds lovely," I said, a renewed surge of hope rushing through my system.

Rusty smiled and nodded.

"As soon as I take care of Chip ... and friends ..."

Following his gaze, I turned to see Chip, cap in hand, with a line of people behind him.

Laughing, I said, "Take your time, Rusty. I'm in no hurry."

12

AMANDA

I couldn't believe my outing—I still couldn't technically call it a date—was still going on. Rusty must have been enjoying my company, otherwise he never would have suggested a walk after dinner. My whole life I'd been told I was a good listener. Comforting. A loyal friend. The type you always knew you could go to with a problem. Most likely, that was why Rusty wanted to stay with me longer. I made him feel better.

And that was okay with me, I guess.

I'd felt so helpless since he'd gotten his devastating diagnosis, and it was a relief to be able to comfort him.

After chatting with Chip and several of his coworkers, Rusty paid the bill, and we headed outside. He seemed in better spirits now, his mood boosted by talking baseball with those fans.

"Thanks for dinner," I said as we walked side by side along the water. "Been a long time since I've had a crab cake that good."

"You're very welcome," he said, blue eyes sparkling with his smile. "You've been terrific company."

A gentle, cool breeze drifted in from across the water, cutting through the heat and making for a pleasant evening. Despite the beautiful weather, there weren't a lot of people out tonight by the harbor. Just a smattering of joggers, some families, and some people walking their dogs.

"Such a shame about this place," I said. "When I was little, we came here all the time. Back when there used to be so many shops and restaurants around."

"I know," Rusty said, shaking his head. "I used to visit here too, with my parents and sisters. We'd come here for dinner after a Bay Birds day game. I remember street performers and people selling souvenirs on the sidewalk, and you could smell all kinds of different foods all over. There's barely anything left anymore."

We walked in silence for a few minutes, but it was a comfortable quiet. I had the urge to reach over and hold his hand. I would never do that, of course. We were just friends. Still, it would have felt natural. At least to me.

An older man walking his adorable golden retriever came near us, and the dog strained on his leash, wanting to play.

"Is it okay to pet him?" I asked the guy.

"Sure," the man said with a smile. "Chase is friendly. Loves people."

Crouching down, I eagerly petted the sweet baby, scritching behind his fuzzy ears. "Hello, Chase. Hello, my little friend. Awww, you do love people, don't you? You good boy."

The dog wagged his tail happily, and I heard Rusty chuckling behind me.

I didn't want to keep the man waiting, so I reluctantly stood. I could have played with Chase all day.

Apparently, Chase still wanted to play, because he

jumped up on Rusty. He barely flinched. I was sure it hurt, though, because the dog's paws landed on his ribs.

"No, Chase. Don't jump on people," his owner said, tugging on the leash.

Rusty laughed. "No harm done. Is there boy? No. You're a good boy, aren't you?"

Crouching down, Rusty played with the dog as enthusiastically as I had.

The man loves animals and *his mother. Why did he have to be so perfect?*

"Thanks, man," Rusty said to Chase's owner when he stood up. "Have a good one."

"You too," the man said with a friendly wave.

"Oh, I love dogs so much," I said as we continued our walk.

"Me too. Do you have a dog?"

"Ugh, I wish. I can't have pets in the apartment building where I live."

"I have the same problem. I got an apartment in Baltimore." He paused for a moment, and that look of sorrow briefly returned. "My family's from West Virginia, which isn't too far away. I guess now I have to figure out where I want to live permanently. I always planned to settle down and buy a house someday. Then I'd get *two* dogs."

"That sounds wonderful. I'd like to do the same. Once I can buy a home. I'm saving up for a down payment on a house. That's why I live in such a tiny place."

"Where did you say you work again?"

"At the University of Timonium."

"Hmm. What exactly do you do there? Sorry, I know you told me before, but I can't remember what you said."

I didn't blame him for forgetting. He'd been preoccupied

that day, and it wasn't like my job was particularly memorable.

"I'm just the assistant to the director of human resources." Yuck. That sounded so unimpressive when I said it out loud. "The director is leaving soon, though, and I'm really hoping to get promoted to her job. Right now, I prepare all the forms and make appointments and stuff like that, but she gets to do the real work. Like interviewing people, helping current employees understand their health benefits, and dealing with conflicts. I'd love to be the one doing all of that."

"Interesting," he said kindly, though I highly doubted he meant it. It was interesting to me, but I didn't think it was to anybody else.

"I like the idea of being able to help people," I said, feeling as if I had to defend my job. "I know how nervous people get when they're at an interview or it's their first day on the job. And I also know that sometimes you can't get a straight answer from HR about your health or dental plan or your vacation days or whatever. I want to try to make things run smoothly and make everyone's job easier on everybody. Do my part to make the workplace as positive as it can be."

Rusty glanced over and grinned at me. "I love that."

My stomach quivered when he looked at me that way. And it had sounded like he'd meant it.

"Working at a college must be cool."

"It is. Sometimes I get to interact with the students, especially if they're interning in one of the academic departments. I just wish I could be more hands-on when it comes to my work."

"Well, I hope you get the promotion."

"Thanks."

We continued on our pleasant walk, stopping to meet and greet every single dog we encountered. After a while, the sky began to darken.

"Getting late, so I guess we'd better head back," I said.

Rusty stopped walking, so I did the same. His eyes met mine. "Tonight was really nice, Amanda. It's the first time I've felt even halfway normal since I left the hospital. And I have you to thank for that."

"I'm glad I was able to help you feel better," I said, unable to tear my gaze away from him. Even here in the dreaded friend zone, I found myself caring more for Rusty by the minute. Being here with him felt so right, as if we belonged together.

I had to stop thinking that way. It would only make it more painful when he dropped me off at the end of the night with a peck on the cheek. Or worse, a handshake. My romantic fantasies about him were no more realistic now than they had been when I'd admired him from the stands at Old Bay Stadium. Sure, now I knew him personally, but he was still way out of my league.

Rusty surprised me by putting a hand on my back for a moment as we walked toward the car. Such a sweet gesture, but I knew I shouldn't read too much into it. Most likely, it was a protective measure to make me feel safer in downtown Baltimore at night.

On the drive home, Rusty flipped on the radio. The sound came blasting out, making me scream and then laugh.

"Sorry!" Rusty said over the noise. He quickly turned the sound down.

"Rocking out the last time you were in the car, were you?"

He laughed. "Yeah."

"What kind of music do you like? Other than just loud music?"

"I like all kinds, but specifically alternative, metal, grunge—that type of deal. Pumps me up when I'm working out or just before a game."

His face fell, and I realized that he was still truly grieving. Just like when somebody you loved died suddenly, and there were a million daily reminders of everything you'd lost.

"In theory, I can still work out as long as it's not too strenuous," he said. "But I can't right now because *somebody* cracked two of my ribs."

I moaned loudly.

He chuckled and winked at me. "I'm only teasin' ya."

"Does it still hurt a lot?"

"I can handle it." he said in an exaggerated, manly voice.

"Oh, I'm sure you can, tough guy."

"Any radio station requests?"

"98 Rock is good," I said.

"Done."

We chatted comfortably on the way back to my apartment, and I loved how easily the conversation between us flowed. I was beginning to hope that our friendship would last. But only time would tell.

Rusty pulled into a parking spot in the lot of my building. I unbuckled my seat belt and turned to face him.

"I had a wonderful time with you tonight," he said in a gentle voice.

"Me too. This was so lovely."

Rusty nodded, gazing intently into my eyes. Before I even knew what was happening, he tenderly stroked my cheek and then leaned in and kissed me.

Shocked didn't even begin to describe how I felt.

Turned out I was very, very wrong about his intentions.

Recovering from my surprise, I eagerly responded, wrapping my arms around him. Moaning softly, I happily got lost in his passionate kiss.

When we finally broke apart, Rusty stroked my cheek again.

"I'd really love to see you again."

Breathlessly, I managed to say, "That could be arranged."

"I'll call you, okay?"

His words sounded so hopeful; I could hardly believe they were directed at me.

I nodded and got out of the car. Rusty waited until I was safely inside before he drove away.

Hands trembling, I texted Wilder immediately.

It was definitely a date.

13

RUSTY

I drove home on autopilot, lost in my thoughts of Amanda and my suddenly surging emotions, not to mention my libido.

I'd kissed my share of women over the years, but I'd never had a kiss like that. The evening had started out with me wanting to hang out with a friend, but it had ended with me desiring Amanda Miller more than I'd ever wanted any woman in my life.

From the beginning, I thought of Amanda as cute. At our first meeting—if you didn't count when she'd saved my life, considering I'd been barely conscious at the time—I thought she was adorable. For our second visit, Amanda had kept me calm and had provided much-needed support, but it had been hard to focus on anything else but my pain.

Tonight had been different. Different from our first meetings, and miles away from what I had expected when I first asked her out to dinner. I felt like I had connected with Amanda on a deeper level than I had with anyone else.

When I went on a date, I normally talked about my

exciting life in baseball. The places I'd traveled, athletic feats I'd accomplished, and the celebrities I'd met along the way. In the blink of an eye, my old life had completely vanished. Everything had been stripped away and all that was left was just ... me. I hardly knew who I was anymore without baseball, and yet with Amanda, I felt like I was still *somebody*. Like maybe there was something left of me after all.

Nobody had ever listened to me the way she did. All evening I got lost in her pretty brown eyes, so filled with concern for me. For a while there I'd been a little worried that she just had a special attachment to me because she'd saved my life. After all, she'd only seen me at my absolute worst. I'd been a hot mess all around. I'd worried that she thought of me as some pathetic lost puppy in need of rescuing.

And then I'd kissed her.

Amanda had kissed me back with passion and heat. I knew I hadn't imagined the spark between us.

When my sister Olivia had first met the man who is now her husband, I laughed at her when she insisted she had found "her person."

But I got it now.

Amanda somehow looked past all my pain and everything I used to be, and she still seemed genuinely fond of me. Being with her felt natural, as if we were truly meant to be together. It was all so weird, but in a good way. I wasn't the type to go for one-night stands, but I hadn't been in a lot of steady relationships either. I had thought I'd been serious about Emily Martindale, but in all the time we were dating, I hadn't felt about her the way I already felt about Amanda.

Tonight we'd had a lot to talk about because of everything that had happened to me recently, and it felt cathartic talking to her about what I was going through, especially since I'd been trying hard to keep up a brave front around my family. The problem was, what else could we talk about besides baseball? I felt like I didn't know anything else. My whole identity was wrapped up in being a successful athlete. What the hell would she see in me if I didn't have that?

I arrived at my apartment, barely remembering driving there. As nice as my place was, lately it had felt like a prison. I'd been lonely, with no ambition, going crazy with nothing to do. But now, for the first time since my baseball career ended, I wasn't feeling depressed.

No, it was more than that. I actually felt *happy*. For whatever reason, Amanda seemed really into me. At least for now she was.

I could still taste her on my lips, and the idea of seeing her again thrilled me. I'd never met anyone as sweet and caring as Amanda, and the way she'd doted on every dog in sight warmed my heart.

And I couldn't get over the way that girl *looked* at me. Like she cared deeply for me and was wildly attracted to me at the same time. Sure, I'd had women lust after me before, but I feared that might never happen again since I was no longer a Major League Baseball player.

But Amanda didn't seem to care about that. She still cared about *me*.

Later, when I settled into bed, my head was filled with fantasies of Amanda. Those brown eyes, petite body, and beautiful smile. I imagined having sex with her, visualizing what her face would look like as I made her come. For the first time since my heart scare, I jerked off vigorously due to attraction and excitement rather than boredom and loneliness.

I fell asleep soon after I came, feeling more relaxed and at peace than I had in a long time.

14

———————

AMANDA

When Rusty had first asked me to dinner, I'd been riddled with confusion and uncertainty. Then he'd silenced all my fears when he kissed me.

And it wasn't only *that* he kissed me. It was *how* he kissed me. His touch had made me feel like I was the only woman in the world.

Rusty had said he would call me, and I knew he would. I just *knew* it. Strange how I'd gone from feeling so insecure about us to having a sudden, deep-seated knowledge that there was something strong and real between the two of us.

He did call me the morning after our date, at about 11am.

"Is it pathetic that I'm calling you already?" was the first thing he said when I answered.

I laughed. "Of course not."

"I hope I didn't wake you. I wasn't sure how late you slept in."

"Not very. I'm so used to getting up early for work that I can't sleep in much, even when I try."

"Whatcha doin'?"

"Making lasagna."

"Damn, you fancy for Saturday lunch."

I laughed again, trying to balance my cell phone while I stirred up the meat and cheese mixture. "It's not for right now. I like to cook stuff on the weekends and freeze it so I'll have food for later in the week. After work, I'm usually too tired to cook."

"Makes sense," he said.

"What are you doing?"

"Puttering."

"Puttering? What does that mean?"

"It means I'm wandering around the apartment aimlessly, feeling sorry for myself. Which I do way too much of these days. I know I need to do something with my time ... and with the rest of my life. I just don't know what yet."

"I get that," I told him.

"Amanda?"

"Yes?"

"Would you like to go out again tonight? And I promise I'm not *only* asking because I'm bored stupid. I really would like to see you again."

I closed my eyes, still hardly believing that this was my life right now. When I opened them, I was still on the phone with the man of my dreams. Yep. This was real.

"I would love that."

"Do you like Italian food?" Then he laughed and said, "Well, duh. You're making lasagna. Which means you'll be eating Italian food all week."

"Correct."

"Okay, forget Italian for tonight. Where do you want to go for dinner?"

"I don't know. Where do you want to go?"

"I picked last night."

I smiled at the way we already sounded like a couple. "Okay, fair. Do you like steak?"

"Hell yeah, I like steak. Do you?"

"Yeah. I like steak and steak houses in general because they always have all kinds of good food. Even chicken at a steak house is usually really good if that makes sense."

"Yes, it does," he said, and I could practically hear the smile in his voice. "I like a girl with a good appetite."

"Then you'll love me. I do like food."

"But you're so tiny. How do you do it?"

"Well," I said as I wrapped up the lasagna in tin foil. "The truth is I'm the type who can eat pretty much anything I want and not gain any weight."

"Wow, lucky you."

"You would think that, wouldn't you?"

I put the lasagna in the freezer and then wandered into the living room to flop down on the couch. The dirty dishes could wait.

"Uh ... yeah?"

"I know I shouldn't complain, and I know I am lucky in that regard. It's just, I don't have *any* curves."

"Oh, you have curves, Amanda," Rusty said. Again, I could tell he was grinning, and his lusty voice filled me with warmth.

"You're sweet to say that, but really, I don't. I have such a boy's body. It's funny—everybody knows it's rude and hurtful to comment about somebody who's overweight, but people have *no* problem commenting on people with super skinny bodies. I couldn't gain weight if I tried. It's not as if I have control over it. Like seriously, jokes about anorexia are not funny. Not only is it a serious illness, but saying that somebody looks anorexic is not a compliment. It means you look frail and thin. Like, the opposite of womanly."

"I think you're very womanly, Amanda Miller," he said, the heat still in his voice. "But I get what you're saying. I never thought about it like that before."

I smiled listening to him speak. I'd bottled up my feelings about all those insensitive skinny-girl comments for so long, but something about Rusty made me feel like I could tell him anything and he would understand. And he did.

"So steak joint tonight it is," he said. "Pick you up around five?"

"Sounds wonderful."

RUSTY ARRIVED RIGHT ON TIME. I came out to meet him when I saw his Corvette pull up.

"Still won't let me see your place, huh?" he said when I slid into the passenger seat beside him.

"Oh. Honestly? I didn't even think about it. Just came out when I saw your car. You can come see it sometime if you want. Believe me, there's not much to see."

"I look forward to it," he said with a sexy grin that warmed my body all over.

I could hardly believe I was going on a date with this incredible man, let alone imagine how it would feel to have him make love to me.

Okay, I *could* imagine. I *had* imagined. Frequently. And from the look on Rusty's face, he'd imagined it too.

We had a pleasant drive to a restaurant in downtown Baltimore. Far more relaxed than I'd been at the start of last night's date, I found being with Rusty was a lot of fun. We listened to the radio, including some of his noisy grunge music. It wasn't too terrible, especially at a reasonable volume.

During the ride, I confessed that I enjoyed showtunes in addition to rock music. Rather than make fun of me, Rusty found a Broadway channel that was part of his radio subscription plan. I warned him about my terrible singing voice, but I felt brave enough to sing along when one of my favorite songs came on. He grinned at me, like he thought it was cute when I sang. I couldn't get over how comfortable I was with him already. We fell into an easy rhythm, as if we'd been dating for months.

Dinner at the steak joint was delightful. The food and conversation were wonderful, and we gazed into each other's eyes a lot during the meal. Though I'd always been attracted to the fantasy baseball celebrity version of Rusty Power, the real person was much better. He was a good man with a good heart, and I simply adored him.

Unlike near the restaurant at the harbor, there was no good place to take a long walk. Besides, it was starting to drizzle as we headed back toward the car.

"Do you want to come back and see my place?" Rusty asked as I buckled my seatbelt.

I turned to look at him, considering.

"Seriously, no pressure or, you know, expectations of any kind," he said. "Just thought you might like to see where I live."

"Sure. That would be nice," I said with a smile. I'd never been one to jump into a physical relationship with a man, and I wasn't about to with Rusty either, no matter how tempted I might be. I appreciated his taking things slow, because I wasn't eager to have this lovely evening come to an end just yet.

Even a simple car ride was fun when I was with Rusty. We enjoyed each other's company tremendously.

"Wow, you have valet service here?" I asked when we pulled up outside of Rusty's apartment building.

"Yup," he said with a smile.

I didn't know why I was surprised. I'd known that Rusty was extremely wealthy. It was just such a different experience than I was used to. I was pleased to see how the valet greeted him by his first name rather than Mr. Power. As usual, there was no arrogance; Rusty treated everybody with kindness.

"Wow," I said when we entered the lobby. It was much larger than I'd expected. The Harbor View gave off a fancy hotel vibe. "I can't believe you actually live here."

"You know this is just the lobby, right?" Rusty said, elbowing me playfully. "I don't actually live right *here*."

"Yes, dear. I realize that. But still ..." I looked around in amazement.

"Here, I'll show you around real quick," Rusty said, taking my hand and leading me toward some closed doors to the right of the front desk. "These are the banquet rooms."

He opened one of the doors to reveal a fancy party room that was suitable for weddings and other fancy events.

"Beautiful," I said, scanning the room. There were several chandeliers and a huge bank of windows.

"And one floor up we have the Aquatics Center."

"What is an Aquatics Center?"

"Pretty much just a fancy term for the indoor pool and stuff."

"You have an indoor pool in this place?" I asked, eyes wide.

"And we have a health club. You know, an exercise room and all that."

"Wow," I said again. "This place is incredible."

"Yeah, I guess it really kinda is," Rusty said, looking around. I got the impression that he felt a little guilty for not realizing how amazing this place was. I supposed it was only natural to get used to living like this after a while.

"Okay, now I really can't wait to see your place," I said enthusiastically.

"Off we go." He gestured with a flourish toward the elevator.

On the way up, I said, "You could fit my entire apartment in that lobby downstairs. I am so not kidding."

Rusty nodded. "I hear ya. I didn't always live like this. I grew up in West Virginia. Not poor, but definitely not rich. My mother's a teacher, and my dad is an automotive technician. I didn't move here until after my first full year with the Baltimore Bay Birds." Laughing ruefully, he said, "I guess I wanted to make sure things were gonna work out with the team. Turns out I didn't wait long enough."

I put my hand on his back, rubbing gently. How I hated it when that look of sorrow crossed his face.

When we got to the fifth floor, Rusty punched in the code to his front door.

"Wow," I said once again when I saw his place. "This is wild!"

I rushed inside like I owned the place, making Rusty laugh.

"Your view is incredible." I quickly crossed the living room and straight over to the huge bank of windows at the corner of his apartment. "You can see the whole city from here."

"Pretty much," he said, walking over to stand beside me. The sun was beginning to set in a spray of orange and red across the city's skyline.

"Must be really amazing at night."

"It is." Rusty and I gazed out the window together, quietly taking in the view for a few minutes. Then I turned around to look at the rest of his beautiful apartment.

"Oooh, I like this kitchen," I said, wandering over to get a better look.

"Yeah, it's pretty cool. I like that I can see the living room TV from in here while I eat."

"That is nice," I said. "I usually read books while I eat, and then I watch TV after."

I admired his fancy granite countertops and shiny kitchen appliances. Everything looked so new that I figured he probably didn't cook much. After I finished exploring the kitchen, Rusty continued the tour.

"And over here is my bedroom," Rusty said in a sly voice that made my stomach quiver with anticipation at the mere idea of seeing it. I glanced at him and felt my face get hot. That made his grin widen and made me blush more.

My eyes grew wide when I saw his spacious bedroom. It had a view of the city as gorgeous as the one in the living room.

"This is huge," I said as I walked around the room. His king-sized bed faced a large wall of windows overlooking Baltimore. "This is amazing."

Rusty chuckled. "Yeah, I guess it is."

I watched his eyes as he surveyed his bedroom. He seemed to especially appreciate how incredible this room was. I'd never seen anything like it in real life. I did look forward to spending more time in his bedroom with him ... Just not quite yet.

But probably soon. Very soon.

I locked eyes with him for a moment, giving him a chance to read my mind. He did. And he grinned.

"Okay, now show me the rest of your place," I said, briskly walking out of the room.

Rusty laughed and rushed to catch up with me.

"There's not a whole lot more to see," he said. His shoulders drooped, and I followed his gaze to a closed door. "Just ... that room over there."

"It's not some kind of Christian Grey sex torture room, is it?"

"And if it was?" Rusty asked, arching an eyebrow and looking deadly serious. Then his face broke into that grin that I loved so much. "Come on, I'll show ya."

He sighed softly as he opened the door. I almost would have preferred a scary sex room over whatever was in there that made him so sad.

It turned out to be a fairly simple-looking office. There was a desk with a computer and a chair. Some papers scattered around, a container that held pencils, pens, and a few Sharpie markers. Nothing unusual at all.

Scanning the room, I started to understand what made him so sad. On the floor, there were several cardboard boxes filled with stuff. Baseball stuff. The first thing I noticed were numerous framed pictures of baseball players, many of them autographed, and all of them dumped unceremoniously into boxes.

The walls were bare except for some hooks and nails still stuck in the drywall. I walked over to get a closer look into the boxes and found they were filled with baseballs, small wooden bats, and souvenir stadium cups. A lifetime collection of memorabilia all packed up.

A lump formed in my throat and I fought back tears. A deep sadness swept over me as I surveyed all of Rusty's most precious belongings. For a moment, it truly felt as if someone had died, and these things were all that were left.

"It's too hard to look at this stuff anymore," Rusty said quietly. "That's why all the walls in my living room are pretty bare now, too."

I nodded, though I hadn't noticed that at all. His apartment was so beautiful; it hadn't occurred to me that anything was missing.

"I used to spend a lot of time in here. Reading up on baseball. Planning strategies for the night's game, that kind of stuff. I don't really come in here much anymore, but when I do ... Well, I don't want to see anything baseball-related anymore. So I'm packing everything up to give away or throw out or whatever."

"Don't!" I cried out suddenly, whipping around to look at him.

Rusty looked quite startled. He probably hadn't been expecting my tears.

I walked over to him, touched his cheek softly, and gazed into his eyes. "Don't get rid of anything yet. I understand you don't want to see it right now. Just ... just get some storage space somewhere and put it away for now. But don't get rid of anything yet. *Promise me.*"

Deep blue eyes wide, Rusty nodded. I'd sounded so insistent that he couldn't say no.

"Okay, Amanda. I promise. I won't get rid of anything permanently. Yet."

I nodded and pulled him in for a hug. I wanted to tell him how sorry I was for everything he was going through, but I couldn't find the words. Instead, I simply held him close. Hopefully, that told Rusty all he needed to know. That I was hurting for him and that I cared.

When I let go of him, he led me back into the living room.

"Did you want to watch a little TV or something? Or are you tired and want to go home?" Rusty asked.

A warm, happy feeling flooded my entire being. I loved the way he asked those questions, because I knew that "watching TV" was not code for him wanting to sit on the couch and feel me up or pressure me into anything. I'd made it clear I wasn't ready to be intimate, and he respected that.

"I'd love to watch TV for a little bit."

"Cool," he said, his eyes lighting up with happiness.

We settled in on the couch together, and he flipped on the television. An action movie was on, and the first thing we saw was some guy getting shot in the head.

I screamed loudly and jerked my head away from the screen.

"Sorry, sorry," Rusty said, quickly flipping the channel.

The scene hadn't been all that graphic. I wasn't even sure it was a rated-R movie. It might have just been a crime show.

Rusty looked both apologetic and confused.

"I know, I know. Look, that's something you have to know about me. I'm super sensitive about stuff like this. Well, I'm sensitive about everything really. Violence, scary things, or even those stupid reality shows and prank shows where people get humiliated on television ... I can't watch it. I know it sounds dumb, but it upsets me."

I tried to laugh it off, but Rusty looked at me with concern. I loved that he took my words so seriously.

"It doesn't sound dumb, Amanda. I'm glad you told me."

I smiled at him, relishing how safe I felt when I was with him.

"Believe me, I know it's kind of weird, but it's how I am. It's like ... I don't know. When I see something upsetting, even when it's fake violence or whatever, it's like I can't shake it off right away like other people can. Especially if it's right before bed. I need to watch something light-hearted, especially late at night."

"Then that's what we'll do," he said.

Then he turned on the digital guide to see what was on instead of randomly switching channels. He scrolled through for a bit to find something Amanda-appropriate.

"Oooh, *Hugh's Shop*," we both called out in perfect unison.

I giggled. "I love that show."

"Dude, same," Rusty said, chuckling as he fist-bumped me.

"I've seen all the episodes a million times, and I never get sick of it," I said.

"Same with me. Except I can't watch it with my dad. He's an automotive technician and he's always like 'That's not how you hold that tool,' or 'That can't be a 2002 model because it didn't come out 'til 2006.'"

"Well, you don't have to worry about that with me. I'm not that into cars."

"I love cars, actually," Rusty said. "I just have no interest in working on them."

"Fair enough."

We snuggled up together on the couch to watch the show. After two or three episodes, I started to nod off.

"Amanda," he said, gently shaking me awake. "You're exhausted. I better get you home."

"Oh," I said groggily. "Okay. Sorry you have to take me all the way home at this time of night."

"It's okay." After a moment, he added, "It's totally up to you, but maybe next weekend you'd like to spend the night?"

I didn't even have to think it over.

"I would love that, Rusty."

He smiled, and then he kissed me softly before helping me up from the couch.

15

RUSTY

All week long I eagerly anticipated seeing Amanda again. And it wasn't only the sex I looked forward to, though that was a big plus. Having her in my life gave me something to be happy about. Something to live for. Being with her made me *happy*. And the idea that she would spend the night at my place thrilled me to no end.

While I was waiting for the weekend to come, I needed something to do with my time. In the past, I'd dabbled some with electric guitar and figured it might be a good time to take it up again. I thought about turning that spare room into a music space rather than keep it as the graveyard to my dead baseball career. As it was, I hated even going in there.

I pulled my electric guitar out of the closet where I'd stowed it when I moved in and plugged it into the new amp I'd bought. I was eager to play some cool stuff so I could show off for Amanda. Not that I had any plans to go pro in the music world, but at least I could prove to her—and to myself—that I had *some* degree of non-athletic talent.

I fired up the guitar and amp and cranked it up. The loudness and vibration got my blood going, and I was ready to rock and roll. Loud, angry music always got me charged up. But then again, I had usually been amping myself up for a baseball game.

I tried to play Metallica's "Enter Sandman" by memory, but it turned out my memory was shit when it came to music. I couldn't even remember those basic notes from "Smoke on the Water," which pretty much everybody knew. Whatever. That was what the Internet was for.

I turned on my laptop and found the music online. Finding the chords was easy. Playing them correctly was not.

"Fuck!" I yelled after screwing up the Metallica song for the tenth time. What the hell was wrong with me? I used to be able to play that song pretty well. Yeah, it was years ago, but still. It shouldn't be this hard.

I fought the urge to smash the goddamn guitar against the wall.

Damn.

I sucked in a deep breath to try to calm down. It was unlike me to get so pissed off. Even when I struck out badly or bobbled a ball at first base, I'd never been the type to throw the bat down or storm off the field. Sure, I'd get frustrated, but I'd still been even-tempered.

I hated feeling like this. The last thing I wanted was to become a bitter, angry person, but I seemed to be well on my way there.

Gripping the guitar, I tried the chords again and messed them up even worse. As much as I hated giving up, the more I practiced, the madder and more frustrated I got. I had to accept that today was just not my day, and this stress couldn't be good for my heart. That, and holding the guitar was aggravating my sore ribs. I flipped off the amp and stalked into the kitchen.

I felt better when I checked my phone and saw a text

from a friend I'd grown up with in West Virginia. He was checking in on me and said we should get together the next time I was in town. Though it was cool of him to touch base, I wondered if it would be awkward the next time I saw him. Like pretty much everybody else in my life, we'd bonded a lot over sports through the years. What would we have in common anymore?

~

IT HAD BEEN one hell of a long week, but Friday eventually arrived and it was time to go pick up Amanda. I drummed my hands impatiently on the steering wheel, and then smacked my fist on it when I hit what felt like the millionth red light on the drive over.

I was honored that she would finally let me see her place, and I hoped she wouldn't feel bad comparing our living spaces. Though I hadn't lived at Harbor View all that long, I had gotten used to luxury living. Watching Amanda wander around my building, her eyes wide with amazement, had reminded me of how lucky I was to live there.

She was waiting outside her building when I pulled up. I wondered if she'd changed her mind about letting me into her apartment. Of course I would respect whatever she'd decided, but I hoped she trusted me enough by now to let me see where she lived.

"Hey," she said with a smile when I got out of my Corvette. "Figured I'd meet you outside so I could make sure you found the right apartment."

"Oh, cool," I said, relieved that we were still on the same page.

Holding up my keys and looking around, I said, "No valet? Whatever." I shook my head dismissively.

Amanda laughed. Good. That was the reaction I'd been going for. She knew by now that I wasn't snobby just because I was wealthy.

"Shut up," she said, playfully punching me in the shoulder.

I bent down and kissed her, and Amanda let out a soft moan, making me feel like she'd missed me all week too. After our hello kiss, she slipped her arm around my waist and we walked inside. Such a simple, intimate gesture, but it meant the world to me. Already it felt like we'd fallen into an easy rhythm as a couple, far faster than any other relationship I'd been in.

Amanda led me up the stairs to the second floor.

"I'm warning you," she said before opening the door. "It's really tiny. I deliberately got the smallest, cheapest place I could find so I could start saving up for a down payment on a house."

"That seems smart."

We walked into her place and I looked around. It was small for sure, but pleasant. Warm and homey, like she'd done the best she could to make it a comfortable place to live.

"I like it," I said.

Amanda laughed and shook her head. "You don't have to say that." Scanning the room, she seemed slightly uncomfortable. Like she was trying to see it from my perspective, wondering what I was thinking.

"No really. I do." I wandered over to the kitchen. The cabinet doors were made of glass, so I could see inside them. She had tons of pots and pans, which didn't surprise me since I knew she liked to cook. She'd made the most of what little space she had, and everything was tidy and organized.

"I lived in a place even smaller than this when I was in the minors."

"Really?" Amanda asked, sounding quite surprised.

"Yeah. With *two other guys*," I said with a chuckle.

"Wow."

Gesturing at the scented candle warmer she had plugged in, I added, "And it didn't smell like roses, I can tell ya that."

Amanda laughed, seeming more at ease.

"It's cozy. Has a warmer feel than my place does."

My apartment had been warmer and homier when I had all my baseball stuff up. Now it reflected how I currently felt. Lost and empty. Being here with Amanda where she lived definitely made me feel a lot less lonely.

"Not much else to see," she said. "Over there is the bathroom, and then there's my bedroom."

She didn't lead me over to the bedroom, but she'd left the door open, so I figured it was okay to take a quick peek.

"Oh wow, what do we have here?"

"What?" Amanda asked, following my gaze.

I walked straight into her bedroom, unable to help myself.

"Oh my God," she said, covering her face with embarrassment. "I cannot believe I forgot to take that down."

Amanda had a signed picture of me hanging on her wall. I stared at it for a moment.

"So I really was your favorite player?" I asked.

"Of course."

"Huh. I'd always wondered if that was true, or if you just said it to be nice."

"You've always been my favorite, Rusty. Ever since you joined the team." She still seemed a little embarrassed as she spoke, but she looked me in the eye.

"Why?" I asked her, genuinely curious

Smiling, she said, "You always had such a positive attitude. In all the interviews, you seemed so nice. I could tell how grateful you were to be on the team. I just loved that. You never played it cool, and you had no problem telling the world how lucky you were to have made it to the majors."

Though her words were so sweet, I was sad to think I was no longer that happy-go-lucky guy. I tried to hide it from her—from everybody—but there were times lately when I got so damned angry, I hardly knew what to do with myself.

"And it didn't hurt that you happened to be incredibly handsome," she added.

Tearing my gaze away from the photograph, I asked, "Had we met before? At an autograph signing?"

Shaking her head, she said, "Oh no. That picture was a gift from my sister. I'm not sure where she got it."

I nodded. "Makes sense. I would have remembered if I'd met you before."

We both knew it was a lie, though. I'd met thousands of fans, and as lovely as Amanda was, most likely I would never have recognized her later.

I sighed heavily. "I wished you'd known me, you know, before."

Amanda walked over to me and gently placed her hand on my back as we both gazed at the photograph of my former self.

"I think you're wonderful just the way you are."

A lump formed in the back of my throat, and so help me, I had to fight back tears.

Because I believed her.

Something in the way she spoke and the way she looked at me made me believe she was telling the truth.

"I'm sorry," she said quietly. "I didn't mean to upset you. I should have taken this down."

"It's okay." I turned to face her. "I think it's kinda hot that you have this hanging in your bedroom."

Amanda laughed and blushed, then she looked away. Her reaction made me wonder if she'd ever touched herself while looking at my picture.

I got hard just thinking about it.

As much as I enjoyed that thought, I didn't want to embarrass my girl any further.

"Thanks for showing me your apartment, Amanda. I really do like it."

She nodded and smiled.

"Are you ready to go back to my place?"

"Absolutely." She grabbed the overnight bag that was sitting on her bed. "Let's go."

We headed toward the door. She turned off the electric candle, then took another glance around to make sure she hadn't forgotten anything.

Such a simple moment, but I was suddenly struck by how lovely she was. Just being near her made me feel happy, like maybe not everything in my life was as terrible as I'd thought.

"What?" she asked, catching me looking at her.

"I just think you're beautiful, that's all."

Amanda's expression softened, and I could have sworn she looked like she might cry. I had the feeling she wasn't used to being called beautiful, which was a damned shame.

I pulled her close and kissed her, loving the way her body melted into mine. I relished the familiar moan she let out when my lips touched hers. It wasn't long before we were hardcore making out. I had to break it off before I wound up taking her right here in her apartment. That wouldn't be a bad thing, but I'd imagined our first time in my large bed in my sprawling apartment.

"You know," I said breathlessly, "we still need to get dinner before ... you know."

"How about we order pizza?" Amanda's face was flushed and her voice was as breathless as mine. "Pizza's probably the quickest way to get food."

Grinning, I said, "I like the way you think."

Amanda ordered pizza online with her phone as I sped toward my place. Fortunately, the food arrived not long after we did, and we sat in my living room to eat our dinner. As much as I hated anything that would delay our lovemaking, I needed the energy for everything I was about to do to her.

I wanted to leap up from my chair and drag Amanda to the bedroom the second I finished my dinner, but somehow I managed a level of restraint.

"Do you want another slice?" I asked her, hoping like hell she would say no.

"No, I'm good. Thanks." She blushed slightly, knowing what our next activity would be.

"Great, let's roll!" I said, jumping up and grabbing her hand. So much for restraint.

Amanda laughed, allowing herself to be pulled toward the bedroom. I managed to pick up her overnight bag on the way, wanting to make sure she had everything she needed to be comfortable.

I put her bag on the floor and then, more gently this time, pulled her toward the bed. She sat down next to me, and I gazed into those pretty brown eyes. My God, I was crazy about this girl.

Tenderly brushing her hair from her face, I kissed her. This time we both moaned. I could tell she wanted me as badly as I wanted her, and it was wonderful to be needed. I often felt so useless these days, but Amanda had a way of making me feel like a man again.

I cupped her face as I kissed her, then slowly slid my hand down to touch her right breast.

"Rusty," she said, pulling back.

I stifled a groan, hoping like hell she hadn't changed her mind about going to bed with me.

"You okay?" I asked.

"Yeah," she said with a smile. "It's just ... the blinds are open."

Glancing behind her, I saw that the shades on my huge bedroom window were indeed wide open. I could hardly blame her for not wanting to have sex in front of the entire city of Baltimore.

Laughing, I said, "Right, right. Sorry."

I grabbed the remote control and lowered the shades. It got seriously dark when they were closed, so with another remote, I clicked until the room was filled with soft lighting more suitable for lovemaking.

Amanda sighed and said, "That's perfect. Now, where were we?"

"Right about here." I pressed my lips to hers and massaged her breast again. Her body melted into mine; the moment felt perfect.

Without breaking off the kiss, I reached behind me and slid open my nightstand drawer.

"I'm on the pill," Amanda murmured in between kisses.

"Niiiice," I said, shutting the nightstand drawer with a flourish.

I gripped her blouse and pulled it over her head, tossing it aside. The briefest grimace crossed her face, and for a second, I wondered if I was moving too fast. She glanced down at her own chest before looking away self-consciously. A sexy red lace bra covered her smallish breasts.

Then I remembered how much all those skinny-girl jokes had hurt her feelings. That, and she was probably painfully aware that my last lover was a beautiful actress. Amanda had nothing to worry about. I was far more attracted to her than I ever had been to Emily Martindale. It wasn't even a close contest. Still, I knew how I would feel if Amanda's last boyfriend had been a male model or something. After all, I was no longer as fit as I was when I played for the Birds. And I had a few cracked ribs, but I was determined to be all man for her tonight.

Rubbing her breasts, I took my time admiring them. She was about a B-cup, and that was perfectly fine with me. Amanda was my girl, and she was beautiful. I hoped I could make her understand that. Touching her chest was such a turn-on, and I couldn't wait to explore the rest of her body.

"I know I'm pretty small," she said quietly, and I was glad she'd voiced her insecurities.

"You're *perfect*." Still staring at her breasts while she watched me massage them, I said, "You know what they say. Anything more than a handful is a waste."

Amanda laughed softly. I lifted my gaze to stare intently into her eyes, willing her to understand how much I genuinely wanted her.

"Ever since our first kiss, I've been fantasizing about making love to you," I told her.

"Really?"

"Oh yeah. And I can't believe I finally get the chance."

I pulled her close again, kissing her hard, wanting her to feel my urgency. Amanda responded eagerly to my kiss and unbuttoned my shirt. Once she got it off, it was her chance to stare at my chest.

"Wow," she said, her eyes wide.

*You should have seen me when I was still an athlete. Not ...
whatever it is that I am now.*

I shoved that painful thought away, reminding myself to
focus on being with my girl.

She squeezed my shoulders and drew in a breath. The
desire in her eyes fired me up. I could hardly wait to be
inside of her.

Pushing her down onto her back, I slid off her jeans to
find a matching pair of red lace panties. They looked expensive—I had to resist tearing them off. Instead, I slowly slid
them down and planted a kiss on the mound between her
legs. Amanda let out a delicious moan. I reached behind her
to unclasp her bra, and at last she was naked lying in my
bed. Just where I wanted her.

I took a moment to admire Amanda in all her luscious-
ness, then I climbed off the bed. Staring directly into her
eyes, I unbuckled my pants and slowly unzipped them. I
took my time, enjoying Amanda's torture as she waited for
me to get naked. At last, I slid my jeans and underwear
down, never tearing my gaze from hers.

"Rusty," she said in a throaty, lusty tone. "I've never been
so wet in my life."

Her face reddened as she spoke; I suspected she wasn't
normally outspoken in the bedroom. I loved that I'd
brought out that side of her.

It was an effort not to jump into bed and ram into her as
hard as I could, but teasing her was too much fun. Instead, I
took my time. Positioning myself on top of her, straddling her,
my gaze bored into her. I reveled in the sight of her pretty brown
eyes widening as I rubbed between her legs with my cock.

"Oh Rusty," she gasped. I could *feel* how badly she

wanted me. I knew I was driving her crazy, and I loved every second of it.

She gripped my shoulders and tugged, as if willing me to penetrate her.

Leaning down, I murmured in her ear, "Do you want me?"

"God yes," she panted.

"Tell me," I said. And then, because I could not resist, I added, "Beg me, Amanda."

"Rusty," she said, desperation in her voice. *"Please."*

That got me so hot, I could have come right then and there. I hadn't thought she would actually say it, but she did. She *begged* for me.

And she deserved to be rewarded for it.

In a quick motion, I smacked my knee against hers to open her legs wide and then rammed inside her. I'd expected her to scream, but she moaned and dug her nails into my back, arching her back to allow me to get deeper inside. Somehow, that was even hotter than a scream. And she was indeed soaking, dripping wet.

Amanda was pretty tight down there. That, coupled with the sex drought I'd had lately, sent me into pleasure overdrive.

"Amanda, baby. Oh God, you feel good," I managed to say while pounding her relentlessly. As much as I'd wanted to maintain my cool demeanor, my hot girlfriend made that impossible. Still, my mission was to make her come before I did, no matter how hard that might be to accomplish right now.

I reached between her legs and stroked her clit. That did make her scream. She dug her nails in even harder. Amanda seemed close to orgasm, but so was I. Dangerously close. My breathing grew heavier, and I had to fight my way back from the brink.

Her body tensed beneath mine. At first, I thought she was starting to come, but then I felt her grip on me loosen. Amanda's face darkened. I wasn't sure what was happening, how she was feeling, or what she needed. I kept thrusting until I was past any semblance of control. Amanda was too damned beautiful, and I couldn't help but surrender to my release. Shuddering and groaning, I came hard inside of her.

Delicious sexual relief swept over me. I caught my breath and rolled off her, laying down beside her.

And that's when the guilt and self-loathing set in.

I lay there in silence for a moment. "Sorry."

"Sorry for what?" she asked in a soft voice.

"I didn't take care of you. You didn't ... you know."

Turning onto her side to face me, she stroked my face and said, "It's not your fault. It's mine."

"No it's not." I was super pissed at myself. This never happened. I *always* got the woman off during sex. *Always.* Figured it would happen with Amanda of all people. She was the girl I wanted to impress the most. There were no second chances when it came to first impressions. I'd had the chance to rock her world, and I'd totally blown it.

"Yes, it *is,*" Amanda insisted. "I just ... lost focus there for a bit."

"What does that even mean?" I asked. Had she gotten distracted by something in the middle of having sex? Could I not even hold her interest?

She looked alarmed at my expression. "No, it's not like ... I didn't mean ..."

I stared at her, desperately needing an explanation for

why she'd apparently found it hard to stay awake during sex with me.

Amanda sighed. She sat up in bed, pulling the sheet up to cover her nakedness.

"Rusty, I was just worried about you."

"What? Why?" I snapped.

She blinked, startled by the sudden anger in my tone.

"Because you were breathing so heavy."

"We were having *sex*, Amanda. Of course I was breathing heavy!"

The rage erupting inside took even me by surprise. My hands shook with anger and frustration at having my manhood questioned.

"I'm not some weak little boy just because I have a heart condition, you know."

"You don't understand," Amanda said, her voice quaking.

I should have realized how upset she was and backed off. But of course I didn't. Instead, I yelled at her.

"Then help me understand!"

Her eyes filled with tears, and she covered her mouth, stifling a sob. When she finally lowered her hand from her face, she said in a quivering voice, "Your lips were *blue*."

"What?"

A sliver of fear rippled through me. Did I look sick? Was I having another cardiac arrest without knowing it?

"No. Not now. I mean ... that day in the ballpark," she said, wiping her eyes with the back of her hand. "When I ran onto the field to check on you. Rusty, you—your lips were blue. Your face was completely *gray*. I thought maybe it was too late. That you were already dead. I still have night-mares about it. It was bad enough when I didn't know you personally, but now it's so much harder, and—"

She broke down sobbing, covering her face.

And I could not believe how utterly stupid I had been.

No wonder she had freaked out when she saw me breathing hard. I knew damn well that Amanda was the type of person who felt things very deeply. She was sensitive, but in a good way. She was so empathetic that she couldn't even watch fictional people on television get hurt without getting upset. I couldn't begin to imagine what it must have been like for her to witness my near-fatal cardiac arrest.

"Oh, Amanda, I'm so sorry," I said, pulling her into my arms. Seeing her cry made my anger vanish in an instant. Upsetting her was the last thing I wanted.

The way I'd flown into a rage so quickly was frightening. I'd felt so out of control a moment ago that it was scary. I hadn't for a moment thought about hurting Amanda physically, but I *had* felt like smashing everything in my apartment.

Damn.

I held Amanda close, stroking her back. Eventually, her sobs began to subside, and her breathing became steadier.

She pulled back from me a bit and wiped her eyes. "I know you must be frustrated with everything that's happened with you."

"That's no excuse for flipping out on you."

Amanda nodded, and I was glad she didn't argue with me. I was allowed to be mad, but I wasn't allowed to take it out on her.

"I just got so scared all of a sudden," she said, her voice barely a whisper. "It could happen to you again, Rusty. Your heart could give out, and—"

"It's not gonna happen again."

"But it *could*. That's why you're not allowed to play base-ball anymore. Because it could kill you."

I sighed heavily, hating that she was right. The thing I loved most in the world could literally kill me.

"Listen," I said, tenderly running my fingers through her hair. "I've talked a lot with my cardiologist, and we went over what is and isn't safe for me. And you better believe I brought up the subject of sexual activity."

Amanda laughed softly and the tension in my body eased. I didn't ever want to see her cry like that again. And I silently vowed never, ever to be the cause of her tears again.

"And sex is safe. I promise. As long as I'm not swinging from a trapeze or something, it's cool. Really. It's actually good for me, believe it or not."

She nodded and looked like she was feeling better.

"You okay?" I asked.

"Yeah."

"I'm really sorry I yelled at you."

"I know you are," she said with a sweet smile. "I know you're angry these days, and I can understand that."

I hadn't realized my pent-up anger issues had been that obvious. I worked hard to maintain my sunny demeanor on the outside. It was both sweet and concerning that Amanda could see through me.

"I still need to take care of you," I said in my most seductive voice.

She looked tired. "I know. Just not tonight."

I could understand why she wasn't in the mood anymore. I still felt like a failure and wished for the chance to redeem myself sexually.

But I knew I had to take care of my girl and give her what she actually needed.

I pulled her close and held her in my arms.

16

AMANDA

I woke up before Rusty the next morning and watched him sleep for a few minutes. His chest rose and fell with each breath, and he looked so peaceful. I worried about him, but after what happened last night, I realized I needed to get better at hiding it. He was obviously super sensitive about appearing vulnerable due to his illness, and I understood that. He'd lost so much after his diagnosis, and I couldn't blame him for being bitter.

Still, the way he'd yelled at me last night had been scary. I'd never seen him so angry. In fact, I'd never seen him get angry at all. Witnessing him fly into a rage had been an eye-opener. Clearly, he had a lot of fury bubbling just beneath the surface.

I absolutely adored Rusty, but I was starting to realize that being with him was not without its challenges. Fortunately, I was patient, and he was more than worth the effort. He was still navigating this new existence of his, and I was glad I could be here to support him. The idea of him going it alone at a time like this broke my heart.

Rusty moved around, then opened his eyes.

I smiled at him, not bothering to hide that I'd been watching him sleep.

"Do you hate me?" was the first thing he said.

"Of course not," I said with a laugh.

"I'm sorry I was such an asshole last night. I hate that I ruined our first time together."

"You didn't ruin anything." I planted a kiss on his forehead.

"I really do appreciate you worrying about me. I know I have a funny way of showing it."

"It's okay."

"Did you sleep well? Are you hungry?"

"Yes and yes," I said decisively.

"Okay." He leapt out of bed with surprising energy. "I'm gonna jump in the shower first, but only so's I can get started making you breakfast. Anything in particular you want?"

Shrugging, I said, "Not really. I like all breakfast foods. Anything you make is fine."

"Cool." He bent down to kiss me where I lay in bed.

He is so adorable. I watched his cute naked butt as he ran off to the bathroom.

Maybe last night hadn't exactly gone according to plan, but I was still happy to be here. Falling asleep wrapped in Rusty's arms had been wonderful, and that was more than enough for me.

After I showered and got dressed, I walked into the kitchen to find Rusty standing over a hot stove, enthusiastically flipping pancakes.

"Could you be any cuter?" I asked, making him smile. I walked over to get a closer look. "This is pretty impressive. Making pancakes is one of those things that's a lot harder than it looks."

"Tell me about it. You shoulda seen my first few dozen

attempts. Made a ton of burned ones, runny ones, and rubbery ones until I finally got it right. Now making pancakes is a breeze."

To emphasize his point, he expertly jerked up the frying pan and managed to flip the pancake over without the use of a spatula.

"Okay, *that* was *really* impressive," I said.

Rusty's brand of entertainment cooking was just the sort of thing that would amuse young kids. I could easily imagine him as a terrific father.

We settled in at the counter and enjoyed an absolutely delicious meal of fluffy pancakes, crispy bacon, and fresh coffee. Rusty's cooking rivaled any breakfast diner, and I was sure to tell him so. He seemed pleased with my compliment and he relished watching me enjoy my meal.

"I'm tellin' ya, don't be too impressed. Breakfast is all I know how to make."

"Well, it's amazing, Rusty."

"Cool," he said with a grin.

I insisted on cleaning up after breakfast, and Rusty reluctantly let me. It was so much fun being with him, and I loved that simply sharing breakfast with him could be so enjoyable. It boosted my spirits to know he was still capable of experiencing joy, even though he was going through a rough time. Once he figured out what he wanted to do for the rest of his life, I hoped everything would fall into place for him. He needed another purpose, but I knew it wouldn't be easy. It was hard to imagine Rusty being passionate about any type of work after baseball. Nothing could possibly compare to the sport in his eyes.

After breakfast, we settled in on the couch to try to figure out what we wanted to do for the rest of the day. I honestly didn't care what we did. I was happy being with him.

Rusty turned to face me.

"You know," he said in a low voice, his eyes dark and his expression intense. "It occurs to me ..."

"Yeah?" I asked uncertainly.

"That I still owe you an orgasm."

My face heated, but I didn't tear my gaze away. He was right. Before I'd gotten so upset, we'd been in the middle of incredibly pleasurable sex. Last night, I'd been too worried about him to enjoy myself. But now, the tingling between my legs reminded me that my needs had indeed gone unsatisfied.

And oh God, I'd been so close last night. So. Close. With Rusty pounding into me and his fingers massaging my most intimate spot, I'd been seconds away from pure sexual release.

"I—I guess ... I guess you're right," I stammered. Rusty's knowledge of how desperate I was right now made me vulnerable. But I needed relief, and after last night, I knew how good he was in bed.

"Then it's time I gave you what you need," Rusty said in a deep, sensual voice. He leaned in and kissed me deeply, cupping my face. Almost instantly I was as wet as I had been last night. Like we'd picked up right where we left off.

Rusty broke off the kiss and moved the coffee table out of the way with his foot in one hard shove. I didn't know what he had in mind, but I couldn't wait to find out.

He reached under me and scooped me up into his arms. I thought he was going to carry me to the bedroom, but apparently he had other ideas.

Rusty laid me down on the carpet and unbuttoned my shirt. I drew in a breath of exhilaration. He was more forceful than he'd been last night. I got the impression he wanted to prove his manhood. That was more than okay by me.

He kissed me as he massaged my breasts, which were covered by my black lace bra. I owned exactly two sets of fancy underwear, and now Rusty had seen them both.

"I want to see you," I said, tugging at his shirt until he pulled it off for me.

I couldn't get over how ripped he was. He might be a former athlete, but he still had the body of a pro baseball player. Even if he hadn't, I would still have been hot for him. Rusty was much more to me than a pretty face and a rocking body.

In no time, we were both naked. The shades of his living room window were open, but I wasn't worried because we were hidden from view by the couch.

That, and I was so turned on that I doubted I would have cared if the entire city of Baltimore were watching us have sex. After Rusty's stellar performance last night, I could hardly wait for the encore. I hoped this time it would end with the grand finale I'd been aching for.

Rusty plunged into me and I cried out in ecstasy, grabbing his shoulders. I closed my eyes, losing myself in the sheer bliss of his large cock pounding the hell out of me.

"Now who's breathing heavy," Rusty murmured in my ear, sending a fresh ripple of bliss between my legs. He knew how much I wanted him, needed him, and somehow that made this delicious experience even hotter.

"Yes," I panted as he drove in and out of me, faster and faster.

When he slipped his fingers between my legs and massaged my clit, I completely lost my mind.

Crying out again, I gripped his shoulders even harder, willing him not to stop. I opened my eyes to see Rusty's gorgeous, piercing blue eyes intense with concentration. It was like his mission in life was to make me come as hard as possible.

And that's when the sexiest thought on the planet flashed in my mind.

Rusty Power is fucking me on the living room floor.

With that, all my wildest fantasies came to life as my body rocketed to the most intense climax I'd ever had.

"Rusty," I cried out as I came, my body quivering and shuddering with delicious release.

He groaned deeply as he found his own release, emptying himself inside me.

I lay there for a moment, unable to move and not wanting to.

"That ...was ... *amazing*," I said.

Rusty grinned, a cocky expression on his face. He was proud of himself. As well he should be. I was thrilled, as it was a far cry from how things had ended last night. The last thing I'd wanted was to make him feel weak, like he was less of a man due to his illness. I had planned to show my enthusiasm the next time we made love in order to build up his ego.

Turned out it didn't take any extra effort on my part. Rusty had truly been amazing, and he had fully, deeply satisfied me. My screams of ecstasy had been involuntary and one hundred percent *real.*

Rusty rolled off and then reached underneath me with his arm and pulled me to his chest. I snuggled up against him happily.

"Wow," I said with a deep, satisfied sigh.

"And I didn't even die."

I laughed. "Nope."

"But if I had, I'd have died happy."

Giggling, I snuggled up closer. I gently traced his naked chest with my finger and then I planted a kiss right over his heart. To me, that simple kiss felt like a promise. My pledge to Rusty's heart that I would always take care of it, physically and emotionally. I'd once helped start it went it gave out, and I felt it was my duty to look after it.

Forever.

I shivered slightly, and Rusty noticed.

"I better let you get dressed, beautiful."

I shivered again, but for a different reason this time. No one had ever called me beautiful before Rusty. And no one had ever made me *feel* beautiful the way he did. I'd always been the type to fade into the background, but he had a way of making me feel valued. Important. Like I was more than just the solid, reliable friend that everyone knew they could count on.

Rusty sat up and put his hands behind his head, watching me get dressed. I could feel his eyes on me, admiring me. Again, not something I was used to. He never looked at me like I was a scrawny, skinny girl. He eyed me up and down like I was a supermodel. I couldn't help comparing myself to Emily Martindale, but I never felt like Rusty was comparing me at all. Somehow, he seemed like he was just into *me.*

Once we were dressed, we settled on the couch again, incredibly relaxed and happy, still reveling in sexual release. Just sitting on the couch with Rusty was fun. Everything was more fun with him.

He clicked on the TV, once again using the guide instead of randomly changing channels. He settled on a sitcom rerun and then turned to me.

"So, whaddya wanna do today?"

"Hmm, good question."

"You know," he said, "you can always stay overnight again tonight if you want."

My body tensed up.

"Oh, um ... well, I would love to. Really. It's just ... I kinda have plans later tonight."

"You do?" he said with raised eyebrows.

"Yeah," I said quietly.

"Oh."

Rusty gazed at me, waiting for me to elaborate. I really did not want to tell him where I was going, but he was gonna think I had a date with another guy if I didn't give him any details.

Sighing heavily, I said, "It's just ... Rusty, I have tickets to the Bay Birds game tonight."

"Oh, I see," he said, his expression a mixture of relief and sorrow.

"I'm sorry. I didn't want to say anything because—"

"I understand, Amanda. You didn't want to upset me. Sometimes I forget what a big Bay Birds fan you are. I mean, you have season tickets. Of course you're gonna go to a lot of games."

Rusty smiled, but it was forced. He was hurting, and I hated it.

"I don't have to go if—"

"Yes," he said firmly. "Yes, you do. I wouldn't dream of keeping you from going to the game. You're allowed to have a life outside of me, you know."

I nodded, grateful that he understood.

"You going with a group of friends?"

"Yeah. I already had a two-ticket season plan, but the Bay Birds gave me a bunch more after I saved your life. That, and my seats got way upgraded."

That made him laugh, and I was happy to hear that sound.

"Niiiice," he said, fist bumping me enthusiastically. "That was cool of them."

"It really was."

"Gimme your feet."

"What?" I asked.

Slapping his thighs, he said, "Put 'em here."

I did as he asked, and he started rubbing my feet.

"Oh damn, that feels really good."

"Breakfast and foot rubs. That's my skill set."

"Works for me," I said.

"So, did you want to do something today before the game or did you just want to head home?"

"We can hang out, sure. Game's not until 7:05."

"Cool," he said with a grin as he massaged my feet.

"What do you want to do?"

Rusty thought for a moment. "Whaddya say we visit the Maryland Science Center and play with all the kiddie science exhibits?"

"Are you serious?"

"As a heart attack," he said and then wrinkled his nose. "Sorry. Too soon for that joke?"

I laughed and shook my head.

"So, Science Center," he said. "Dumb idea?"

"Not at all. I kind of love it." Doing such a thing was totally unlike me, but that was what I liked about the idea.

"Let's do it!" Rusty said with a boyish grin.

17

AMANDA

"I haven't been here since I was a kid," I said with a smile as Rusty paid our admission to the Maryland Science Center.

I watched lots of little kids running around excitedly, many of them making a beeline toward the dinosaur exhibit, which had a huge T. rex model on display.

"Really?" Rusty said as he wrapped the paper wristband on me that proved we had paid to get in. "I come here all the time."

"You do?" I asked, eyes wide.

Chuckling, he said, "Nah. I've been here exactly once. With my sisters and their kids. They were in town to see me play with the Bay Birds and we did some sightseeing."

"That sounds fun."

"Yeah, it was," Rusty said, his blue eyes sparkling with happiness. He obviously enjoyed being an uncle. "Let's go see the dinosaurs!"

He grabbed my hand and pulled me toward the exhibit. I laughed heartily, enjoying his enthusiasm. We amused ourselves by stepping into giant dinosaur tracks to see how small our feet were and reading up on various dino facts.

Next up, we checked out a biology exhibit where we learned all kinds of gross things about germs.

"Stand here," Rusty said, gesturing toward an exhibit entitled How Far Do Germs Travel?

Before I knew it, I heard coughing and a wet puff of air hit in me in the face. This science experiment was to show how far and fast a sneeze could expel germs.

Cackling, Rusty clapped his hands.

"You jerk," I said, laughing and punching him in the arm.

"Yeah, I found out about that one the hard way last time I was here," he said with a grin.

Rusty and I checked out the bed of nails experiment next.

"They had this here when I was a kid," I exclaimed. "I totally remember laying on it when we were here on a class field trip."

"Lay down," Rusty said.

I stretched out on the flat surface and he pressed the button to raise up the nails to lift me up.

"Always feels so weird," I said.

He nodded and seized the opportunity to kiss me while I was lying down.

A kid walking by saw us and muttered, "Ew. Gross."

I laughed with Rusty's lips still on mine. When he lifted his head, he glanced over at the kid and chuckled.

"Check out his shirt."

Sure enough, the kid of about six years of age sported a Bay Birds shirt.

"That is hilarious," I said, happy to see that Rusty still had a sense of humor when it came to the Bay Birds.

We finished up our little field trip with a visit to the planetarium, which I found particularly romantic. It was as if Rusty and I were sitting under the stars together. This was the best date I'd ever been on, and it wasn't even over yet.

We left the Science Center and went out into the hot and humid air to head over to the Hard Rock Cafe nearby. I held Rusty's hand and gazed out at the Chesapeake Bay as we walked the same route we had on our first date. I marveled at how quickly and pleasantly our relationship had progressed since then.

"Do you usually do crazy stuff like visit a children's museum for fun?" I asked.

"No. Never. I just knew you would be cool and up for something goofy like this," Rusty said with a smile.

"This was the most fun I've had in a long time," I said, squeezing his hand.

Sighing happily, I thought about how easy it was to imagine spending the rest of my life with Rusty already. I could see us as an old couple, married for, like, forty years and still having fun and doing goofy things together.

Over juicy burgers at the Hard Rock Cafe, I broached the subject of Rusty's future.

"So, have you thought any more about what you might want to do now?"

"You mean, after this? I thought you had a game to go to."

"No, I didn't mean immediately after this. I meant, you know, in general. Like, have you come up with any ideas for what you might want to do for a living?"

"Oh," he said, looking depressed as he bit into his cheeseburger. He swallowed and wiped his mouth with a napkin. "Not really. Definitely having a hard time with that."

Gazing at him from across the table, I said, "I know there will never be anything that you love as much as baseball."

Rusty nodded, and the warmth in his eyes was so lovely.

"It means a lot to me that you understand that."

"Can I ask you a personal question, Rusty?"

He laughed. "Baby, we had sex on the floor this morning, and you're asking if you can get personal?"

I laughed too, but I still waited for him to answer the question.

"Beautiful, you can ask me anything you want."

As always, a shiver of delight rippled through me when he called me beautiful.

"How much money do you have?" I asked bluntly.

Rusty chuckled. "A fair question."

"I mean, do you have enough money that you can take a year or so finding your way and figuring out what you want to do? Or do you have enough money that you could pretty much go into any business that interests you?"

He thought for a moment and then said, "That second one, I guess."

"Well, that's good, right?"

"I know I should be grateful," he said in a low, sad voice.

"I'm not saying you're not grateful, Rusty." I reached across the table to squeeze his hand.

"I have a lot of money. Like, you know, *tons*. But I would give it all up if it meant I could still play baseball."

"I know you would." I gave his hand another squeeze and let go so he could eat his lunch. "But even if you can't play anymore, there must be stuff that's baseball-related you can do. You could be a TV or radio sports announcer, or a journalist. You could even be a coach or a trainer as long as the job doesn't get too physical."

He sighed deeply. "Yeah, I know. I've thought about all

that. Believe me, I have. And I've always known that there would be life after baseball and I would have to figure out what to do with the rest of my life. But I always thought that would happen after I got to play for years. I'd play ball and retire at the ripe old age of forty, and *then* I'd have to find something to occupy my time. I just never dreamed I'd be washed up in my twenties."

I nodded sympathetically as I listened.

Eyes narrowing, he said sharply, "That's what I am, you know? Washed up. I fuckin' hate that term, but that's what I am."

I flinched. Rusty was good at keeping his anger in check, but it was always there, waiting to burst out at any moment. It occurred to me that speaking to a therapist might help him, but I knew better than to bring it up right now.

He drew in a deep breath and let it out slowly, as if willing himself to calm down.

"The idea of doing something baseball-related ... It just hurts too much. I can't do it. I could never be a sportscaster and go to all those games, day after day, watching guys play ball. It would ..." He swallowed hard. "Amanda, it would kill me."

The catch in Rusty's voice tore my heart to pieces.

"I understand," I said, fighting back tears. I wanted to help him figure out an alternative as fast as humanly possible. Give him something, anything, to focus on besides his pain.

"You could start any kind of company you want. After all, you have that business degree to fall back on."

Eying me curiously, he asked, "How did you know I have a business degree?"

"I told you, I read every article there was on Rusty Power.

You got a bachelor's degree from West Virginia State University."

Rusty grinned at me. "Very good."

"You must be at least somewhat interested in business if you got a degree in it."

He shrugged. "Eh, kinda. Learned some interesting stuff. It was mostly because it seemed like a good idea as a backup plan."

"But you hoped you would never have to use it."

"Exactly," he said before stuffing a french fry in his mouth.

"I'm trying to think of businesses for you; things you know about and would be good at, but all I can think of is sports stuff. Like you could open a sports memorabilia store. Or maybe even open a gym!"

"I guess I could. I don't know. Sports memorabilia would just be more baseball stuff. And for the gym idea, I think it would make me feel bad too. I can't work out like I used to, so ..."

I nodded sadly.

"Hey," Rusty said gently. "I don't mean to shoot down all your ideas."

"I know you don't."

As much as I wanted to help him, a tiny part of me wished we could talk about me for once. I felt bad for even thinking it, but it would be nice to vent about my own job. Though I was sure Rusty would listen and support me, I didn't feel right about burdening him. He was dealing with enough.

"You like cars, right?" I asked.

"Yeah. I do."

"What about opening a car dealership?"

"Huh," Rusty said, considering the idea. A glimmer of

hope blossomed inside me, and hopefully in him as well. I knew he would be so much happier if he had a goal in life, something to pursue. He was not the type who could sit around doing nothing without going crazy.

"Think about it. You could start by opening one dealership, and if things go well, before you know it, you could have a whole bunch of stores."

"That's true. I could do that," he said, seeming to really warm to the idea. "I've always liked cars. Reading about them, going to car shows, even tinkering with some repairs."

"And isn't your dad an automotive technician?"

"He is. And damn, would he be thrilled if I owned a car dealership."

"You think he would?"

"Well, it certainly can't compare to having a son playing in the major leagues," Rusty said, that familiar tone of wistfulness in his voice. "But yeah, I think he would get a kick out of me owning a dealership, since he's been in that business for so long. He could give me some advice, and after hearing him complain about work all these years, I'd be able to see things from an employee's perspective. I wouldn't want to be a mean boss, you know?"

"Of course you wouldn't."

I couldn't even imagine Rusty being mean. Other than his infrequent bouts of anger that were due to the recent upheaval in his life, he was always sweet. He always treated restaurant servers, strangers on the streets, and even random dogs with kindness.

"There's something to be said for owning your own business." He chewed on a french fry thoughtfully. "I remember as a kid my dad would take us to his company holiday parties. He had worked for some pretty shitty dealerships in his day, but he's been with his current company for, like, twenty years. Anyway, I remember going to his work's annual Christmas party and they'd have little games and prizes for the kids. Then the boss would get up and make a speech to thank all the workers and would recognize all the five-year, ten-year, and twenty-year work anniversaries. Stuff like that. It was nice, you know? As I got older, it made me realize how much of a difference it makes when you have a good boss."

I nodded, thinking of a hundred things to complain about when it came to my current job. There was a lot that I liked, but definitely many other things I didn't. Mainly, I hated how little control I had over my work. That was why I needed to get that promotion, so I could start making a difference in people's lives.

I wanted to tell Rusty all of this, but I figured it was best to wait. Maybe if this car dealership idea worked out, he'd have something good to focus on. Then perhaps he'd be a little more emotionally available for me.

"I really like sports cars," he said excitedly. "Maybe I could start with something like that."

"That sounds wonderful," I said as relief swept through me. "And you have the perfect name for it. You could call your company Power Automotive or something."

"Hey, yeah," he said, his eyes lighting up. "That's a great idea. Thanks, Amanda. For everything. For your support. Listening to me whine. I really appreciate it."

"I know you do."

I couldn't help hoping he would ask me about my work now, but he didn't. I guess I should just bring it up on my own—there was no sense being a martyr. That was stupid. And yet, I still wished he would think to talk to me about my life without my prompting.

"Ugh, my work has been driving me crazy lately," I said.

"They're implementing this new payroll system, but nobody's making an effort to learn how it works. And believe me, that will be a major headache down the road if people don't start taking it seriously."

Rusty nodded thoughtfully, which made me feel like he was invested in what I was saying.

"That sucks," he said. He was quiet for a second, and I thought maybe he was trying to figure out what advice to give me. "You know, there really is a lot of history with sports players owning car dealerships. There's that pro football guy that owns all those shops in Pennsylvania."

I blinked, needing a second to follow the sudden change in subject.

My heart sank. This conversation made me genuinely worried about what would happen in our relationship once Rusty got his life back on track. As much as I wanted him to succeed, would he just dump me once he no longer needed my comforting? My problems might not be as tragic as his, but was I not ever allowed to be upset?

"So who knows?" he continued, oblivious to my emotions. "Maybe this actually will work out. Thanks again for helping me figure stuff out, Amanda."

Rusty's pretty blue eyes were filled with such gratitude that it was hard to stay mad. He needed me right now, and that wasn't his fault. I'd have to ride out this storm with him and see where it took us.

I just hoped he wouldn't abandon me at sea.

We finished up our lunch, stopping to look at some of the rock music memorabilia in the restaurant before heading back to my place.

As we pulled into the parking lot, I said, "You can hang out here until it's time for me to leave for the game."

I regretted those words the moment they came out of my

mouth. Though I wanted to spend as much time with Rusty as possible, I'd forgotten that if he hung out with me until I had to go, he would meet Wilder.

"Cool," Rusty said. He parked the car, and we headed toward the building.

Of course I wanted Rusty to meet my best friend. But this was *Wilder*, my ridiculously *attractive* best friend. When she was around, guys stared at her and instantly forgot that I existed. It hurt enough when strangers did it. With Rusty, it would be excruciating.

Oh well. Too late now. Wilder would be here soon. I was sure she would love to meet Rusty, and it had to happen sometime.

Once we got inside my apartment, I flopped down on the couch.

"My feet hurt from all the walking," I said, lifting up my feet and wiggling them at Rusty. He got the hint and sat down to massage them.

Rusty did take good care of me, and I felt guilty for being annoyed at him for not reading my mind at lunch.

"Today was so wonderful. I really needed the distraction since work is so stressful lately."

"That's too bad," he said with concern. "I thought you liked your job."

"I do for the most part, but I feel like I'm gonna be totally useless if I don't get that promotion."

"Oh yeah. I remember you mentioning that a while back. Some kind of director position?"

Okay, he got serious bonus points for remembering that. Points for that *and* the relaxing foot rub he was giving me.

"Director of human resources."

"That's the one. They're really draggin' their feet making a decision on the promotion, aren't they?"

"They sure are. Well, it's mainly because the current one, Denise, wound up staying on the job longer than she expected. There was some delay in the job she was leaving us for."

"Hmmm." Rusty wrapped up my foot massage, then leaned over and kissed me, sending all kinds of erotic sensations through me. Hard to believe we'd had incredible sex just this morning, because my body reacted to his touch as if I was in a sex drought.

"How long until you have to leave?" he asked.

I let out a sharp, frustrated sigh. "My friend will be here any minute."

"Kind of makes it more exciting, don't you think?"

My nipples hardened in response. "Yes, but we really can't, Rusty. There's just not enough time. I'm not gonna be caught naked with you when Wilder gets here."

"Oh, I think there's enough time," Rusty said seductively. "And we don't have to be naked."

With that, he unzipped my jeans and slid his hand between my legs.

"You've been a wonderfully supportive girlfriend, Amanda," he said huskily. "And you deserve a reward."

He slipped two thick fingers inside me, massaging my vagina until I was good and wet. I gasped when he stroked my clit. I wanted to protest, but I was already too far gone. All I could do was moan as Rusty pleasured me. I bit my lip, doing my best not to cry out too loud in case Wilder was already approaching the door.

Rusty was right. That *did* make it more exciting.

"Oh Rusty," I panted. "Oh God. Don't stop ... don't stop ..."

I was so close, and if he stopped, I would die right there of sexual frustration. At that point I wouldn't have cared if

Wilder was watching us through the window. Rusty simply had to finish what he'd started.

"Ah ... ah," I cried softly as I came hard beneath his thick fingers.

"That's my girl," he said smugly as he watched my body quiver and spasm with release.

Panting, I whispered, "That was ... incredible."

There was a knock at the door.

Rusty chuckled and said, "Oh shit."

He jumped up and ran to the kitchen sink where he washed his hands and splashed water on his face. I felt bad that I hadn't had the chance to return the sexual favor, but right now I had to compose myself. My face flushed, I zipped up my jeans and straightened out my hair.

Wilder knocked again; I had to hurry, or she would get suspicious. My apartment was tiny, so it wasn't like I had to walk far to get to the door, no matter where I was.

"Do I look okay?" I asked Rusty, tugging at my clothes.

He chuckled again and shrugged. He was messing with me, but there was nothing I could do about it now.

I opened the door, doing my best to act like I wasn't out of breath.

"Hey," Wilder said with a sweet smile. She didn't seem to notice anything out of the ordinary. It helped that she spotted Rusty and was immediately distracted.

"Oh wow, it's so great to meet you finally," she said, her pretty face lighting up with excitement. I loved her for being so happy to meet my new boyfriend, but my heart sank. The woman really was insanely beautiful. I dreaded Rusty's initial reaction when he saw her. I wished I'd warned him that she was gorgeous, to give him a chance to at least pretend he wasn't impressed.

I watched carefully as Rusty dried his hands on a towel in the kitchen and headed over to Wilder.

Extending his hand, he said, "So great to meet you too, Wilder."

Rusty smiled warmly as he shook her hand. As always, he was cordial and kind, but his eyes were hardly popping out of his head like every other guy who saw my supermodel friend.

"Wow dude, you are *tall*," Wilder said admiringly.

"You're no slouch yourself," he said. Though he eyed her up and down, it seemed like he was only checking out her height. He didn't leer or stare at her boobs like an idiot.

"True," Wilder said. Turning to me, she asked, "So what did you guys do?"

"Ah ... wh—what?" I asked, my face getting hot.

"What did you guys end up doing today? Last I heard from you was your text this morning saying you hadn't decided."

Rusty shot me a knowing grin, and I loved sharing our secret about what we had *just* done on my couch.

"Oh, we had a blast," he said, taking over the conversation while I got ahold of myself. "We wound up going to the Maryland Science Center and playing around with the exhibits."

"Did you really?" Wilder asked.

"Yeah," I said, finally finding my voice again. "It was so much fun. We went to the planetarium, too."

"Wow, I haven't been there since I was a kid," Wilder said.

"Me neither," I said. "Then we went to the Hard Rock Cafe."

"Cool. Sometimes it's fun to play tourist in your own town," she said, gazing at me with a sweet smile. She knew how much Rusty meant to me, and she clearly enjoyed seeing my happiness.

"Oh hey, how did your audition go this morning?" I asked her.

"Pretty well, I think. Hard to say, but I feel good about it."

"Are you an actress?" Rusty asked.

"Trying to be," Wilder said with a laugh. "I majored in theater in college, and my hope is to make it to Broadway someday."

"Nice," he said with interest.

A twinge of jealousy rose up in me, and I hated myself for it. Rusty was showing a genuine interest in my best friend's career aspirations, and it was very sweet of him. Part of my problem was this conversation reminded me that his last lover had been a gorgeous Hollywood actress. Between Emily Martindale and Wilder Price, there was no way I could compete.

"What was the audition for?" he asked.

"A local production of *Little Shop of Horrors.*"

"Cool. Well good lu— ah, I mean, break a leg."

Wilder laughed. "Thanks."

"I don't wanna hold you guys up," Rusty said. "I know you need to get going."

He looked over at me, meeting my gaze. And just like that, my insecurities melted away. He hadn't ogled Wilder like every other dude on the planet. No. But he *did* look at me with a delicious combination of desire and fondness that made me feel like I was the only woman in the room.

I couldn't have put into words how Rusty made me feel. I couldn't describe the deep connection I felt with him, but it was there. And it was *real.*

I was falling in love with Rusty Power. Not my celebrity

crush Rusty Power, the famous baseball player. But the real flesh and blood guy standing before me.

And, unless I was crazy, I thought he was falling for me too.

"Should I just go, or ..." Wilder said, making Rusty and me burst out laughing.

We had lost track of how long we'd been staring into each other's eyes. The fact that Rusty seemed to have literally forgotten Wilder was there for a second meant more to me than he could ever know. I was always the one who was ignored and forgotten.

But not anymore.

"Sorry," I said. "We can get going now."

"Have fun you guys," Rusty said, looking only at me.

He kissed me tenderly on the lips, then I kissed him on the left side of his chest where his heart was. Rusty smiled softly at me. I loved that he got the message. Instead of getting angry, he appreciated my concern. He understood that I didn't think he was weak, but that I worried because I cared deeply for him.

The three of us walked out to the parking lot, separating when we reached our respective cars.

Rusty never took his eyes off me.

18

RUSTY

The following Friday night, Amanda stayed at my place. We made love in my bed that night and again in the morning. I couldn't get enough of her, and she seemed to feel the same way about me. It was glorious.

We slept in on Saturday. After breakfast, we decided the weather was far too gorgeous to stay inside. Since there wasn't much within walking distance of my place in the city, we drove to a park a few miles away.

As soon as we got out of the car, Amanda drew in a deep breath of fresh air.

"I love that smell of fresh cut grass. Smells like summer," she said as she gazed up at the trees and around the park.

"Me too," I said, though that smell, like so many other things, made my chest feel heavy with sorrow. The sights and sounds of summer reminded me of baseball. But then, pretty much everything did.

Amanda fell into step with me, and we started up the walking trail. Now that I took a moment to breathe in the fresh air, I found a sense of calm. I always did love being outdoors. I supposed I would get used to doing things that didn't involve baseball, but it would take a while. I had to completely rewire my brain—and my heart—to adjust to the fact that baseball was no longer a part of my life.

"You okay?" Amanda asked.

"Yeah. Fine," I lied.

"Did you make any progress this week on the car dealership idea?"

"I did, actually. Started researching stuff about how to start a car business. It's pretty interesting."

"That's great," she said with a smile.

It was sweet that Amanda really wanted the dealership idea to work out for me. I loved that she worried about how I was doing, and that she was aware I desperately needed some kind of goal to work toward.

I also thought it was cool that Amanda had asked me how much money I had, solely because she wanted to explore my career possibilities. Now she knew for sure that I was loaded, but she didn't seem to care. She never asked for anything—not expensive jewelry or help with paying her rent or anything. Of course, I was more than willing to help her with anything she needed, but I also didn't want to insult her. Amanda had a job, and she worked hard to pay her bills. From what I could tell, she didn't need my help.

The one thing we had decided early on was that I would pay for our dates. I could easily afford it, and it was silly to make her pay half. We could enjoy everything from fancy dinners to pizza at home, and she would never have to worry about the extra expense.

Besides, from the way our relationship was blossoming, I could easily imagine her moving in with me. Then she *really* wouldn't have to worry about her finances ever again.

"That would be cool if the whole Power Automotive thing worked out," she said.

"I do like that name," I said enthusiastically. "So perfect for an automotive business."

"Did you tell your dad what you're thinking of doing?"

"I did. He seemed pretty excited about it. My mom is thrilled too. You've seen how she is. She worries so much about me, and I think she'll sleep better at night knowing I've got something to focus on."

"You mom is so sweet," Amanda said.

"Yeah, she is."

I glanced over at my girl, watching the soft breeze ruffle her pretty hair. Being with her brought me such a sense of peace. Whenever I was with her, it felt like everything would be okay. Everything here felt peaceful. Such a nice respite from the city, with the birds chirping and the sound of kids laughing and shouting in the distance. Baltimore had a bad reputation with all the violence from drugs and guns. Unfortunately, that reputation was based on truth. But there was so much more to this place than that, even if a lot of work had to be done.

"I hope you guys had fun at the game last week," I said sincerely, even though it would be hard for me to hear about it.

"It was okay."

I grinned. "Beautiful, I saw the highlights. It was more than just okay." It warmed my heart that she was trying to protect my feelings.

Amanda laughed. "You're right. It was more than okay. It was incredible!"

Her eyes lit up, and I couldn't help but find it sexy that she was so into baseball. Sometimes I forgot that, since she was careful not to discuss the topic around me.

"Did you stay for the whole game?"

"All twelve innings," she said proudly. "And we were really glad we stayed."

"I bet."

With two outs, Brady Keaton had hit a three-run blast in the twelfth inning. Baseball didn't get much more exciting than that. Though I'd been happy for my buddy when I watched the highlights on TV, it had hurt like hell to see all my former teammates celebrating and fist bumping one another.

I should have been with them.

Normally, I avoided watching sports news, but I'd made an exception since my girlfriend had been at the game.

Amanda's expression fell, and I realized my heartache was showing on my face. Damn. The last thing I'd wanted was to make her feel bad.

"It was nice getting to meet your friend last week," I said, changing the subject as we started up a small hill on the walking trail.

"What did you think of her?"

"She was nice."

"Just nice?"

"Uhhhh ... very nice?" I asked, confused by the question. Wilder seemed pretty cool, but I'd only spoken to her for a few minutes. I wasn't sure what Amanda was getting at.

I glanced over at her, searching for clues. I came up empty.

She was quiet for a moment. Then she said, "The truth is, I was afraid to have you meet her."

"Really? Why?"

"Because she's so beautiful." The deep sadness in her voice took me by surprise.

I thought back. Sure, Wilder was pretty. Tall, blond, blue eyes. Or maybe green. I couldn't remember.

Well, yeah. She was very pretty, now that I thought about it. But I wasn't attracted to her. Especially not with Amanda standing right there. She was the only woman I wanted.

"Are you jealous of her?" I asked as gently as I could.

Amanda sighed. "Yes. Well, sometimes. And I feel awful about it because she is my nearest and dearest friend. I mean, it's not just that she's so much prettier than I am."

"Amanda, she is not pr—"

"Yes, she is," she said firmly. There was no point in arguing with her. "It's not that it bothers me that she's more attractive than me. I'm not *that* superficial."

"You're not superficial at all."

That got a small smile out of her, which made me happy.

"It's just ... you wouldn't believe the way people act when we're out together. It's one thing that guys stare at her. That I can understand. But I'm so plain next to her that people literally forget I'm there when I'm with her."

"I'm sure that's not true, beautiful."

Amanda abruptly stopped walking, so I did too.

Facing me, she asked, "Do you know what happens when we go to bars together?"

I shook my head. The pain on her face made my stomach hurt.

"Guys use me to get to her. They sit down and chat me up. Sometimes it's obvious what they're up to. The guy's talking to me while staring at Wilder, so I know the score. But sometimes they get me into a real conversation. And then, just for a minute, I start thinking they might actually be into me. Next thing I know, they say something like 'Is it okay with you if I ask your gorgeous friend over here for a date?'"

I stared at her, horrified. "They don't really do that ... do they?"

"Hell yeah. Happens all the time."

I had no idea what to say. I hated all those nameless, faceless bastards who had hurt my precious Amanda like that. She deserved so much better.

"I'm serious. It's like I turn invisible when Wilder is around. So I was afraid—really afraid—of what would happen when you met her."

I saw the fear in Amanda's eyes. She wasn't kidding.

My mind raced back to the moment I met Wilder. Had I stared at her? Dear God, I hoped not. If only I'd known about Amanda's insecurities, I would have been careful about how I reacted.

Tears sprang to Amanda's eyes, and my body tensed.

Oh God, I hope I didn't screw this up.

"But Rusty, when you saw her, you didn't even blink. You shook her hand and talked with her, but you kept looking at *me.*"

Thank God.

I remembered Wilder's joke that maybe she should leave because Amanda and I had been staring at each other so long.

"That's never happened before," she said, tears spilling from her eyes.

"Oh, baby." I pulled her into my arms. "You never have to worry about stuff like that with me. You're the only girl I want."

"I know it's stupid to get so upset."

"It's not stupid, Amanda. Nobody deserves to be treated like that. Like they're invisible." Pulling back to look at her, I said, "For what it's worth, you're the most beautiful woman in the world to me."

"That's worth a lot, Rusty," she said with a smile.

The more I thought about what she had just told me, the more pissed off I got.

"You okay?"

"Yeah, I just hate those guys for being such jerks. I hate that anybody would ever make you feel so awful."

Amanda shrugged and sighed, as if resigned to her lot in life as second fiddle. We started walking again, but I was still stewing.

"I'm gonna pick you up in a bar," I said.

"What?"

"I mean it. Some day when you're out with Wilder at a bar, I'm gonna hit on you in front of everybody in the place."

Amanda laughed, but I saw the delight in her eyes.

"That is really sweet, Rusty. Seriously, even if you never actually do that, I love that you even thought about it."

"I'm *totally* gonna do it," I said.

"Okay." She laughed again, but I didn't think she really believed me.

As we continued walking the trail, enjoying the perfect weather and the gentle breeze, I thought about what Amanda had said about her friend. Now that I thought about it more, Wilder truly was an attractive woman. Tall, blond, and with a terrific figure. She had much bigger boobs than Amanda, and could probably have been a model.

I smiled to myself when I realized that I still wasn't attracted to her. Objectively, I could see that she was prettier than Amanda, but I wasn't hot for her the way I was for my girl. Emily Martindale was prettier too, I guess, but I'd never been as turned on by her as I was by Amanda. Turned out I needed more than just physical beauty to be attracted to a woman. And as far as I was concerned, Amanda was the whole package. She was intelligent and sweet and tons of fun to be with, not to mention super-hot in bed.

I could not get the image of Amanda being repeatedly used and rejected in public out of my head. The mere thought made me so damned angry. I never wanted to see that look of pain and rejection on her face again. I wanted to fix it. *Now.*

I knew exactly what I could do to lift her spirits.

My chest ached just thinking about what I was going to say, but I knew in my heart it was the right thing to do. It was an idea I'd been kicking around for a while, and knowing it would make Amanda happy made any pain I would suffer totally worthwhile.

"So I've been thinking," I began. "Since I got to meet your best friend, maybe you'd like to meet some of my friends."

"That sounds great. I would love to meet some of your friends."

Clearly, she hadn't quite grasped my meaning yet. My stomach tingled with anticipation, and I was already confident that I'd have no regrets about this. She was gonna flip out. In a good way.

"The team's in Boston right now, but they'll be back soon."

Amanda gasped, covering her mouth with both hands. Now *there* was the reaction I wanted.

I chuckled.

"You mean I can meet some of the Bay Birds?"

"Yup," I said.

Not only had Amanda never asked for any money from me, she'd never asked for autographs or any other favors from my famous friends. My girl really was amazing.

"Rusty, that would be incredible!"

"It'll be fun." Her happiness would be a true joy, even if it hurt like hell to be around a bunch of baseball players who were living my dream while I'd been sidelined forever. I hadn't hung out with any of the guys since I'd been forced to hang up my cleats, but many of them had stayed in touch. It was mostly through text and the occasional phone call, but of course they were all crazy busy right now. Still, it was nice that they hadn't forgotten me.

Not yet, at least.

We looped around the walking trail, winding up where we started.

"Wanna try out the swings?" I asked.

"Sure," she chirped excitedly.

We found two empty swings and hopped on like we were a couple of kids.

As we pumped our legs, swinging higher and higher, we managed to carry on a conversation. Meeting the players was all Amanda could talk about, and for once, it didn't hurt so much to talk about baseball. Her giddy excitement was contagious, and making her happy was the only thing that mattered to me right now.

Because I was in love with her.

19

RUSTY

During the baseball season, the players frequently hung out at Brady Keaton's place when they needed to chill and take a break from the fans. This was especially true for Brady himself—he was so well-known, he got mobbed everywhere he went.

Amanda and I drove over to the house in Baltimore that Brady shared with his wife, Lyric. Though Amanda was excited about meeting the guys and she'd assured me she still wanted to go, this past week she'd gotten increasingly nervous about seeing so many famous people at once, terrified that she would somehow make a fool of herself.

"They're famous, Amanda, but they're still just people," I reminded her as we neared the Keaton residence.

"I know, I know," she said, still sounding super jittery.

"Are you especially nervous about meeting Brady?"

"Yes. But technically, I have met him before."

"Really? At an autograph signing?"

"No," she said softly. "It was the day you collapsed. Oh God, I was such a mess. It was right after I'd managed to get your heart started again. Then the trainers took over, and they got the ambulance for you and everything."

Amanda's voice shook, but now for a different reason—it was still hard for her to talk about.

"I was on the field during all the commotion, so Brady came over and took care of me."

I couldn't look at her because I was driving, but I felt better that I could hear the smile in her voice.

"Brady was very sweet. He put his arm around me and led me over to the dugout to sit and got me some water."

"That was cool of him."

"Yeah. Matt Jovey helped too. Took me to Julia's office, and she sat with me a bit until I calmed down."

"They're a great bunch of people," I said with pride, happy to hear how kind my friends had been to Amanda that horrible day.

"Yeah." She still sounded nervous.

"You have nothing to worry about, Amanda. These are my *friends*. They're gonna be nice to you."

"I know," she said.

I knew no matter what Amanda said or did, my buddies would never laugh at her or make her uncomfortable. There was a code among ballplayers; you always respected the wife or girlfriend.

As it turned out, she got more than respect when we entered the large, fully furnished barroom.

"There she is!" Brady exclaimed, rushing out from behind his beautiful dark wood grain bar to greet Amanda.

He engulfed her in a big bear hug, practically swallowing her up in his arms. He looked *huge* next to her. Amanda blushed and laughed.

"Nice to see you too," she said when he released her.

"Way to ease her into it, Crush," Lyric said, shaking her head as she walked over to us from one of the many tables.

I was glad to see her here. Lyric was such a sweetheart and much more low-key than her boisterous husband. If anyone could put Amanda at ease, it was her.

"Hi, Amanda," Lyric said with a gentle smile. "It's so nice to meet you. I'm—"

"Lyric!" Amanda blurted out excitedly. "Of course I know who you are. How's medical school?"

Lyric's pretty smile widened, and her blue eyes sparkled. It was the perfect thing for Amanda to ask. Lyric was too often treated as Mrs. Brady Keaton. She was crazy smart and had a perfectly good identity of her own.

"It's been going well," Lyric said. "I'm on summer break right now, but still working a ton at the hospital and doing research, that kind of thing."

"That's amazing," Amanda said, visibly calmer.

Yep, Lyric had that effect on people. I knew she was going to be a terrific doctor.

"Come on over and sit down," Brady said, gesturing to the bar. "Have a drink."

I put my hand on Amanda's back and ushered her over. I murmured in her ear, "I told you everything would be fine."

She smiled and nodded. I'd been so busy taking care of her that I hadn't had time to deal with the fact that I was in a room full of people who were living the dream as professional baseball players. As long as Amanda had fun, I knew I would be okay.

Still, it hurt to be here. I was an outsider. An invited guest—no longer one of them.

Brady slid me a beer as soon as I sat down. The simple gesture made me feel welcome. It meant a lot that he'd remembered my favorite beer. He asked Amanda what she wanted and got her a glass of wine.

"I was at last Saturday night's game," Amanda said enthusiastically to Brady.

"Really?" Brady looked pleased. As well he should be, given his performance that night.

"Yeah. I thought it was all over when poor Matt Jovey struck out on that nasty slider," she said.

"Hey," Matt said from a few seats over. With mock hurt, he added, "I did the best I could."

Amanda blinked for a second, not having noticed his presence. I was afraid her worst fears had come true—that she would be embarrassed in front of the players. Her response took me by surprise.

With a smile, she told Matt, "Hey, with a batting average up near .300 right now, you've got nothing to feel bad about."

Matt grinned, looking impressed.

Turning to Brady, she continued. "But then with two outs in the twelfth inning, you got hold of that hangin' curveball and just launched it. It was incredible."

Both Brady and Matt glanced over at me and then back at Amanda, impressed with her sports knowledge. I realized Amanda was really in her element when she was talking baseball.

And yet I'd made it clear that no baseball talk was allowed around me. Like I'd been silencing her voice or something. I knew she understood why it upset me to talk about it, but I still felt guilty about the whole thing.

Amanda was happily chatting with Brady and Matt about baseball, so I turned to Angel Jimenez, who was sitting on the other side of me. He was one of our starting pitchers. Or rather, he was one of the starting pitchers for the Bay Birds. I couldn't really refer to it as "our" team anymore.

"How's it going man?"

"Doin' great," Angel said, before taking a healthy swig of beer.

"How's that young lad of yours?"

That got a huge grin out of Angel, as I knew it would. He adored his wife and son, and he was notorious for showing pictures of them to anyone and everyone. It was a running joke that we—well, the players on the team—would mockingly run and hide when we saw him coming with his phone out, ready to show off the latest photos of his kid.

"Enrique's doing great. Starts preschool soon."

"Wow. That was fast."

"Tell me about it," Angel said. "It all goes so quickly. So how've you been?"

"Good," I said.

"You're such a liar."

"What?"

Angel's dark brown eyes narrowed as he scrutinized my face. "This whole thing sucks. I can't imagine what you've been going through since this all went down."

I nodded, grateful that my former teammate had seen right through me. Pretending I was fine could be exhausting sometimes.

"I want you to know I understand exactly what you're going through," he said, his grim tone taking me by surprise.

"You do?"

"Yeah. When I was still in the minors, I got in a real bad car accident. Was in recovery for a long time, and through it all, I wasn't sure if I'd ever pitch again."

"Damn. I had no idea."

Angel's fastball was a killer. I'd never have guessed that he'd been injured.

"I'll never forget how that felt." Angel's eyes locked on mine. "It was hell. I don't know what I've would've done if …"

I'd seen that look before on many of my friends' faces. Deep down, they all knew that what had happened to me could happen to them. That thought haunted everybody who played sports for a living.

"I just … I don't know what to say, Rusty. Except I'm real sorry this happened to you."

"Thanks, man. I appreciate that."

Angel slapped me on the back and took another sip of his beer. Grinning at me, he said, "And I know meeting the right girl won't magically make it all better, but it sure as hell helps."

"True," I said.

"Amanda sure looks like a natural holding that baby," Angel said with a chuckle.

"Baby? What baby?" I turned around to look.

I hadn't seen our catcher, Trace Ridgerton, enter with his girlfriend and new baby. Amanda certainly had—she was already holding the tiny infant in her arms and sharing a laugh with his mother, Sarah. Trace had met Sarah through the Bay Birds organization. She worked on community service projects with the team. I worked on some events with her in the past, and she was a real sweetheart.

I couldn't take my eyes off Amanda as I watched her cooing over the baby. Angel was right. She *was* a natural. Remembering how much fun we'd had at the Science Center and swinging at the park like a couple of kids ourselves, it was easy to imagine having children with her.

Suddenly, my life didn't seem so bleak. Being surrounded by all these ballplayers felt like a knife had been plunged into my heart, but seeing Amanda like this was like a balm to my wounds. I *loved* this woman, and more than anything right now, I wanted a future with her. I wanted to buy a big house and adopt a bunch of dogs and have a lot of kids and build a life together. It wouldn't erase the pain of losing baseball, but it was a wonderful future to look forward to.

Trace waved at me from across the room, shooting me a knowing smile. He knew his precious little son was irresistible to my girlfriend.

"I'm gonna go say hi to the baby," I said to Angel, who lifted his glass in response as I stepped away.

"Hey man." I gave Trace a slap on the back in greeting. "How you doing?"

"I'm tired," he moaned. "So ... tired. But good, you know? Things are good."

"I can see that." I looked down at the baby in Amanda's arms. The little guy was fast asleep. Cute little thing.

"Isn't he precious?" Amanda asked, gazing up at me dreamily.

"Yeah, he is."

"I'm gonna go sit down over there for a minute, okay?" Sarah also looked weary but happy. She gestured over to where Lyric and Julia sat at a table.

"Of course," Trace said, kissing her on the cheek.

"Do you want me to take him back? Or ..." Sarah asked Amanda.

"No way." Amanda clutched the baby closer, making Sarah laugh.

"Cool," Sarah said, sounding grateful for a break. "Come on over with us."

Amanda smiled and followed her over to join the women. Trace and I headed to the bar.

Brady slid Trace a beer and glanced at my empty glass. I nodded, and he got me another. Though he could have easily afforded to hire a full-time bartender for his place, Brady enjoyed serving the drinks himself.

"So, what have you been doing with yourself these days?" Trace asked. I tried to ignore that familiar expression of pity and fear on his face.

"Been kickin' around some ideas."

"Yeah?" He waited for me to elaborate.

"Thinkin' about starting a business. Maybe a car dealership."

"Nice," Trace said, looking genuinely interested. "That could be cool. Sports cars, I assume?"

I grinned, pleased that he'd remembered my automotive preferences.

"Naturally. I haven't decided for sure about doing it. Right now, I'm just kinda looking into it."

"You're bored out of your skull, aren't you?" Trace said, seeing right through me just as Angel had.

Slumping my shoulders exaggeratedly, I said, "You have no idea."

Trace chuckled and nodded.

"Amanda and I are doing great. I don't know what I would have done without her."

"She seems really cool."

"She's incredible. Like, I can't believe how quickly we connected, you know? And at the time when I needed that the most. But she's got a life outside of me. I mean, as well she should. She works full time and all of that. I can't expect her to keep me occupied all the time. I gotta figure out what I'm gonna do for the rest of my life."

"I hear ya. Give it some time. Dude, you had the rug ripped out from under you with no warning. You'll land on your feet. Just might take a while."

"Yeah," I said somberly.

"Can I make a suggestion?" Trace asked, setting his glass down on the bar.

"Please." I already felt like I'd run out of options. The car dealership thing was a good idea in theory, but I was having trouble finding the motivation to make it work. And I still felt like a total idiot every time I picked up my guitar.

"You should learn to ride a motorcycle," he said.

I laughed. "I should have expected to hear that from you."

Everyone knew about Trace Ridgerton and his beloved Indian motorcycle. The first outfit Sarah had bought for the baby while she was still pregnant was a teeny black onesie with a motorcycle on it.

"I know," he said with a grin. "But for real, they don't call it wind therapy for nothing. Getting out on the open road and just ridin' hard ... Dude, there's no feeling like it."

I shrugged.

"Rusty," he said sternly. "I know you gotta be goin' through hell right now."

I swallowed a huge gulp of beer. After a moment, I said, "Yeah. I really am. I know I should be grateful just to be alive, but ..."

"I get it, man. I do. I'm just sayin' you need something that's just for you right now. I'm telling you, learn to ride. Buy a motorcycle. I know you can afford it."

I nodded, feeling renewed guilt over my self-pity. I did have my health, and I did have lots of money. What right did I have to be upset?

"Just promise me you'll think about it," Trace insisted.

"I'm tellin' you, riding has helped me sort out all kinds of stuff in my life. I don't know. Somehow it just helps. Clears your mind."

"That does make sense."

"No feeling like getting out on the open road, blasting your music the whole way. Gets your blood goin', ya know?"

Now that *did* appeal to me. I couldn't play my music too loud in my apartment, but I cranked it up in my car. Riding a motorcycle might be a way to release some of the fury I had bottled up so much of the time. Funny how loud, angry music had a calming effect.

"Sounds pretty cool, actually."

"You let me know. I'll get you signed up for riding lessons. Help you pick out a bike. Whatever you need."

"Cool, let's do it," I said, clinking my glass with his.

I tried not to contemplate what Amanda might think about my learning to ride a bike.

Even worse, what would my *mother* say?

20

AMANDA

I couldn't take my eyes off the sweet baby in my arms.

"Oh, Sarah. He's beautiful," I said to her across from me at the table. Lyric sat to my left and Julia was to my right. I felt like I was sitting in the baseball players' wives' section. It was fun, especially since the women all made me feel welcome, as if I'd always been a part of their group.

"Thanks," she said with a tired smile. "I love him, but I'm happy he's asleep right now."

"I'm sure," I said, reminding myself that holding a sleeping baby for a few minutes didn't give you any idea what it was like to be a mother. I wanted kids, but from everything I'd heard, it was an incredibly demanding job.

As exhausted as she was, I could see the joy in Sarah's eyes when she gazed at her tiny son. With her lightish blond hair and gentle blue-green eyes, she had soft beauty that made her look like the definition of a loving mother. And Trace seemed to be a doting father, judging by the way he kept glancing over to check on Sarah and their child.

Until today, I hadn't been sure I liked Trace Ridgerton.

He always came off as kind of a jerk in interviews, like he thought he was better than everybody else. But I'd already changed my mind about him. Not only did Rusty seem to be having a good conversation with him, but it was clear that Trace was very much in love with Sarah. Now that I'd met him in person, I got pretty good vibes from the man.

"So, you guys make an adorable couple," Julia said as she looked over my shoulder at Rusty.

I laughed. "Thanks."

"Amanda," Lyric said, putting a gentle hand on my shoulder. "I have to tell you, what you did for Rusty that day was incredible."

"Oh, I'm just glad he's okay." I flashed back to Rusty's ashen face as I so often did when someone mentioned the incident.

"From what I hear, you don't have any medical training," Lyric said, sounding impressed. She let go of my shoulder and picked up her wineglass, shaking her head in amazement.

"No, not really. Just one CPR lesson."

"Amazing," she said. "Not only do you need to know how to perform CPR, but you have to keep your cool under pressure. Believe me, a lot of people freeze up in that situation. It's totally understandable of course, but it can have tragic consequences."

"Yeah," I said, feeling tears form in my eyes. "And to think I almost didn't run down there because I was afraid of making a fool of myself. I saw him collapse, but I wasn't really sure what was happening. But God, when I saw him … I knew something was horribly wrong."

My voice quavered a little as I spoke. It had been hard enough when I had watched a virtual stranger in peril, but now I was in love with Rusty. Thinking about what could have happened still haunted me.

"He's doing great now," Julia said with tremendous empathy in her voice. She had seen firsthand how shaken up I'd been that day.

I nodded.

"So what do you do for a living, Amanda?" Lyric asked, clearly trying to steer the conversation toward something cheerier.

"I work in human resources. Over at the University of Timonium."

"Oh, nice," Julia said. "It must be cool to work at a college."

"It is for the most part. I love working in HR, but I'm feeling a little stifled career wise. Right now, I'm just the HR assistant, so I don't really get to *do* much, you know what I mean?"

"Yeah, I get that," Lyric said. "You feel like you're on the sidelines."

"Exactly," I said, grateful for the chance to vent about work. "I know that HR is supposed to protect the interests of the company, but what I want to do is be a true liaison between the workers and the employer. Really listen to concerns that the employees have and try to negotiate a solution. I want to make having to work forty hours a week as pleasant as possible for people, you know?"

"I love that," Julia said, tipping her beer at me. "And I think you're right. HR can do a lot to make workers happier, and that's good for the company and the employees."

"If I can just get the promotion I'm dying for, then I can do everything I've been wanting to do. But the director of human resources keeps putting off her resignation date, and

I'm going crazy waiting for them to make a decision about the promotion."

"That sucks," Julia said before chugging her beer.

"Well, I hope you get the promotion," Lyric said.

"Me too," Sarah said. "I'd toast you for good luck, but your hands are full with my child."

I laughed with the other women. I already felt so at home with this group.

I turned to check on Rusty at the bar. He had been watching me hold the baby. His smile sent shivers of delight through my body. Of all his gorgeous features—tall and muscular with broad shoulders and stunning blue eyes—it was still his smile that attracted me most. I hoped I would always feel that thrill when he smiled at me.

"You're thinking about having children with that man, aren't you?" Julia asked bluntly, making me blush.

"*Julia,*" Lyric admonished, making us all laugh.

"I'm only teasing," Julia said. "I just think it's sweet the way you guys look at each other. And Rusty's a doll. He would make an amazing father."

I couldn't help smiling.

"Yeah. Yeah, he sure would."

I glimpsed at Rusty again and saw a worried expression on his face as he spoke to Trace. Then he winced and touched his chest. My anxiety ratcheted up, and I had the impulse to toss Sarah's baby in her lap and rush over to check on him.

My common sense kicked in, and I realized it was just his ribs bothering him. Letting out a deep breath, I wondered what toll all this worry was doing to *my* cardiac health.

21

RUSTY

We were chilling at Amanda's apartment, relaxing on her couch, when I floated the motorcycle idea past her.

Her face fell and she groaned. "Oh, Rusty. *Really*?"

I'd been prepared to do battle with her over this, but I wasn't prepared for the way her reaction made me feel. Amanda looked at me like I was the most precious thing in the world to her.

Her agonized expression was all too familiar to me. It was the same look she'd given me when we had sex for the first time and she was afraid I was having another cardiac episode. It was the same haunted look she had after yet another nightmare about finding me dead on the baseball field. Like the idea of losing me was too much to bear.

I gazed into her eyes, utterly overwhelmed by my feelings for her. I'd had lots of adoring fans stare at me, and I was lucky to have a bunch of great friends in my life who cared about me. But nobody had ever looked at me the way she did.

Finally, I couldn't hold it in any longer.

"I love you, Amanda."

"Wh—what?" she asked, her eyes wide.

"I love you," I repeated.

Amanda's expression softened, and I already knew by her reaction that she felt the same way about me.

But that didn't make it any less momentous when she said, "Oh, Rusty. I love you too."

I dipped my head and kissed her, loving the sound of that familiar moan. Still cupping her face, I gazed into her sweet brown eyes.

"This better not be your way of emotionally manipulating me into letting you get a motorcycle."

I laughed. "Of course not."

Amanda's laugh and the adoring look in her eyes told me that she'd only been joking. She knew me well enough to know I was sincere and that I was not the emotionally manipulative type.

"I just ... I hate that you worry about me, but I also kind of love it at the same time."

She laughed again. "I know what you mean."

"I don't mean to worry you, beautiful. I just feel like learning to ride would be good for me, you know? Like it's something I should do."

She sighed. "Well, it makes sense. You love sports cars, and I'm sure you would have a lot of fun with a motorcycle."

"I will," I said, getting excited about the idea all over again.

"Hmm." She shook her head.

"What?"

"To think ... just when I was starting to like Trace Ridgerton."

I laughed. "Yeah, he can be kind of an acquired taste. But he's a good guy."

"I guess," she grumbled. "But if anything happens to you, I'm coming after him."

"Fair enough."

Amanda rubbed my chest, then she leaned over and kissed my heart as she so often did.

A renewed rush of love for her washed over me. I'd never know what I did to deserve a woman like her in my life.

"You know," I said. "We've never done it in your bedroom before."

"You're right," she said, gazing into my eyes with an irresistible combination of love and lust.

"We should fix that."

Though I did want to christen her bedroom, it was more that I wanted to *show* her how I felt.

"We should," she said in a husky voice, making it clear that I was forgiven for the whole bike thing. For now, at least.

I got up, took her hand, and led her to the bedroom.

When I undressed her, I took my time admiring her body. It broke my heart to think of the way she compared herself to Wilder, and I wanted to erase any doubts and insecurities she might have. I wouldn't trade my Amanda for the hottest supermodel in the world. I couldn't imagine being more attracted to any other woman. Not when I had the perfect girl right here.

I teased and tantalized her once I slid inside her body, allowing her to get close to release but not quite.

"Rusty," she cried, pleading with me to make her come.

"Not just yet, my love," I murmured in her ear. She sighed softly, temporarily placated by my romantic words.

I sped up, making her cry out again. Her bed was smaller than mine, not to mention squeakier. The noise the bedsprings made was kind of hot. The sound of vigorous, athletic sex made it even more exciting. More pleasurable. More ...

I'm not gonna last much longer.

"*Please,* darling," she said breathlessly.

She knew by now that her begging drove me crazy.

I had to give Amanda an orgasm; I wouldn't let myself finish first. Not again.

I shifted my body, thrust hard, and massaged between her legs with my fingers. I knew her body well and could make her come whenever *I* was ready.

She screamed my name as her body rocked underneath me. Just hearing her come was enough to push me over the edge. I yelled her name too when I came.

Amanda lay beneath me, flushed and panting. "Oh, Rusty. Now I *really* love you."

She knew just what to say to make me feel like a man.

Her man.

I rolled over and pulled her into my arms. We held each other, skin to skin. As always, I felt more at peace with her. Having her close made me feel like everything would be all right.

She leaned forward and kissed my chest near my heart, that familiar worried look crossing her face. She no longer feared for my health in bed, but I knew what she was fretting about now.

"I'm gonna be fine on the bike, Amanda. I promise."

She nodded but didn't look convinced.

"Trace has been riding safely for a long time, so he's gonna help teach me."

He'll help when he has time, anyway. Unlike me, he still has a baseball career.

"I'm gonna sign up for riding lessons, and they make you

do, like, thirty hours of classwork and a whole bunch of actual riding training."

A "whole bunch" was technically only six hours, but I didn't think that would be enough to make Amanda feel better.

"And they don't make you take the separate motorcycle safety class unless you're under eighteen, but I'm gonna take it anyway. Okay?"

"Okay," she whispered.

"Sweetheart," I said, stroking her hair. "It's gonna be fine. I swear."

"I know," she said wearily. "But you already cheated death once, Rusty. It feels like you're tempting fate here."

"I hate making you worry." I didn't entirely mean it. Sometimes it annoyed me when Amanda fussed over me, and sometimes it felt good that somebody loved me enough to care. My parents worried of course, but having my girlfriend worry felt different.

I wasn't trying to be reckless or anything. This was just something I really wanted to do.

"I need something to occupy my time right now," I told her. "And the way Trace describes it, riding is a great way to clear your head, you know?"

"I guess that makes sense."

Another reason I always felt good around Amanda—she always understood me.

"Are you hungry?" she asked, gently trailing her fingers around my heart and running them down toward my stomach.

"Don't go any further south there, girl, unless you're up for round two."

Giggling, she said, "No way. I can't handle any more right now."

The sexual satisfaction in her voice filled me with pride.

"Then yes. I am hungry."

"Cool. I can make us dinner." She got out of bed, giving me a lovely view of her nude body.

"You sure you don't mind?"

Amanda shook her head. "Nope."

I felt a little guilty having her make dinner, but she seemed to genuinely enjoy cooking. I loved when we ate a home-cooked meal together. It was like we were already a family.

I SPENT a lot of time that week studying the motorcycle manual. Finally, I felt a sense of purpose with a new goal to work toward. They gave you the option to take online classes or attend the school, so I chose the latter. It felt good to get out of the apartment and interact with other people. The class was a nice mix of all ages learning to ride, so that was cool. A few of the students glanced at me curiously as if they recognized me from somewhere but they weren't sure how they knew me.

Considering just a few months ago I was recognized everywhere I went, it sucked that I was already being forgotten.

I met up with Trace one morning at the Indian dealership since he wouldn't let me buy a Harley. He was an Indian motorcycle guy all the way, and I trusted his judgment.

The place had a whole bunch of gorgeous bikes, and I enjoyed having something to be excited about again. We explored the dealership, checking out all the different types of bikes. The Springfield, the Challenger, the Roadmaster, and more. It was awesome, yet hard to pin down exactly what I wanted. But that was what the sales guy was for. To help me figure out what would suit my purposes.

I planned to get a bike that was suitable for two people. But no way in hell would I put my precious girl on the back of my motorcycle until I'd had tons of practice riding. Meaning way more than just the required six hours. I needed to be totally confident that I could keep her safe. Eventually, when the time was right, I envisioned taking lots of motorcycle trips with her.

The sales guy noticed us looking around and sauntered up to us. The man was tall and slender, with dark black skin and a winning salesman smile. He looked dapper in his expensive suit and tie, which I took to mean that he was a *successful* salesman. I owned a couple of similar suits that I only wore on special occasions.

"Good morning, gentleman," the man said, flashing his pearly whites. "I'm Drew. What can I help you with today?"

"I'm looking to get my first motorcycle," I said as I shook the man's hand. "I'm doing the classes and all that now."

Drew nodded, listening carefully.

"So, I'm not exactly sure what I'm looking for. Just something safe and not too crazy, but comfortable for two. I'm hoping my girlfriend will eventually ride with me."

"Okay, okay," Drew said, nodding again as he spoke.

"My buddy here is a hardcore rider, and he insists that Indian is the way to go."

"Your buddy is right," he said, turning to shake Trace's hand. Suddenly, his eyes lit up. "Trace Ridgerton!"

Trace chuckled. My stomach tightened. Just when I'd thought I'd found a distraction from baseball.

"Great to meet you, man," Drew said, shaking Trace's hand vigorously—so much that I started to wonder if he would ever let go. For a few seconds, his slick sales demeanor disappeared. He was just another overexcited Bay Birds fan.

One who clearly had no idea who I was.

Drew and Trace got into a discussion about the Bay Birds and their chances of getting into the Wild Card race this year. I'd been utterly forgotten, which was particularly annoying since I was the one looking to buy.

I noticed two other customers, a youngish couple, who heard the commotion and turned to see Trace talking with the salesman. They, too, recognized Trace. After watching from a distance for a couple of minutes, they tentatively made their way over. Before I knew it, the four were engaged in a lively discussion about baseball.

The man and woman had even made eye contact with me, smiling politely as they brushed past to get to Trace and Drew. Not even a flicker of recognition, even though they were clearly Baltimore Bay Bird fans.

After a few months away, I might as well have never played baseball at all.

Physically painful grief stabbed me through the heart. It wasn't that I cared so much about being famous, though that had been a lot of fun. I missed the random conversations with people who loved the game as much as I did. I missed being a part of baseball.

I wished like hell that Amanda was here. She would have gazed into my eyes and seen my anguish. She would have pulled me aside, comforted me. Distracted me. Done whatever she could to make me feel better.

But Amanda wasn't here. So rather than stand here like an idiot feeling like a knife was sticking out of my chest, I wandered around the dealership. I tried distracting myself by looking at all the shiny bikes, trying to remind myself of how lucky I was that I could buy any one of them outright. No need for financing, I could pay for it and walk away with a shiny new toy. There were probably lots of people who came in every single day just to look, longing to buy but not having the means.

I tried to be grateful. I really did. But I didn't want a shiny new bike. I wanted my fucking life back. The thing I wanted most in my life—baseball—was the one thing I could never, ever have.

I simply had to find a way to accept that. I had to move on. I tried to focus on being inside a dealership since that was what I was supposed to be working on for my future. I wandered down to the service department, smiling politely at the cashier, who smiled back.

"Can I help you, sir?" the service adviser asked from behind the desk. He squinted at me curiously, and I realized I'd better get used to that look. That expression of hazy recognition. The "Don't I know you from somewhere?" look.

I'm a nobody. A has-been. Don't bother trying to figure out where you know me from. I'm not that guy anymore.

"Oh, no. I'm just kinda wandering around. Looking to maybe buy a new bike."

"Wonderful," the man said brightly. "Well please do let me know if you have any questions."

"Will do," I said with a salute.

Everybody seemed nice around here. Owning a dealership seemed like a pleasant enough plan. I thought about how it would feel to be the big boss in a place like this. The cashier, the service advisers, and the auto technicians would know me as The Owner when I came here for a visit.

I don't want to be Rusty Power, business owner. I want to be Rusty Power, first baseman for the Baltimore Bay Birds.

That dream was dead. But I wasn't, so I needed to figure out how to live.

As I headed back up the steps toward the sales area, Trace came rushing toward me. His left shirtsleeve was still rolled up, so I could tell he'd been showing off his Indian motorcycle tattoo to all his adoring fans.

"Dude, I'm so sorry about that." His dark brown eyes flashed with guilt.

"Ah, it's fine," I said, lying through my teeth.

I was pissed. I couldn't help it. This kind of bullshit was exactly what I did not need right now. What I wanted was a distraction from the agony of missing my old life. Trace could talk to goddamn baseball fans anytime he wanted.

Trace knew damn well he'd screwed up. Let me down. But there was no undoing it now. He hadn't meant any harm, and it was hard not to get caught up when people started talking baseball. I knew that better than anybody else.

So we might as well move forward.

"I'm leaning toward maybe the Roadmaster or the Indian Pursuit," I said simply, my way of letting Trace know he was off the hook. "Whaddya think?"

"Let's go take another look." We headed back toward the showroom.

Drew rushed over when he saw us. To his credit, he spent the rest of the time fawning over me. As a customer, not as a former ballplayer.

It was better than nothing.

22

AMANDA

Rusty was planning to go visit his family in West Virginia for the day, and he asked if I wanted to go with him. His simple request meant a lot to me. We had already professed our love for each other, and going to see his family felt like another huge and wonderful step in our relationship.

"So you should know," Rusty said while we were en route, "I haven't exactly told my parents that it's you I'm dating."

"Oh." I was unsure how to take that news; maybe his family liked it better when Rusty was dating a famous actress. Rather than fret in silence, I figured it was best to straight up ask him about it. "Why? Are you ashamed of me or something?"

Rusty laughed heartily, banging his hands on the steering wheel. "*Quite* the opposite, my dear. I just want to see the look on my mother's face when she finds out my girl-friend is the woman who saved my life."

Remembering his mother's reaction to meeting me that day in the hospital, I understood exactly what he meant. It made me feel better to think that rescuing their son would beat being famous any day.

"It also might soften the blow for when I tell my mom I bought a motorcycle."

"You haven't told her yet?" I asked, though I was hardly surprised. Like me, Jane Power worried constantly about Rusty. The man was taking years off both of our lives.

"Not yet. I figure she might take it better if I tell her in person."

"I guess."

I had to admit that Rusty did pick out a beautiful bike. He chose a blue Indian Pursuit, with plenty of room for two riders. I was willing to ride with him, but he'd told me he didn't want me anywhere near the thing until he was completely confident in his ability to ride safely. His concern for me was sweet, and it did make me feel better to know that he was taking a lot of time to practice riding on various types of roads.

We enjoyed a luxurious drive through the lush green Appalachian Mountains and arrived at his parents' house just before noon. No doubt it would make a lovely motorcycle trip for us someday. His family home was nice but modest, big enough to have raised three children in but not so huge as to be too much for a couple of empty nesters. Rusty had told me he'd offered to buy them a new house, but they'd declined. They had, however, gratefully accepted his offer to pay off the rest of the mortgage. I saw the joy in Rusty's eyes when he'd told me about that. He loved his mom and dad dearly and was happy to be able to repay them a bit for all the love and support they'd given him over the years.

Standing at the front door, Rusty raised his hand to knock, but his mother flung it open before he even had a chance. Her pretty blue eyes lit up when she saw him, and I was once again struck by how much Rusty resembled his mother. Well, except for the fact that he towered over the tiny woman.

"Hi, baby." She threw her arms around him and squeezed him tight.

"Hi, Mommy," he said, making her laugh.

Releasing him, she turned to me and said, "And this must be your girl—"

Jane's eyes flew open wide, and she screamed. Actually screamed. "This is who you're dating?" she yelled.

It almost sounded like she was mad about it, but I knew better. Rusty chuckled beside me.

His dad came running up to the door, looking understandably confused. There was a slight resemblance to Rusty in his face and he was nearly as tall as his son, but otherwise he didn't look a lot like him. He had dark hair that was beginning to turn gray and blue eyes that were darker than Rusty's.

"This is who you're dating?" she repeated, still waiting on confirmation from Rusty.

Looking utterly bewildered, his father asked, "Uh ... who is this?"

"Allen! This is Amanda Miller!"

I would never forget the look on that man's face. The instant recognition. The sheer and utter gratitude in his expression. He knew my name, all right.

"Amanda," he said with such deep reverence that it nearly made me cry. He took my hand in both of his. "It's so nice to finally meet you."

"You're dating?" his mother asked once again, as if afraid to hope.

"Yes, Ma. Amanda is my girlfriend," Rusty said with a grin.

His mother gasped and said, "Marry her!"

"Mom!" Rusty said, looking slightly embarrassed.

I laughed. "It's okay. I don't scare that easily. At least not about stuff like that."

"Come in, come in, come in," Jane said, pulling us both inside.

We sat down at the table in their warm and sunny kitchen. Everything about this experience felt warm and sunny, and I could see where Rusty had gotten his good-natured disposition.

I couldn't help thinking what an amazing grandmother Jane would be. But she already was one—Rusty's sisters both had children. I smiled just thinking how spoiled those kids must be, having grandparents like the Powers.

"So how have you been?" Jane asked Rusty, looking worried.

"Good," Rusty said with forced cheerfulness. I could usually tell when he was faking enthusiasm. As lovely as it had been driving through the countryside today, seeing his old high school and childhood baseball fields on the way through the neighborhood hadn't done him any favors. He hadn't said anything, but I'd seen that dark look in his eyes.

All his childhood dreams were gone, and now he was here in his parents' house pretending everything was fine.

"Really?" his mother asked him suspiciously. Like me, she knew him better than that.

"Yeah, I got all kinds of plans in the works. Been working a lot on the car dealership idea."

"Good for you," his father said with great interest. That made Rusty smile.

"Maybe start with sports cars. Something cool like that.

And then, you know, maybe branch out into more boring stuff like Toyota or Honda. The kind of cars that are likely to sell steadily."

"Makes sense," Allen said.

The two of them chatted about the car business until his mother eventually cut in. "Okay, okay enough car talk. You're probably boring poor Amanda to death."

"It's fine," I said, though she wasn't wrong. The sad part was that I found the conversation boring because *Rusty* sounded bored. I knew nothing would ever compare to baseball in his heart, but I wished he could at least be a little excited about the car dealership idea. But he didn't seem into it.

Jane stood and put a hand on my back.

"Amanda, honey, why don't you make yourself more comfortable on the couch while Rusty and I fix lunch for everybody."

Rusty smiled as he watched his mom usher me over to the living room, which was just off the kitchen.

"She's a mother hen," he called out to me. "You better get used to that."

"I think it's sweet," I said.

I sat down on the big fluffy couch that was as warm and cozy as the rest of the house. I felt so comfortable here. The only thing missing was a dog.

Rusty's dad came to sit with me on the couch.

"We're really glad to have you here with us, Amanda." His eyes had the same friendly sparkle as Rusty's.

"It's lovely to be here."

Allen glanced over to where Rusty was helping his mom in the kitchen and then he looked back at me.

"I know your relationship is still new, but Rusty seems real happy with you." I saw the relief in his eyes when he said, "And believe me, my wife will sleep better at night knowin' you're around to look out for him."

I nodded, smiling at his dad.

I did feel pressured to look after Rusty sometimes. I cheered him up when I could, but his happiness was ultimately up to him. And he was really struggling with that.

Though I felt guilty for even thinking it, sometimes I got tired of things feeling so one-sided. Rusty was going through a hard time, and I understood that. And yet it felt like I wasn't allowed to have bad days. Sometimes I'd start to complain about my job, and it seemed like Rusty was only half listening. Admittedly, my problems paled in comparison to his. Yes, I was increasingly unhappy with my day job, but he'd suffered a life-threatening, dream-killing medical nightmare. He had won a contest nobody wanted to enter.

Rusty suddenly said loudly from the kitchen, "I don't care *what* you say, Mom. I love Amanda, and I want to be with her no matter how much you don't like her!"

My head whipped in the direction of the kitchen.

"Rusty, will you stop that!" his mom said, swatting him on the shoulder.

He cackled madly, making us all laugh, including his mom. She couldn't help herself. He had that effect on people.

I rolled my eyes and waved at his mom to show I understood that her son was just being an idiot. He grinned and blew me a kiss, reminding me of all the reasons I loved the man. Sure, he was fairly high maintenance right now, but he would find his way. I adored his sense of humor and the way he loved joking around and making people smile. I needed to remember that I met him on the very worst day of his life. If we could love each other during this rough patch, it simply meant the best was yet to come.

"Thanks for putting up with him," Allen said, chuckling and shaking his head.

"Ah, he's not so bad," I said affectionately. As I watched Rusty help his mom in the kitchen, I fell in love with him all over again. He might have been joking around, but he *had* said that he loved me in front of his parents. That made me really happy.

Allen reached over and grabbed the TV remote. "Mind if I turn this on?"

"Not at all," I said. Rusty's dad was nice, but I wasn't sure how much we had in common, so it was hard to think of things to say. Having the television on made things more comfortable.

The TV was tuned in to a cable sports channel when Allen turned it on. With a quick, nervous glance over at Rusty, he changed the channel with lightning speed. I realized his dad, too, felt he had to avoid the topic of baseball around his son. My heart sank, and I wondered if he and Rusty had talked sports before everything went down.

Jane chatted with Rusty in the kitchen, but I only caught bits and pieces of their conversation. Until I heard his mom exclaim, "You bought a *what*?"

Allen sighed. "I guess he finally told her about the motorcycle."

"He told you about that?"

Nodding, Allen said, "Yeah. He wanted to prepare me for the battle."

"Maybe I better go help him," I said, getting up. I figured I was the perfect middle ground since I both understood his need for a distraction these days while I endured the agony of worrying about him. As usual, it was my job to swoop in and smooth things over and try to make everyone feel better.

THE FOUR OF us sat at the table and enjoyed a pleasant meal together. Jane was still upset, but she'd seemed to feel better once I'd gotten Rusty to discuss all the reasons he wanted to ride a motorcycle. He'd been through so much, and his mother did seem grateful that he had something in his life to look forward to.

I was overwhelmed by the pure love I felt in this house. Rusty's parents clearly doted on him, and the house was filled with photographs of him, his two sisters, and their children. I couldn't begin to fathom the unimaginable grief his family would have suffered if Rusty hadn't survived his cardiac arrest. I was humbled to be in the presence of such love, and I vowed to remember how it felt to be here the next time I had that terrible recurring nightmare about finding Rusty dead on the field. He was okay, and that was what mattered.

After I helped clean up after lunch, Rusty went out to the car to grab his cell phone, which had pictures of his new bike he wanted to show off. His dad went with him, giving his mom a chance to corner me.

"Tell me the truth, Amanda," she said, her blue eyes turning serious. For a moment, I thought I was in trouble for something. "How is he doing?"

Her worry and fear were palpable. Parenthood wasn't for the faint of heart. And yet Jane was the kind of mother I wanted to be someday. One who loved and fiercely protected her children.

"He's doing all right," I said, gently touching her arm. "I mean, he's definitely still grieving the loss of baseball."

Jane nodded sadly, but she seemed to be grateful that I

was leveling with her. She knew her son probably better than anyone; she could see the pain in his eyes.

"He'll find his way. It'll just take some time. He still needs to mourn a bit and then figure out what he wants to do with the rest of his life. But he's gonna be okay. I promise. You'll be glad to know that he's been really good about following doctor's orders, going to his checkups and all that."

Jane sighed with relief, nodding again. It made me happy to help set her mind at ease. I knew how awful it was to worry.

"I'm so glad he has you around to take care of him," she said, squeezing my arm.

"Me too," I said, suddenly feeling quite tired.

23

RUSTY

My buddy Charlie called me the day after I went to my parents' house. Apparently, my mother had let it slip that I'd been in town.

"I can't believe you didn't come see me, you prick," he complained, and rightfully so. I'd thought about taking Amanda to meet him. I really had. I just still felt so lost in my life that I hadn't been ready to face any of my old gang. It was stupid. It wasn't as if I'd flunked out of college and was slinking back home. But I knew I'd feel better when I actually had something real going on in my life that I could talk about. Once my car dealership plans were firmed up, then yeah. I'd go back and spend more time in my old stomping grounds.

"I know, I know," I told him. "But you know how it is. Bringing the girlfriend home to meet the parents."

He laughed. "Yeah, I get it. So you two are pretty serious, huh?"

"Yeah we are." We talked for a bit, and it was nowhere near as awkward as I'd expected. I wound up regretting not meeting up with him.

Over the next few weeks, I did the best that I could to stay busy. I attended all my motorcycle riding lessons, both in class and on the road, and I took the extra motorcycle safety class, as I'd promised Amanda I would. Trace and I met up a couple of times to help me prepare for my test.

I passed the first time, which was awesome. I realized Trace had been totally right about wind therapy. Being out on the open road calmed me and helped clear my head. The more I rode, the more at ease I became navigating all kinds of terrain. The first few times I went out, I had to concentrate hard on the actual riding of the bike, but after that, I was able to let my mind wander.

My new bike was beautiful, and opening her up out on the road always eased my tension and stress, but I was still struggling with how to move on from baseball. I was hurting all the time, no matter how much I tried not to think about my old life.

When I wasn't on my bike, I threw myself into research on how to open a car dealership. I mostly worked in my home office, which was depressingly bare without my baseball memorabilia. I studied the websites of local car companies to figure out how they ran their businesses, and I lost track of how many times I nodded off at my computer. I tried to remember some of the business stuff I'd learned in college, but most of my classes had been a blur. My grades were pretty good, but I never gave a damn about the classwork part of school. I'd gotten in on a baseball scholarship, and of course sports were all that ever really mattered to me.

I was fortunate that I'd gotten a business degree, but I hated like hell that I now had to use it. A fallback plan is great to have and not need.

When I was desperate to get out of the apartment, I visited a few dealerships in the area. The owners were helpful and friendly, especially once they found out who I was. What sucked was having to *tell* them. I missed the days when my face was automatically associated with baseball. The people I spoke with gave me lots of tips on how and where to open a business, and it helped to see which dealers were located where. I didn't want to open a Porsche store anywhere close to another successful one.

After all that time online doing research, going on field trips to other dealers, and studying up on business tactics, I found myself completely and thoroughly miserable. Deep down, I'd always known I was kidding myself with this car dealer bullshit.

I had absolutely no idea what my future held, but this wasn't it.

The day I had that stark and depressing revelation, I angrily shot up out of my office chair so hard I knocked it over. Leaving the damned thing where it fell, I stalked into my living room.

I flipped on the television to watch an infomercial or a game show or whatever daytime TV garbage that unemployed losers like me watched during the day when everyone else was out having a life. I turned on the local news, figuring I was already depressed, so why not see what horrible things were going on in the world?

Staring blankly at the television, I barely heard what the newscaster was saying. I felt guilty for wallowing in my own self-pity while terrible things were happening, even if I wasn't really listening to what those things were.

Then the sports report came on. Good news, everybody! For the first time in years, the Baltimore Bay Birds were in serious contention in the Wild Card race.

Dear God, that hurt.

I wanted to be happy for my friends. They'd worked

their asses off all season, and God knew the Baltimore fans deserved to be rewarded for their years of loyalty to a losing team.

I should have been there for this. The Birds were my team too.

My chest hurt so bad that it scared me. For a few seconds, I feared I was having another cardiac arrest. I drew in a few deep and steady breaths to calm myself, and the pain lessened. Physically, anyway. Most of my agony was emotional heartbreak, not a physical heart problem.

I would survive, whether I wanted to or not.

Leaning forward, I put my head in my hands. I was utterly lost and alone.

I needed Amanda more than I'd ever needed her before.

24

AMANDA

When I got into work in the morning, I was surprised to see a new meeting on my schedule.

The meeting was for the whole department, which was relatively rare.

Poking my head out of my cubicle, I asked, "Hey, Bell, do you know what this meeting is about?"

"Not sure," she said, sitting at her desk, buffing her nails. She looked so much like a stereotypical lazy secretary that I nearly laughed out loud. Bella did an okay job overall, I supposed. She usually answered the phone by at least the third ring, and she answered most of her emails in a relatively timely fashion. More or less.

"I can tell you what the meeting is about," Denise said as she dramatically swept into the room. "At last I'm leaving you, my darlings."

It's about damn time.

Denise was nice enough, and she was a decent boss, but she'd been saying she was leaving for so long that I was starting to believe it would never happen.

My stomach quivered with excitement. Finally, I would get the promotion I'd wanted for so long. Every day I'd been growing more and more frustrated with the limitations of my current job. Being the HR assistant mainly meant dealing with a ton of forms, scheduling appointments, and tending to minute details. I wanted to work directly with *people*. I wanted new hires to come to *my* office so I could welcome them personally and help them get comfortable in their new jobs.

I was jittery and excited all morning long, watching the clock and waiting for 11:30. Then, at the last damned minute, the meeting got postponed until the end of the day. It was positively *maddening*; I wasn't sure my jangled nerves could handle the wait.

Finally, at 4:30 we all convened in the conference room. We went through all the agonizing formalities of a company meeting: Denise went over a few business items, then she took a few minutes to thank us all for our hard work. Then, after giving a short speech about how great it's been working with us and how much she was going to miss us and blah, blah, blah, at last she got to the point.

"So," she said, drawing in a breath and letting it out. "That just leaves the matter of the position of human resources manager."

My body tensed and I leaned forward.

"As you know, there's a lot that goes into being the HR manager. There's experience and know-how, but there's also personality and, you know, what they call people skills."

I frowned, not entirely sure what the woman was talking about or where she was going with this. There was only one person who had years of experience with the employee database, the job postings, coordinating the orientation and training sessions, and all the forms and policies associated with the HR department at the University of Timonium. And that person was me.

"This was not an easy decision," Denise said, making my body grow even more rigid and tense.

It should have been an easy decision. I was her assistant, and my performance and attendance were impeccable.

"But I think it makes the most sense to promote Bella to serve as human resources manager," she said with a smile.

I couldn't breathe.

"Omigod, I can't believe it," Bella gushed excitedly.

Neither can I.

And neither could anybody else. All the heads, at least the ones that didn't belong to Bella and Denise, slowly turned to look at me.

I'd never been so angry and humiliated in all my life. Everyone knew I deserved that promotion, but instead, Denise had given it to her favorite bar-hopping buddy, Bella.

The promotion, like so many other things in life, was nothing more than a personality contest. And I never won personality contests. Not in high school, not in college, and certainly not when I was sitting in a bar next to Wilder. Sure, I was competent and hardworking, and I knew my job inside out, but I wasn't *fun*. Denise and Bella were tight outside of work, and apparently that was enough to get the job.

Denise was right that people skills mattered in a human resources job, but I didn't think doing belly shots off a hot bartender qualified. I hated how petty I sounded inside my head, and yet I knew I was right. I wasn't being petty because another woman had gotten the job instead of me. I was righteously angry because I'd been passed over for a promotion that I genuinely deserved. The people skills required for the job were kindness, understanding, and patience.

At the moment, I was furious, impatient, and heartbroken. I fought back tears as hard as I could, refusing to give anyone in this horrible place the satisfaction of seeing me cry.

Having the meeting at the end of the day turned out to be a blessing. Not long after it was over, I got the hell out of the office.

I managed not to cry until I was safely out of the parking lot. Instead of going home, I headed straight over to Rusty's place.

More than anything, I needed his love and support right now.

❧

RUSTY LOOKED ALARMED when he saw me. Not only had I shown up unannounced, which I never did, but my face was a blotchy mess from crying.

"Amanda! Are you all right?"

"Yes, yes, I'm okay," I assured him, realizing too late that I should have given him some warning that I was coming over. "I mean, I'm not okay. I'm very upset, but nobody died or anything."

"That's good, I guess." Rusty still looked worried as he pulled me over to the couch.

Wiping my eyes, I sat down next to him. I scanned the room and saw a bunch of Chinese takeout containers and trash on the floor.

"I know, the place is a mess," Rusty said apologetically. "It's been a bad day."

My stomach clenched. I knew that dark look. Rusty was

spiraling again—it seemed to happen more and more these days. Though I was sorry he was having a rough day, I did not have the mental or emotional energy to deal with his issues.

"Amanda, what the hell happened?"

"I didn't get the promotion," I said, a fresh wave of devastation washing over me. I hated saying those words out loud, especially after fantasizing for so long about how much fun it would be to tell my family and friends about my exciting new job.

"Oh, thank God," Rusty said with a sigh.

"What?"

"No, I didn't mean ... I just thought something terrible had happened."

"Something terrible *did* happen, Rusty," I said, my frustration building all over again. Of course, I knew what he had meant. When somebody rushes in when they've been crying, you can't help but think the worst. That someone had died in a horrible accident or had been diagnosed with a terminal disease. Though I understood his relief, saying *Thank God* about my troubles wasn't the proper response.

"I didn't mean thank God you didn't get the promotion. I just meant it's not that big of a deal."

I stared at him with absolutely no idea how to respond to that. After a few seconds of icy silence, I said, "What do you mean it's not that big of a deal?"

"I mean it sucks that you didn't get the job, but you can always get another one. A different job in the same field. I'm sure lots of people are hiring in HR."

"I don't *want* another job. I want *this* one. Because I deserved it. I worked my ass off for this promotion, and they gave it to somebody who was completely unqualified."

"Yeah, but at least you get to go out and get another job

doing the exact same thing," Rusty said, sounding frustrated. He acted as if I was bothering him with my petty problems when he had "real" problems. "I'm just saying it's not like the position I'm in. Where I can't do my job ever again."

"I *know*, Rusty," I snapped angrily. "Your situation is much worse. You win. You *always* win."

"What is that supposed to mean?"

"It means your problems will always be worse than mine, but that doesn't mean I don't have problems too. You just don't give a damn about them."

"Of course I do, Amanda. I'm just sayin'—"

"I understand exactly what you're saying," I said, shaking with anger. "You don't have to ever feel bad for me because you will always have things worse. You get a lifetime free pass from having to care about stupid, insignificant problems because your life sucks worse than mine."

Rusty seemed shocked by my fury, which only made me madder. I felt like I was being gaslighted. Made to feel like I was crazy for wanting a little bit of love and sympathy after giving so much of it to him. I always tried my best to make other people feel better, but there was more to me than just a bottomless pit of sympathy. I had feelings too, dammit.

"Well, my situation is different. Very different," he said, rolling his eyes dismissively as he spoke.

"You know, I got used to the fact that you never ask me about my work and that your eyes glaze over with boredom if I dare mention my job, but it would be nice to think you actually cared. Even a little bit. God knows, I've done everything I can to help you through your situation."

"You just don't get it, do you?" Rusty roared, his eyes flashing in anger. I'd seen that dark look many times before, but this was the first time it had been directed at me. "I'm a goddamned has-been at age twenty-six. No matter how long I live, my obituary will say 'He played for the Bay Birds for a couple of years' because that will be my greatest accomplishment. And it's over. I'm completely washed up already!"

His fists were balled up in fury; I was genuinely afraid he might punch through a wall or something.

"But at least your obituary might be when you're eighty years old! It could easily have read 'Rusty Power died tragically at the age of twenty-six after collapsing on the baseball field.'"

My anger and disappointment and frustration threatened to consume me. I'd come to the man I loved for comfort. I couldn't believe how he'd managed to make everything so much worse. I'd always done my best to empathize with him. I understood that he had lost so much so quickly, but sometimes I could not comprehend why he wasn't more grateful for the things he *still had.*

"I really needed that promotion, Rusty. I've never had a lot of money, but you have *millions.* I can't even imagine what it feels like not to have to count every single penny. It's *awful* that you can't play baseball anymore, but do you have any idea what happens to people who get sick or injured who don't happen to be millionaires? People who suddenly can't work end up entirely dependent on family and friends or they wind up homeless. Do you even get that?"

Rusty's steely glare told me in no uncertain terms that I was not getting through to him. Not even close.

My voice shaking, I said, "You knew how much I wanted this promotion. Or at least you should have known. How can you look me in the eye and tell me this is no big deal?"

He shook his head, laughing bitterly. He was still acting like I was the crazy one, daring to bother him with my tiny little problems.

"My whole life, so many people have made me feel insignificant. Plain. *Invisible.* But I never thought you of all people would ever do that to me, Rusty. I feel terrible that you lost your dream. I really do. But that is no excuse to treat me like this.

"You just don't get it, Amanda."

"I guess I don't," I said, grabbing my purse from where I'd dropped it and slinging it over my shoulder. "I'm sorry I'm too *ordinary* to understand what you're going through."

I stormed out, slamming the door hard on my way out.

Heartbroken and angry, I called Wilder for support. After I got home and stopped crying, anyway. Part of me kept wondering if maybe I *was* the crazy one.

Wilder didn't get off work until 10pm, but she was more than willing to meet me for drinks to talk. She even said she would come pick me up so I could drink all I wanted without having to drive. Thank God I had at least one supportive friend in my life. Wilder would listen to me, and she would understand why I was upset. She always did.

Sitting on my couch, all alone, wiping my eyes, I went over and over my conversation with Rusty. Every time I started to wonder if maybe I was wrong, I reached the same conclusion.

No. This fight was not my fault.

Of course I knew that Rusty's job situation was far worse than mine. I'd never denied that. But that didn't mean my problems—and my pain—didn't matter. He shouldn't have made it a contest in the first place. When you loved somebody, you were supposed to support them, not one-up them with your own sob story. The more I thought back on all the times I'd held my tongue, listening to him vent about his problems while ignoring my own, the more I realized this confrontation had been inevitable. Sooner or later, it had to be my turn to be upset. And if Rusty couldn't handle that, then, well, I didn't know what would happen. All I knew was I couldn't go on like this.

Wilder and I went to a local bar and sat at a high top table for two so we could talk. The first thing that struck me was how she reacted when I told her the news about my promotion.

"You have *got* to be kidding me right now," Wilder said, eyes wide. She lowered the martini from her lips and stared at me. "Bella. They made *Bella* the freakin' HR manager? That's insane!"

And right then, I felt less crazy. Now *that* was the normal human reaction to what had happened. I didn't have to explain to Wilder who Bella was and why it was nuts to give her the promotion. Wilder already knew because she actually *listened* when I spoke.

"I know, right?" I said before taking an angry gulp of beer.

"Wow," Wilder said, shaking her head. "If I'm this stunned, I can't imagine how you must feel. Never in a million years did I think you wouldn't get that job. It should have been a slam dunk. You're by far the most qualified! You've been Denise's right-hand woman for years. Who else knows the HR job like you do?"

"Exactly." I felt slightly better already, which showed the importance of a sympathetic ear. Wilder couldn't change the situation for me, but she could provide comfort and support.

"I'm so sorry that happened, Amanda. You deserve so much better."

"There's more," I said dryly.

"Really?" she asked, eyes filled with worry.

"This is nice," I told her. "I mean, everything sucks right now, but I can't remember the last time somebody actually took the time to sit and listen to me."

Wilder nodded sadly, waiting for me to continue.

"Right after work, I went over to Rusty's because I needed a shoulder to cry on."

"Good idea."

"You'd think, right?" I said bitterly.

"Uh-oh."

"Wilder, he looked me right in the eye and said 'It's not that big of a deal.'"

She gasped. "No he did not." Her eyes wide and mouth open, she looked every bit as shocked as I had felt. Once again, she made me feel less insane.

"Oh, yeah. He said I can always get a new job, and it's not like his situation."

Wilder let out a sarcastic laugh and mimed pulling out a playing card and slapping it on the table. "Pullin' out the trump card, as always."

"Yes! Exactly!"

"Ugh." Wilder shook her head again. "I feel bad for the guy. Really, I do. But is he gonna compare everything that happens to everybody else for the rest of his life to what happened to him? I mean, we get it. You win."

"That is *precisely* what I said to him. Yeah, Rusty. You win. Congratulations. Your life is worse. But does that mean I never get to complain about anything ever again?"

"That is so wrong. I'm so sorry he acted that way. I really thought he was better than that."

"Me too. I've always done the best I could to support him, you know? I don't think I even realized how much I've been censoring myself until now. Rusty kept saying 'You don't understand.' Well, maybe I don't understand exactly what he's going through. How could I? But I've always been there for him. What else could I do?"

I drained the rest of my beer. "I love him, but I can't be in a relationship like this. It can't be so one-sided. It's not fair to me. Am I out of line here? If I am, tell me."

"No," Wilder insisted. "You're not wrong. I know I've been guilty about dumping on you with my problems. Like when I don't get a part or if I'm upset about my family. I feel bad about that, Amanda. You're one of those really kind, sweet, giving people who sometimes gets taken advantage of."

"You've never taken advantage of me," I assured her. And it was the truth. "We dump on *each other*. That's the difference. You do come to me with your problems, as well you should. You're my best friend. I want to be there for you. Just like you're always there for me. You always listen to me when I'm upset. You're doing it right now. And you have *never once* belittled my problems and made me feel like they don't matter."

I stared at my empty beer mug, debating whether I should go to the bar for a refill or wait until our server remembered we existed. Then she approached our table.

The server set a fresh martini in front of Wilder and said, "Compliments of the gentleman at the bar." She walked away, ignoring my empty glass.

Wilder looked down at her drink and then she slowly lifted her gaze to me. By then, I was crying.

"Oh honey, I'm so sorry."

"Forget it," I said, wiping my eyes. "It's stupid. It's so

stupid."

"It's not stupid," she said softly, her sweet blue-green eyes so filled with empathy that it made me cry harder. "This is exactly what you've been sad about all night." With an angry look at my empty beer mug, she said, "Feeling ignored and invisible."

I nodded, dabbing at my eyes with a tissue and hoping my makeup wasn't a total mess. Wilder understood exactly what I was going through because we'd had this conversation many times. And she always *listened* when I spoke about how unappreciated, unnoticed, and cast aside I felt sometimes.

Right now, I felt cast aside by Rusty, my workplace, the server, and some unnamed horny guy at the bar who had his eyes on Wilder.

Gazing tearfully at her, I said, "Thank you for being such a good friend. Seriously, I don't know what I would do without you."

She smiled gently at me. "I wish I could do more."

"You get me, Wilder. And believe me, that's more than enough."

Her eyes narrowed as she looked behind me. She was giving somebody her death stare, which was rare for her. She was usually Suzy Sunshine, but someone had pissed her off.

"What is wrong with you?" I asked.

"That skeevy guy from the bar was about to make a move. I think I scared him off."

Giggling, I wiped my eyes again.

"I mean, seriously?" she said angrily. "I'm obviously talking to someone who is visibly upset, and he thinks it's a great time to hit on me."

If only those jackasses knew they didn't stand a chance

with Wilder when they disrespected me. As always, this girl had my back.

Like Rusty should have.

"It's funny. I told Rusty about what happens to me in bars when I'm with you. The way men use me to get to you."

"Really?" she said, looking guilty. Wilder always felt bad when that happened, even though it was in no way her fault. "What did he say?"

"He was kind of horrified, believe it or not. It really made him mad. Not at you, of course. But just the idea that guys would treat me like that."

I let out a sad sigh. "He even said that he'd come out to the bar one day when we were hanging out so he could buy me a drink and 'pick me up.'"

"That's adorable," Wilder said with a smile.

"It really is. So Rusty is capable of empathy, I suppose. I know he's going through a rough patch, but I don't know how much longer I can deal with it. I feel like a terrible girlfriend for saying that."

"You're not a terrible girlfriend, Amanda."

I nodded, knowing deep down that I had done my best.

"I might be boring and ordinary, but I still know my worth. I always swore I would never be with a man who treated me with disrespect."

"Yup. You did always say that, and you're one hundred percent right," Wilder said firmly. "So, do you think you can forgive him?"

"I *could* forgive him, but I don't think that's really the issue. The question is ... is he even sorry?"

Wilder nodded sadly.

My heart sank. I already knew what I had to do.

If Rusty could treat me like that with no remorse, I had no choice but to walk away.

26

RUSTY

An argument with my girlfriend was the very last thing I'd needed after the horrible day I'd had. My life was falling apart. I couldn't stand the thought of opening a car dealership anymore, the Baltimore Bay Birds were headed to the playoffs without me, and Amanda was complaining about some stupid job. Human resource jobs were *everywhere*. I knew this, because I'd looked at tons of job listings over the last few months, both trying to figure out this crappy car dealership thing and when I'd been looking for ideas on what the hell else to do with my life. She could easily find a new job in her field. What was her problem?

After stewing in my apartment, wearing a path in the carpet from pacing, I knew I had to do something with my pent-up rage before I punched a hole in the goddamned wall.

I stormed out and headed for my motorcycle. Just revving the engine made me feel better. I roared down the road with no real idea where I was going. I rode down the highway for a while and wound up in Owings Mills, which was about twenty minutes outside of Baltimore. Being out on the bike helped, but not as much as it usually did. I was still ramped up and angry.

What I needed was a drink, so I stopped at a bar. I plopped down on a stool and realized too late that I was sitting directly in front of a television that was showing the Bay Birds game. Of course. I should have expected that shit after the day I'd had.

How I *hated* this gut-wrenching reaction every time I even thought about baseball. It was a far cry from the excitement and euphoria I used to feel just thinking about playing. I missed those carefree days when I'd paced my apartment with nervous excitement on game day instead of pacing with restlessness, boredom, and now rage.

I ordered a beer and glanced up at the screen while I waited. The score was 4-4 in the tenth inning. I hoped the Birds would win, but I still didn't want to see the game.

I downed half my beer in one long swig. Since I hadn't eaten anything in several hours, it didn't take long to get a buzz going. God, I hated being so angry all the time. It was exhausting. My body wasn't used to it. I missed my old life so much—those days when I was happy most of the time.

Finishing the first beer in record time, I quickly secured another one. I finished that beer quickly, and then ordered yet another one.

I hated my life. And I hated how it felt like nobody understood what I was going through. It took all my energy to hide my sorrow and rage from my family and friends—both my former teammates and my old school buddies. But it was supposed to be different with Amanda. She was supposed to be the one I could turn to. The one who understood me. But I guess that was all bullshit. As soon as one damned thing went wrong in her life, her sympathy for me disappeared.

I looked up at the TV to see that the ballgame had ended at some point. Now they were doing the post-game wrap up. I heard all the voices talking animatedly, but despite the fact that they said the score a bunch of times, I still couldn't figure out whether the Bay Birds had won or not.

I paid my tab, or at least I think I did, and I stumbled to my feet. I got on my bike without even considering that I was in no condition to drive a regular car, let alone a motorcycle.

Then I hit the open road.

27

RUSTY

With little memory of how the hell I got there, I staggered up the steps to a familiar house. I rapped on the door a bunch of times, and somebody finally answered.

"Heyyy, mannn," I slurred. I tried slapping the guy on the shoulder, but I missed.

"Rusty?" Brady asked, eyes wide. He looked upset for some reason.

"Yeah, it's Rusty. Who'd you think I was?" I asked, swaying back and forth.

Brady looked behind me, then glared at me.

"Why do you look so pissed off?" I wondered if maybe the Bay Birds had blown the game after all.

"You got drunk and rode here on your goddamn *motorcycle*?"

"Oh yeah. That. Yep. I guess I did."

"Get the hell in here," Brady said, grabbing me roughly by the collar and dragging me into the house. "You better not let Lyric see you in this condition. You wouldn't believe the shit she sees in the ER because of drunken idiots like you."

Brady led me through the house by the collar like I was a dog. He tossed me into some room with a bed.

"*Sleep it off*," he hissed at me.

Damn. I'd never seen Brady so mad. Actually, I didn't think I'd ever seen him mad at all.

Brady hated me. Amanda hated me.

I hated me.

I staggered to the bed and passed out.

WHEN I WOKE UP, it took me a while to figure out where I was and how I wound up in an unfamiliar bedroom. Then the memories came crashing back.

My head hurt and I felt a little queasy, but I'd had worse hangovers. I tentatively wandered down the hallway, worried I might run into Lyric. I found Brady sitting outside on the back porch by himself drinking coffee and reading something on his phone.

"Well, look who's awake," he said, setting his phone aside. He still didn't look thrilled with me, but he was decidedly calmer than he had been last night.

I glanced around nervously.

"Lyric's at the hospital," Brady added. "She saw your motorcycle, and I told her you came over and had too much to drink and stayed over." He winced with guilt. "I didn't lie to her exactly, but I made it sound like you started drinking after you got here."

"Thanks, man." I collapsed into a lawn chair across from Brady. "I'm sorry about last night."

"Look," Brady said grimly. "I used to do a lot of dumb

stuff when I was younger too. I used to be stupid and reckless and drove drunk too. Then I met Lyric, and as if it wasn't enough to straighten up for her sake, she came home from work one day sobbing because she had a dead sixteen-year-old on a slab because some fuckin' prick drove drunk and fuckin' killed her."

My blood ran cold. It wasn't just Brady's words, but the dark look in his eyes.

"That could have been me," he said. "I could have been dead, or I could have killed somebody else's baby. I never drove drunk again. And you better not, either."

"I swear," I said, holding up my hand to promise.

Fresh shame washed over me when I thought about how I'd managed to take an awful situation and made it worse. And I realized now how much worse it could have been; it was dumb luck that I'd made it to Brady's house alive. I could not remember driving here, and that was terrifying.

"Jesus, you already cheated death once," Brady muttered.

"That's exactly what Amanda said when she found out I wanted to learn to ride," I said, shaking my head ruefully.

"What's goin' on, dude?" Brady asked.

"Everything sucks, and I'm not handling it well."

"Is this about the Wild Card?"

An odd sense of relief swept over me at that question. Brady wasn't just a baseball player. He was exactly the type of ballplayer that I used to be. The type who wasn't in it for the money or the fame. We played because baseball was a part of our souls. Brady, probably more than anyone, would understand how deeply I was mourning my loss.

"Partly," I said. "I mean, it's not that I don't want you guys to win. You know, I—"

"I know," Brady said, waving off my explanations. Because yeah. He did know.

"But that's not why I'm such a mess right now." I put my head in my hands for a moment. Then I looked up and said, "I had a huge fight with Amanda last night."

"Oh damn." He looked nearly as disappointed in me as I was in myself. When Brady and the other guys met Amanda, I could tell they all really liked her. That, and they treated her with special reverence because she had saved my life.

"I'd had a horrible day between the Wild Card news and other stuff. I was not in a great place. Then she comes over and starts complaining about her job—some promotion she didn't get—and I kinda snapped. I just ... I guess it sounds mean, but that's so insignificant compared to what I've been through."

"Hmmm." Brady frowned. I got the feeling he didn't agree with me. Odd, since I figured he of all people would understand my point of view.

"And I accused her of not understanding me. And I think in a lot of ways she really doesn't understand, but that's not her fault, I guess. I told her she could go out and get another job, but it's not like I can ever go back to baseball."

Brady nodded thoughtfully. He was uncharacteristically quiet, and I wondered what he was thinking. Then he pulled out his phone.

"I want to show you something," Brady said. I waited while he searched for whatever he was looking for.

He handed me his phone, and I stared at a photograph of Lyric. She had tears running down her face and her hand covered her mouth. Her eyes were filled with deep shock and sorrow. There was only one word to describe the way she looked.

Grief.

"God, what the hell happened to her?" I asked, looking up at Brady, wondering why he had shown me such a personal photograph.

He shook his head. "It's not what happened to her. It's what happened to *me.* Somebody managed to snap her photo right as she watched me make the final out for Richmond, ending our playoff hopes."

"Wow," I said, staring back down at the photo. Clearly, Lyric had grieved Brady's loss as deeply as if it had been her own.

Amanda looked at me like that all the time when I talked about the pain of losing my dream. I remembered when I'd wanted to toss all my baseball stuff and she'd begged me not to. Because of her, I still had it all in storage.

I handed the phone back to Brady and sat back wearily in my chair.

"When I first met Lyric, she definitely didn't get why I loved baseball so much. And honestly? I don't think she completely understands how I feel about it even now. But she doesn't have to. She *cares.* Baseball is a huge part of my life, and she totally supports that. Hell, I don't understand why anyone would want to be a doctor," he said with a grimace that made me chuckle. "But I totally support her, and I find her drive and passion as a future doctor sexy as hell."

I could hear the pride in Brady's voice as he spoke of his wife. He had an excellent point. It wasn't Amanda's job to understand exactly how I felt. All she needed to do was support me. That's what you did when you were in a relationship. Except in our relationship, she had done more than her share while I had done exactly nothing. No, I'd done worse than nothing. Rather than comforting her in her sorrow, I had viciously *attacked* her.

What in God's name was wrong with me?

Amanda's tear-stained face flashed through my mind. A heavy sense of dread settled in my stomach when it hit me just how horribly I had treated her.

I remembered her telling me on our first date about that promotion and how much she'd wanted it. That she longed for the power to help people directly rather than just assist the HR manager. And now, after she'd waited all these months for them to make a decision, they'd given the job to somebody else. Despite the fact that she was next in line for it and was undoubtedly the most qualified.

And I'd looked her straight in the face and told her it was no big deal.

I'd been so blinded by my own pain that I had completely ignored, belittled, and even insulted her. My darling girlfriend had come to me in tears seeking love and understanding. Not only had I not given her the support she needed, I'd *yelled* at her.

Here I'd been feeling so sorry for myself because Amanda didn't understand me, but what had I ever done to try to understand her?

I thought about all those AITA threads online where people would post about a situation they were in, asking the question "Am I the Asshole" here?

Oh yeah. I was definitely the asshole here.

The gravity of what I had done to Amanda kept washing over me in wave after horrible wave. That poor girl had had the misfortune of meeting me at the absolute lowest point of my life, but that was no excuse to be the worst boyfriend on the planet. I was lucky she had stayed with me this long, considering all I ever did was bitch and moan about my lot in life.

And what exactly was my lot in life when I really thought about it? Like she'd said last night, I had plenty of money, and I lived in a luxury apartment. I was healthy enough to work, yet I didn't. Instead, I'd been hiding out and feeling sorry for myself while Amanda worked like hell in a place that didn't appreciate her.

Nobody appreciated her.

I thought about how I'd gotten too drunk to even think of calling her to apologize. She'd probably spent a horrible, sleepless night wondering how the man she loved had turned out to be such a cruel jerk.

I felt like a monster, but somehow Brady was able to look at me with empathy.

"Dude, I get why you're such a mess. I do." Then he said quietly, "I don't know what I would do if I couldn't play baseball. I'd go crazy too. I would. I know this hurts real bad, Rusty, and I wish like hell I could fix it. But unfortunately, there's just nothing that can be done."

I nodded, grateful that Brady understood why I was losing my mind.

"And now it's time for some tough love," he said.

"Uh-oh."

Brady chuckled. "All I know is you gotta somehow get your shit together, man. You could have fucking died on that motorcycle last night. Think of your mother, jackass. Think of Amanda."

"You're right." A sudden deep fear gripped me. "Oh God, I don't wanna lose her."

Hearing the panic in my voice, Brady leaned forward in his chair and spoke firmly. "You're not gonna lose her. You can fix this, but you gotta make sure it never happens again.

Amanda's a sweet girl, and she deserves better than the way you've been treating her."

"I know."

"Just go talk to her. Tell her you're sorry for everything you said and then do your best to be better from now on. You might not understand everything she's going through either, but you don't have to. All you have to do is listen to her and let her know you care." Then he added in a somber voice, "She's been through a lot."

"What do you mean?"

"God, she was terrified that day when you collapsed. But she was so brave, the way she ran out onto the field."

"Amanda told me you took real good care of her that day. Thanks, man."

Brady smiled. "Glad I could help. And I'm just happy you're okay."

"She still has nightmares about that day. Says in her dreams, sometimes I survive and sometimes I don't. But she always wakes up in a cold sweat."

"Damn," Brady said with a wince. "Poor thing."

"Yeah."

Amanda's fears for me were another thing I'd often dismissed. Why she'd put up with me this long was a miracle. The woman was a saint.

No.

She wasn't a saint, and she wasn't an angel. Amanda was a real, living woman who needed love and support just like everybody else. Too bad I never gave it to her. Until now. I *had* to do better. Not just to keep her in my life, but because, like Brady said, it was what she deserved.

"It's gonna be okay, Rusty."

"How can you be sure?"

"Because when you brought her over here, I could see

how much she loves you. Look, I know I haven't been married all that long, but I've learned a thing or two about happy relationships. It's actually pretty simple. Between my baseball and Lyric's crazy school and work schedule, we're apart a lot and we hate it. But when we finally are together, we easily fall back into the same rhythm. She vents to me about everything going on in her life, and I tell her more than she ever wanted to know about baseball. Then we have sex like a bunch of horny teenagers and fall asleep in each other's arms."

I laughed as Brady grinned.

"The secret to a happy relationship is to always have each other's back and never stop having fun," he advised.

"That's very wise," I said.

"Yeah. Now go get your girl."

28

RUSTY

I left Brady's house and rode home—very carefully—on my motorcycle. I still couldn't believe how incredibly stupid and reckless I had been. Once I got home, though, I hated the idea of puttering around inside my apartment all day, especially since the weather was beautiful. I wanted to see Amanda as soon as possible, but not before I figured some stuff out. I figured I'd go for a walk, to think about what I would say to her.

I found walking nearly as cathartic as riding a motorcycle had been. Even strolling through the city still afforded me time alone with my thoughts. It was late morning on a Friday, so the streets weren't terribly crowded since most people were at work already.

Talking with Brady had helped a lot. As pissed off as he had been with me, he had been able to forgive my stupidity. Hopefully, Amanda would too. Like Brady, she didn't have a short fuse. Of course, I never thought I had either. I hated how *angry* I had become since losing baseball. I needed to work on that before I lost something even more precious.

Amanda.

My heart wrenched in my chest as I pictured her tearful face.

I hated like hell that I'd hurt her, and I wracked my brain to figure out what I could possibly say to explain how sorry I was for being such a jerk. The more I thought about her getting passed over for that promotion, the madder I got. Amanda tended to be quiet and reserved; some damned loudmouth had probably got the job instead of her.

I lost track of how far I'd walked, but somehow I'd made it all the way to a huge cemetery in the outskirts of the city. It seemed to stretch for miles, and it was actually the perfect place to walk along paved paths away from city traffic. And of course, it was quiet.

Though this was a place of sadness, it was also a place of calm. I walked down the winding paths, gazing up at the lush summer trees and feeling the soft breeze on my face. Maybe taking long walks was a good way to tame my anger when I got fired up. Physical activity was also good for my health, and that would make Amanda happy.

Assuming she still loved me, that was.

I still couldn't believe how badly I'd let her down. My chest ached when I remembered her expression of sheer rejection and sadness when she'd told me how men treated her when she was out with Wilder. How, over and over again, random guys told her how beautiful they thought her friend was while utterly ignoring her. No, they didn't simply ignore her. They *used* her to get to Wilder. I'd been so mad about that, and I specifically recall thinking I never wanted to see that look of pain on her face again.

And yet, last night I'd seen that expression of pain and rejection, and it had been all my fault.

Try as I might, I couldn't think of any words to explain to Amanda how awful I felt about the way I'd treated her. I started to realize there was no sense in trying to come up with a prepared apology speech. Maybe it was better to just speak from the heart.

Wandering off the path and onto the grass, I looked at some of the tombstones. Funny how some of them were large and elaborate, while some were humble and plain. Kinda made me think how, in the end, it didn't really matter how much money you had in life. Sooner or later, we all ended up in a place like this.

I smiled when I saw the graves that held couples who had probably been married for a long time and had died at ripe old ages, and I sighed and said a silent prayer when I saw the occasional grave of a child or a baby. One tombstone caught my eye. It was made of shiny black stone and had the image of a young man etched into it. He smiled warmly in the image they had chosen; the type of picture that gave you the feeling he was a good guy. I inspected the date on his gravestone to find that he had died just last year, at only one year older than I was now.

A sharp, frigid chill rippled through me, and I dropped to my knees in front of the headstone.

For the first time, I understood—*really and truly under-stood*—that I could have died. If Amanda hadn't seen me collapse, or if she'd decided not to go to batting practice, my heart would have stopped for good. The trainers would have found me too late. Instead of hauling me off to the hospital, the ambulance would have taken my body to the morgue.

I broke into a cold sweat, breathing heavily. If Amanda could have seen me now, she would have freaked out and called 911. I wondered if I was having another cardiac arrest.

Given the circumstances, I figured out that this was most likely just a panic attack. I figured if I didn't feel better in a minute or two, I would call for help to be safe.

I shifted off my knees and gingerly sat down in front of the young man's grave. Oddly, gazing at the etching of the man's face calmed me. Patrick McDonald was his name. I felt a strange connection with the man. Like he was telling me everything would be okay.

I calmed down enough that I no longer felt the need to call anybody.

Staring at the grave, I wondered who Patrick had been and what had happened to him. Had he died from a long illness? Was he killed in an accident? Had he gotten hooked on drugs? Perhaps, saddest of all, had he taken his own life?

As I wondered about his death, I also pondered his life. Who had he been, and what might he have done had he lived longer? His tombstone was a beautiful tribute, and I found myself thinking about all the people who had loved him.

And I thought about all the people who loved me. So many people cared about me, especially the women in my life: my mother and Amanda. My health scare had probably taken years off their lives. Yet I'd treated their constant worry over me as an annoyance. Or worse, like an ego boost. I'd never given much thought to how awful it was to worry about somebody you loved.

Right there, I swore to God and to Patrick McDonald that I would never do anything so stupid as drinking and driving again. Not only could I have dropped dead at Old Bay Stadium, I could have come home in a box after last night. Plus, like Brady said, I could have sent someone *else's* baby to the graveyard.

Shuddering, I pictured Amanda's face if she'd gotten a call that I'd died in a motorcycle accident. I didn't have to imagine it. I *knew* that expression because it was the same way she looked when she woke up from one of her nightmares. And I would never forget the look on my mother's face when she arrived at the hospital after my collapse.

For the first time, I realized how lucky I was to be alive.

Patrick was gone, but I was still here. I felt unworthy, with no understanding of why I had survived and this guy hadn't. All I knew was that I had a second chance at life.

The question was, what was I going to do with it?

I still had no idea, but for once, I was actually okay with that. Lots of people my age had no clue what they were doing. And there was nothing wrong with that.

Amanda had been spot-on when she'd called me ungrateful. Yes, losing baseball was a huge blow, and it was one that I would never get over. But that didn't mean I couldn't move on with my life. In spite of everything, I was one of the lucky ones. I'd been able to pay all my hospital bills without a second thought, and I had enough money in the bank to hold me until I found a job I wanted. I had an amazing family and wonderful friends. And, unless I had completely wrecked everything, I had an incredible woman who loved me.

So what in the hell was I still bitching about all the damn time?

I got to my feet, filled with renewed energy. Though I couldn't explain it, I genuinely felt like it was no coincidence that I'd stumbled upon Patrick's grave. In a weird way, I'd felt drawn toward the cemetery and toward this particular spot. It was as if this stranger had somehow reached out to me from the spiritual world.

"Thanks, Patrick," I said as I gazed down at his final

resting place. I gently touched the top of his gravestone. With a catch in my voice, I added, "I'm real sorry for your mom, dude."

With that, I turned to leave the cemetery, to start the next part of my life.

29

———

AMANDA

I wrapped up a particularly demoralizing day on the job, and I couldn't wait to get out of the building. Denise was still in her position of HR manager for two more weeks, but she had spent the day training her new protégée, Bella. Between my shock at not getting the job and Rusty's horrific indifference to my pain, it hadn't even crossed my mind until I walked into the office today that Bella would now be my *boss*.

There was no doubt in my mind that I would not be staying here any longer than I absolutely had to. When it came to boyfriends and workplaces, I had no intention of being treated with disrespect. I knew my own goddamned worth, even if it felt like nobody else on the planet did. And, despite Rusty's nasty words, I couldn't just "get another job." That would take time; I was stuck in this demeaning position until I could find something else. Not all of us had the luxury of sitting around and feeling sorry for ourselves when we were out of work.

I grabbed my purse and stormed out of the office. I'd been perfectly polite and cordial to my coworkers all day, but I refused to hide my anger. Denise and Bella were giggly best buddies while Bella allegedly learned the job, but it would likely be a different story in a few weeks. Eventually, Denise would be gone, and Bella would realize there was a lot more to the job than she'd thought.

I stepped outside the building and heard the roar of a motorcycle. I turned to see Rusty's unmistakable Indian Pursuit and sighed, unsure of what to make of his presence here. Emotionally exhausted, I lacked the energy to hash this out with him right now. I knew I was right, he was wrong, and that was all there was to it. I didn't have it in me to defend myself or to explain once again that even though his situation was infinitely worse, it didn't mean my feelings weren't valid.

And if he couldn't understand that, then, well, we had a serious problem. As in a serious, relationship-ending problem. I loved Rusty, but I couldn't be his around-the-clock psychological support system anymore.

I stood there and watched him park his bike and climb off it. My heart skipped a beat when he took off his helmet. His shirt, like his bike, was a deep blue that matched his eyes. I wondered if he'd chosen that shirt on purpose to wear down my defenses. It was working; Rusty looked annoyingly handsome and rugged, even on that stupid bike that had caused me many sleepless nights.

Rusty walked up to me and said simply, "Hi."

"Hi," I said, refusing to say anything else. If he had something to say, fine. But I wasn't gonna be the one to get the ball rolling. Not this time.

"Can we talk?" he asked, sounding hopeful.

"I guess," I said wearily. "Come over here."

I walked over to a nearby bench and he fell into step

next to me. Just then, Denise and Bella came out of the building.

I heard Bella mutter, "Damn," when she saw Rusty with me.

That's right. Eat your heart out.

I didn't even know if Rusty was still my boyfriend, but I was glad to see Bella looking jealous of me for once. Everybody in the office knew I was dating him, but they'd lost interest in him once he was no longer a celebrity baseball player. And yet, I didn't think they'd realized how gorgeous he was until they'd seen him up close.

We sat together on the bench, and I was acutely aware of Denise and Bella watching us until they got into their respective cars and drove off.

Wiping his hands on his jeans, Rusty said, "I don't even know where to start."

"Well, are you here to defend yourself?" I asked, getting right to the point.

"No, no. I'm only here to apologize."

"Good," I said, fixing a steely glare at him. I saw a glimmer of pride in his expression, like he was proud of me for not putting up with his bad attitude. I guess we both knew I deserved better.

Gazing at me with those irresistible blue eyes of his, he said, "Amanda, I'm sorry you didn't get the job, and I'm so sorry I made things worse. I never meant to be so cruel to you."

"You really were cruel, Rusty." I was heartbroken all over again. "I didn't know you had it in you to be so awful."

"Neither did I," he said quietly.

"It was scary. Made me feel like I don't even know who you are if you're capable of being so nasty."

"That's fair." He sighed. I could see he was disappointed

in himself. "It's so weird. I always thought of myself as this friendly person. Now I'm starting to realize that it's easy to be kind when your life is going great. It's much harder when you're going through a lot of shit. Please understand, Amanda. I'm not saying there is any excuse for being so mean to you, because there isn't."

I let out a breath; my anger and tension began to dissipate. Rusty was saying all the right things. *Thank God.* I didn't want to lose him. I could be patient, but he had to be willing to try to change.

"From the very beginning, you have supported me through everything. Then the one time you asked for the tiniest fraction of support from me, I totally let you down. I'm so sorry, sweetheart."

I nodded, still sorting through my churning emotions.

"Again, I want to make it clear that I'm not trying to make excuses, but I do want to try to explain why I snapped like that. I was having a horrible day. After all this time, I realized that the car dealership thing isn't gonna work out. It's not for me, you know?"

I nodded. "I can't say I'm surprised. You didn't seem all that invested in it."

"Yeah. And then it's like right after I figured out I'd have to scrap that whole idea and start over with something else, I turned on the TV and found out the Bay Birds are in serious contention for the Wild Card race. They might make the playoffs for the first time in years."

"I heard," I said quietly. My instinct was to reach over and pull him into my arms. I couldn't help it. Helping people was in my nature, and I knew how badly that news must have hurt him. The Baltimore Bay Birds could potentially wind up in the World Series, and all he could do was watch from the sidelines. I understood his anger—I wanted to lash out on his behalf. It just wasn't fair. "That must hurt so much, Rusty. I'm sorry."

"Thanks, beautiful. So anyway, as usual, I was all wrapped up in self-pity and I took my frustration out on you. I didn't mean what I said, Amanda. This job meant a lot to you, and it's a huge deal that you didn't get it. I should have said that instead of dumping all my problems on you."

"Sometimes I worry that's all I am to you. A fucking therapist."

Rusty blinked in surprise. He'd never heard me cuss before.

"I'm sure I made you feel that way. But I want you to know you are so much more to me than that."

I wanted to believe him, but it was tough. Everybody used me as a therapist. My sisters, my coworkers, and even Wilder to a degree, though she was pretty good at returning the favor. Sometimes I worried that people only liked me because I made them feel better about themselves. Though I thrived on helping people, that wasn't all there was to me.

"I admit, I did get kind of addicted to the way you always supported me. Talking to you was like taking medicine or doing a strong shot of whiskey to kill the pain."

My heart sank. That was what I feared. That Rusty only loved me for the way I bolstered his spirits. So what happened when he figured out what to do with his life and didn't need me anymore?

Gently caressing my face, he said, "But that's only a small part of why I'm in love with you, Amanda." With a smile, he insisted, "I've never had so much fun with anyone in my life. Whether we're goofing around at the Science Center or watching TV and eating pizza or playing with random dogs in the park, I'm happy just being with you."

Rusty's eyes lit up with joy as he spoke, and I found

myself believing his words. Because I felt the same way about him. We weren't just lovers. We were the best of friends.

"And I've never been more attracted to any woman than I am to you."

I audibly scoffed at that one. He spoke convincingly, but I couldn't believe it was the truth.

"I mean it, Amanda." Rusty sounded offended that I was skeptical.

"There's no way that's true."

"But it is! Okay, how can I explain this without sounding like an ass?" he said, making me laugh. "Look. I'm gonna level with you. God, this will sound awful, but hear me out. Of course there are more beautiful women out there than you ... just like there are better-looking guys than me."

"Are there?" I asked.

Rusty chuckled at that but plowed ahead. "There might be more conventionally pretty girls out there. Take Wilder, for example."

Oof. That hit me where it hurt, and it must have shown on my face.

"No, no, no. *Listen.* It's like when I see Wilder, my brain knows she's pretty. I can see that. But I don't *feel* anything. She's attractive, but I don't feel physically attracted to her. Same deal with my ex-girlfriend, Emily. The actress. She was gorgeous, but I was never as attracted to her as I am to you. It's like I didn't even know what was missing until I met you. You *are* pretty, Amanda, But you're also smart and gentle and sweet and fun. You love pizza and steak and baseball and animals and you like swinging on a swing set. And you are the kindest, most loving person I've ever known. And all of those things together make you the most beautiful woman I've ever laid eyes on."

My eyes welled up with tears as I gazed at his earnest face. I couldn't help but believe his wonderful words.

"I need to hear stuff like this, Rusty. Not all the time ... Just once in a while. I don't mean to sound needy—"

Rusty laughed as he wiped my tears with his thumbs.

"Sweetheart, you are the *least* needy person I know. You barely ever complain about anything. And that's why I need to remember to take it upon myself to look out for you and to say all the things you deserve to hear. The squeaky wheel really does get the grease, and the quiet ones get ignored. Amanda, baby, I know how much it hurts that you feel invisible sometimes, and I hate like hell that I made you feel that way too. I'm so sorry I ignored you. I promise I won't ever do it again." He kissed me gently. "I'm sorry."

"I forgive you," I whispered.

Rusty nodded, looking as relieved as I felt. We'd hit another rough patch, but we were gonna be okay.

"And I still want you to tell me how you're feeling, okay?" I assured him. Gazing into his eyes, I worried all over again. The Wild Card thing must have felt like a knife in his heart, and I wished so much that I could heal his pain. "We love each other, and that means we should be able to lean on each other during the hard times. And right now, you need to do more of the leaning, and that's okay."

"I love you so much, Amanda."

"I love you too."

"You sure?"

Laughing, I said, "Yes. I'm sure. It's okay to be sad, and it's fine to yell sometimes, just don't yell *at* me, okay?"

"Yeah. I promise. Never again."

I nodded, considering the matter closed. I was ready to move on.

A college kid with an athletic bag slung over his shoulder walked up to us, looking at Rusty curiously.

"Are you ... Rusty Power?"

Rusty glanced down at his arms and legs and then back up. "Oh my God, I think I *am!*"

I laughed and Rusty did too. The college kid grinned as Rusty extended his hand.

"Nice to meet you," Rusty said.

"Oh man, you too! I'm Adam Dempsey."

"You play college ball?" Rusty asked, gesturing at the guy's athletic bag with the school's baseball team name on it.

"Yeah, I do," Adam said, his brown eyes lighting up with the same joy I used to see in Rusty in his old TV interviews with the team. The kid was so excited. I hoped he would have a long and successful baseball career.

Rusty and Adam chatted awhile about baseball, and for once, it didn't bother me to be ignored. Rusty was in his element talking about the sport, and he gave the kid lots of great insight into the college draft process. Rusty had the inside scoop on how to make it into the majors. Adam gratefully soaked up every word, and it seemed being recognized was good for Rusty's ego.

As the two chatted animatedly, I saw how happy Rusty was, talking about baseball. The topic had been forbidden around him for months, and now it was as if the floodgates had opened again.

As they wrapped up the conversation, Adam turned to me and said, "I'm sorry. I didn't mean to interrupt you guys and take up so much of your time."

Rusty's face fell; he looked horrified that he practically forgotten I was there.

"Oh my God, I'm so sorry. Adam, this is Amanda."

"Nice to meet you," Adam said with a warm smile, shaking my hand. I considered myself an excellent judge of character, and I really liked this kid. He gave off good vibes.

"She's the one who ran onto the field and saved my life," Rusty said.

Eyes wide, Adam said, "You're kidding! Wow. That's incredible."

I shrugged, not sure what to say to that.

"Amanda works here at the college. In HR," he added. I appreciated that. Like he was saying I was more than just the girl who'd saved his life.

"Cool," Adam said politely. "Well, I'll let you guys go."

He seemed reluctant to leave but didn't want to overstay his welcome.

"Good luck, man. I'm rootin' for you," Rusty told him, making him grin ear to ear.

"Thanks. Hey, would you mind if I got a picture with you? Otherwise nobody will believe my story."

Chuckling, Rusty got up from the bench. "Sure."

Adam was going to take a selfie with him, but I reached out for his phone. "Here, I'll do it."

"Great, thanks," Adam said excitedly.

I snapped several photos to make sure he got some good ones.

The kid thanked us both profusely before heading on his way.

"That was fast," Rusty said bitterly.

"What do you mean?" I asked, thinking he was spiraling downward again due to all this baseball talk.

Turning to me, he said, "I started ignoring you already. God, Amanda, I'm so—"

"No, no." I laughed, waving his apology off. "This is different. Really, it's cool, Rusty."

"If you say so," he said, still looking apologetic. I wasn't mad at all, but I was glad to see him making an effort already.

"You seemed to really enjoy talking with that guy about baseball. I'm surprised."

Rusty shrugged, but I could see the exchange had made him think, too.

"I wonder if you're going about this job thing the wrong way," I said.

"What do you mean?"

"I think cutting baseball totally out of your life might be a mistake."

"Oh."

I could see he didn't believe me, but the more I thought about it, the more I felt I was on to something.

"I know talking about baseball hurts you sometimes, but I think trying to avoid it all together is hurting you more. You're always gonna be sad about not being able to play anymore. It's awful, but it's the truth. And yet, it's such a huge part of your life. It's in your blood. It's who you *are*."

The despair on Rusty's face threatened to tear my heart into pieces. I went on because it was for his own good.

"I hope you'll at least consider a future that includes baseball somehow. I don't know. It's kinda like when someone dies and you're grieving. Talking about the person doesn't remind you that they died, because it's not like you could ever forget. Instead, talking about them keeps them alive in a way. If your day job included baseball, that part of your life would still be alive, even if it's in a different way. Does that make any sense at all?"

"Yeah. I guess so."

"All I know is that when you were talking baseball with that kid, you looked happier than I've seen you in a long time. I think you're afraid to talk about it because you think it will cause you more pain. But what if you're wrong? What if it actually makes you feel better? Like you're still involved in the game in a way?"

"Aaaaand here we are talkin' about my problems again, Amanda," he said. "That's not right. I came here so you could lean on me for once."

"Just promise me you'll think about it, okay?"

"I promise. So, do you feel like going out?"

I shook my head. "Not really. I'm kinda tired."

Between losing out on my promotion and my fight with Rusty, I was emotionally wrung out. The last thing I wanted was to go out anywhere.

"Oh, okay."

Rusty looked disappointed, and I realized he'd taken my words to mean I didn't want to hang out with him right now.

"I'd rather just go back to your place and order food."

He grinned, making my whole body feel lighter. I loved when that boy smiled.

"Sounds wonderful."

As we headed to the parking lot, Rusty said, "I'm gonna tell my mom you dropped the F-bomb."

"You wouldn't!" I said with mock horror, making him cackle wickedly. "I'll tell her you've been a bad influence."

"Oh damn. You win. Never mind."

I kissed his cheek before I got into my car. Rusty rode home on his bike, and I followed him. I couldn't help thinking how nice it would be if we lived together. The thought of having dinner together every night, cuddling and watching TV, and falling asleep side by side made me smile.

When we got to his apartment, I immediately collapsed on the couch.

Standing over me with a sympathetic expression, Rusty asked, "Pizza okay?"

"Perfect."

He placed the order for delivery and sat on the couch with me.

"Gimme," he said, gesturing at my feet.

I rested my feet on his lap and he gave me one of his famous foot rubs.

"Oh, that helps," I moaned, feeling my tension drain away.

"So tell me what the hell happened with this promotion, and whose ass do I need to kick?"

I laughed. "They gave the job to Bella."

Rusty winced with guilt, fully aware that he should know who Bella was but clearly didn't.

"She's the administrative assistant. The one who—"

"Oh yeah, yeah, yeah! The one who spends more time doing her nails than answering her messages," he said.

"That's the one."

"Seriously? They gave *her* the job? Isn't she, you know, under you? Seniority-wise, experience-wise ... *intelligence-wise?*"

I laughed, feeling relieved that Rusty finally understood why I'd been so upset.

"Yeah, pretty much. Like so many other things in life, it's a popularity contest. Bella and the boss, Denise, are best buddies. They go out drinking together on the weekends and stuff like that. I guess I should have realized I never had a chance."

Shaking his head, still massaging my feet, Rusty said, "Sucks, because that's what you get for giving them the benefit of the doubt. Daring to think they'd actually do the right thing."

I sighed. "Yeah. It does suck, because I *would* have done the right thing, you know? That's why I like working in HR. In that position, I get the chance to try to be fair to everybody. The company *and* the employees. But I'll never get the damn chance as long as I'm stuck in a lower-level job."

"I hate the thought of you working for those assholes anymore. They don't deserve you."

"Thanks."

Rusty thought for a moment. "Look, I know you're more than capable of taking care of yourself. But I can take care of you, you know, financially until you find a better job. That way you can tell them to fuck right off if you want to."

"Hmmm, that is tempting ..." I said, seriously considering his offer. I wondered if he'd meant he would cover my rent, or did he want me to move in here?

I decided I'd rather live with him because it was what he wanted, not because he had to take me in for financial reasons.

"I appreciate it, but I'm sure I'll be able to find something else soon. Though I hate being stuck there, hopefully it won't take long to leave for something bigger and better. Besides, petty as it sounds, I kind of want to be around to watch them fail. I'm sorry, but Bella has no idea what she's doing. She and Denise are having a great time in her office now, giggling and allegedly 'training' Bella, but soon enough that girl will be on her own. Of course I'll help her, but I look forward to her having to ask me."

Rusty grinned. "Good point."

I moaned again as he found a tender spot on my foot. I was so comfortable in his place, physically and emotionally, that I didn't ever want to leave.

30

RUSTY

Lately, I'd been relishing early morning walks as a way to clear my head and to live in the moment. This morning, I chose to take a long walk after breakfast. It was early September now, and the temperature was perfect with the hint of a chill in the air.

Strolling through the streets of Baltimore, I pondered my life and my future. I was incredibly grateful to have Amanda's love and vowed to work hard every day to deserve it. Talking with Brady and Amanda, and even keeping the late Patrick McDonald in my mind helped me feel better and made me see things more clearly. In a strange way, I wanted to honor Patrick's memory even though I'd never known him. His life was cut short while mine continued, and I wanted to make the best of whatever time I'd been gifted with.

Learning to be grateful for everything I had in my life made a huge difference, but it wasn't a miracle cure. Many days, I still felt lost, unsure of my purpose. The Baltimore Bay Birds were still in the Wild Card race, though it was turning into quite a nail biter. Any day now, they could be eliminated from contention or they could advance to the playoffs. I was happy for my friends, but that didn't heal the deep ache in my soul, the knowledge that I'd never experience a playoff game or a World Series. In fact, I'd never play again.

Sometimes, I walked along the waters of the Chesapeake Bay in the quiet, early morning hours. As I always did when I was with Amanda, I stopped to pet any dog whose owner would allow it. Though I enjoyed this time of solitude, I missed the busyness of my old life. I wanted to *do* something, I just had no idea what.

Until today. Strolling along the water, the answer hit like a bolt of lightning to my brain. Right there near the Chesapeake Bay at Harborplace downtown stood the answer.

The idea struck me full force. The vision was clear; I could actually *see* my future.

"That's it," I whispered.

And that's when I knew, really *knew*, exactly what I wanted to do with the rest of my life. As sure as I was, the idea wouldn't feel real until I'd told Amanda about it.

I rushed home, planning to call her around lunchtime so as not to disturb her at work. But she had other ideas.

Amanda texted me before I could call, to ask if I wanted to come over to her place for dinner. She said she would cook.

"Perfect," I said out loud as I texted it.

I couldn't wait to go see my girl and tell her about my idea, my future, and what I wanted to do for the rest of my life. All afternoon I paced the apartment, as excited as a child. I couldn't get over my plan—so simple and so profound at the same time. It was *perfect*.

Well, at least it was perfect for me.

I parked my motorcycle and knocked on her apartment door.

"Hey, beautiful," I said the moment she opened the door.

"Hey yourself," she said with a pretty smile. "Dinner's almost ready."

"Hot damn, that smells good," I said, wandering into the kitchen. "Whatcha makin'?"

"Chicken fettucine alfredo and roasted broccoli." She lifted a lid off a pot on the stove to stir the sauce.

"You spoil me, woman. I don't know how you have the energy to cook after working all day."

"It really depends on my mood, so don't be expecting this kind of service every night, pal."

I chuckled. "Fair enough."

I set the table for two while she put the finishing touches on dinner. I was antsy as hell to talk to her, but figured it was better to wait until we got settled.

We sat down and I was about to tell her my plans, but she spoke first.

"I'm so glad you could come over tonight because I really wanted to talk to you," Amanda said.

"Everything okay?"

"Oh yeah. Nothing's wrong. It's just ..." She drew in a deep breath, clearly excited about something. "You'll never guess who called me today."

"I dunno. The pope?"

She laughed. "No. Lyric."

"Really?" I dug into my pasta and twirled it around my fork. "And what did she say?"

"She called to tell me about this job opening at the hospital where she works. It's an HR job, very similar to the one I wanted to get at the university."

"No kidding?" I said, deciding right then and there that I

wouldn't say a word about my idea. Not tonight. Amanda's life had been overshadowed enough by all my issues. My news could wait. She was excited right now, and I didn't intend to dull her shine. "So it would be doing HR stuff for the employees of the hospital?"

Amanda took a bite of food, nodding happily.

"Well, damn. That's kinda perfect for you, isn't it? I know how much you want to use your HR skills and stuff to help people, and in a hospital, you would be helping people to help other people."

I paused for a moment, wondering if my rambling made any sense.

"Exactly," Amanda said softly. It was so easy to make my girl happy. All I had to do was listen to her, and I appreciated that it meant a lot to her. "My only problem is I want this job so much. After what happened last time, I'm afraid I'll get crushed all over again, you know?"

"I know. But if the hospital operates—you know, no pun intended—more fairly than your current place, then you have an excellent shot at getting the job."

"God, I hope so."

"So what happens next?" I asked her, and we spent the rest of the meal talking about Amanda's upcoming interview, how she would prepare, how nervous she was, and what it would mean if she got the job.

I enjoyed every minute of our conversation, as I always did. It never mattered where we were or what we were doing. I had so much fun with this woman.

It also didn't hurt that we wound up having fabulous sex after dinner.

Cradling her in my arms in her bed after we were both satisfied, Amanda said in a sensual voice, "I certainly feel a lot more relaxed now."

"Glad I could be of service," I told her.

Holding Amanda close, I was glad I'd finally learned to be less selfish in our relationship.

Besides, I decided rather than just telling her my news, it might be best to show her.

31

AMANDA

The hospital must have been desperate to fill that position because they scheduled an interview within days of my application. I did the interview on a Friday morning and had the rest of the day off. I called Rusty as soon as the meeting ended, and he listened intently as I told him all about it. I'd been nervous as hell, but over-all, I had a good feeling. About my chances of getting the job, and about the hospital itself as a working environment. "Cautiously optimistic" was the catchphrase of the day.

"That's great, sweetheart," Rusty told me over the phone. "I hope like hell you finally get to work in a place that will treat you with respect."

"Thanks. So I've got the rest of the day off and no plans. Are you busy? Do you want to do anything?"

"Yes, I want to do something," he said enthusiastically. "And I've got just the thing. Do you want me to pick you up at home?"

"That'd be great."

"Do you want to try riding on the motorcycle?" Rusty asked earnestly, making it impossible for me to say no. I was nervous about riding on his bike, but I trusted him, and I did want to share that part of his life with him. Riding had become pretty important to him lately.

"Sure, Rusty."

"Great!" he said so happily that I no longer had any regrets.

In no time, Rusty came roaring up to my building. I met him outside, loving how sexy he looked on his bike.

He jumped off and removed his helmet. Rusty was clearly in a great mood, and I loved seeing him look so happy.

"I have something to tell you."

"Is that so," I said, eying him curiously.

"I wanted to tell you before, Amanda. Believe me, I've been dying to. But I wanted to get a few things in order first. It's about what I want to do with the rest of my life. I'm pretty sure I know now."

"Oh, Rusty, that's amazing!" I already had a feeling that this time it was going to work out. He hadn't looked so confident and excited about anything since I'd known him. "What is it?"

"I don't want to just tell you. I want to show you. Come on." He gestured toward the bike.

"Okay," I said, feeling excited for him.

Rusty gazed lovingly at me as he tenderly fastened my motorcycle helmet.

"You ready?"

"Yeah."

"You scared?"

"A little," I confessed.

"Don't worry. I got you."

"I know you do."

Rusty climbed on, then held out a hand to help me get settled behind him.

"Just hug onto me and lean into the curves, okay?"

"Okay," I said breathlessly.

The ride was both frightening and exhilarating. I enjoyed hugging onto my precious boyfriend and, after my initial adrenaline had subsided, found myself loving the experience. I hadn't even thought to wonder where we were going—I was so focused on my first time on a motorcycle.

As it turned out, we didn't go all that far. We parked in the same parking garage we normally used when we were visiting downtown Baltimore when it was too dark to walk. Today, though, the weather was lovely.

I couldn't begin to imagine what Rusty's plans might be. It occurred to me that we weren't all that far from Old Bay Stadium. Had he gotten a job in baseball after all?

"What did you think?" Rusty asked the moment his helmet was off.

"It was fun. Also scary, but mostly fun." My body was a bit shaky from the rush of riding, but otherwise I was fine.

"You were holdin' on pretty tight there, girl."

"Did you mind?" I asked in a teasing voice.

"No," he said decisively, pulling me into his arms and squeezing me tight for a moment. "Okay, come on!"

Laughing, I put my helmet inside the bike's trunk and fell into step with him.

I was eager to find out what had gotten Rusty so excited. Whatever it was, I liked it already since it put a smile on his face.

We walked the same route we always did at the Baltimore Inner Harbor, with the Chesapeake Bay on our left and the old storefronts on our right.

"Here," Rusty said, grabbing my hand and pulling me up the steps to the old Harborplace building.

The place was depressing, with only the dilapidated remains of old stores and restaurants of Baltimore's glory days gone by. The last I'd heard, some developer had finally bought the joint and allegedly had plans to fix it up, but clearly nothing had been done yet.

He pulled me into the first empty storefront to the right inside the building and flung open the door.

I brushed past him to see inside. It had once been a restaurant, an old wooden bar still remained. There was a large mirror behind the bar, but no stools in front. It was dark, musty, and old, but that didn't bother me.

"It's mine," he said. "I bought it."

"You own this place?" I asked, whipping around to look at him.

"Yeah. I know it looks like shit now," he said defensively.

I walked over to him and gazed lovingly into his eyes. "What do you plan to do with it?"

Rusty's expression softened. Just by looking at me he knew he had my unconditional support.

"I want to open up a sports bar and grill. Specifically, a baseball bar," Rusty said, blue eyes wide.

He had me at *baseball.* I'd always known he could never truly be happy until he found a way to bring the sport back into his life.

"You were right, Amanda," he said earnestly. "I miss talking about baseball. For years and years, I lived, drank, ate, and breathed baseball. It *is* who I am, and trying to fight that just made me angry and bitter. I know buying this place won't fix how I feel about not being able to play, but nothing will. This is the next best thing."

Rusty walked around, surveying the place. "It's crazy

how clear my vision is for this place. It's like I can *see* it. It'll be kinda like the Hard Rock Cafe, only for baseball instead of music. I'm gonna hang up all my autographs and memorabilia ..." Grinning at me, he said, "You know, all that stuff you wouldn't let me throw away."

That made me smile. Thank God he'd kept all those precious items.

"And I can always be on the hunt for more cool stuff, you know? Like a hobby. Finding sports stuff to add to the collection. People can come here to have a beer and some food and talk about baseball, look at all the stuff on the walls, and watch the games on all the TVs I'm gonna have here."

As Rusty spoke, I could clearly see his vision, too. And it was wonderful.

"I love being associated with baseball," Rusty said wistfully. "Like that college kid we spoke to. That guy recognized me. He took one look at me and thought ... *baseball*. And he walked right up to me and started talking sports with me. I still want to be that guy. And if I name the bar after me and have my picture here, people will know I'm the former Baltimore Bay Birds player who owns the place. And if they see me hanging out here, they'll know they can still walk up to me and talk about baseball."

I scanned the room, visualizing a lively and happy sports bar filled with like-minded people bonding over their mutual love of baseball. And Rusty would be in the center of it all, hanging new autographed pictures on the wall, joking around with the patrons, and yelling at the televisions when the Bay Birds were on. At last, Rusty had found his new calling. I was so utterly overwhelmed with emotion that I hadn't even noticed the tear sliding down my cheek.

"Amanda?" Rusty asked, looking worried.

"I love it," I whispered. "It's just so ... *you*."

"Right?" Rusty yelled so loud that it startled me, making us both laugh. "And it could be like part of the revitalization of downtown Baltimore, you know? Damn, you should hear Brady talk about what this joint was like in its heyday. And that's the way I remember it too. We can bring that back. I really think it's possible. If people start coming to the sports bar, then maybe more shops can open up and all of that."

"That would be lovely," I said.

"Okay, so I need help with the name." Rusty sounded as giddy as a schoolboy. "I thought about Rusty's, but that's too close to The Rusty Scupper."

"True," I said with a nod. The Rusty Scupper was a famous seafood bar and grill in Baltimore.

"And I figure Power is too good of a name to waste, you know? I mean, *Power*. It's a very sporty word."

I giggled at his infectious enthusiasm. "Also a good point."

"So, I've got it narrowed down to Power Bar and Grill or Power's Bar and Grill. What do you think?"

I considered for a moment. "I think I like Power without the 'S.' Packs more of a sporty punch. Makes you think of a power hitter in baseball. That, and you also kinda get the play on words of a PowerBar. You know, as in the snack an athlete might eat."

Rusty grinned widely. "I never even thought of that. I love it, love it, *love* it! Power Bar and Grill it is."

"I can just hear people saying 'We're going to Power Bar downtown,' or 'I'll meet you at Power after the game,'" I said.

He stared at me. "Exactly, Amanda. Exactly."

Rusty seemed on the verge of tears himself. My heart was so filled with joy for him, it could have burst.

I wandered over to the dusty bar and began wiping it down with my hands.

"And you could serve all kinds of local foods, like crab dip and crab cakes," I said.

"And put Old Bay on everything," Rusty added.

"Of course. You could also do ballpark foods. Hot dogs, naturally. French fries. And Old Bay fries."

He nodded enthusiastically as he came over to the bar.

Rusty towered over me, grinning, then bent down to kiss me. Even his kiss was different—somehow even better than usual. He was all hyped up, excited, and happy. I wrapped my arms around him, eagerly returning his kiss. After so many dark days, we could both finally see and *feel* the light breaking through.

I could also feel the hardness practically breaking through his pants. I was glad we weren't too far from his place—I would certainly be up for some afternoon delight. Considering the mood he was in, he'd be even more enthusiastic than normal.

"I swear, I could bend you over this bar right now, Amanda," he murmured in my ear.

I giggled. "You're crazy."

Rusty stared at me intensely.

"You are kidding, right?"

"We could christen this place, you know?" he said in a husky voice that made my knees go weak. "Make it ours before all the construction guys start showing up and working on it."

Hesitating, I glanced around.

"Think about it." He ran his hand slowly up the inside of my leg. "We could do it right here on the bar, and nobody but us would ever know. And every time we come in here, we'll remember what we did ..."

The desire in his voice alone turned me on enough to weaken my resolve. And the notion of semi-public sex, something I'd never done, was even more arousing.

"Do you wanna?" Rusty asked, the hope in his eyes destroying any possible chance I had of saying no.

"Okay," I whispered.

"Really?" he practically yelled.

"Shhh! And yes. But go lock the door and hurry up before I lose my nerve."

"Yes, ma'am!" He skipped over to lock the door.

The windows were mostly boarded up, so nobody walking by could see in. Not without standing on their tippy-toes and peering in, anyway. However, it was still possible we could get caught.

Which, I had to admit, made it all the more exciting.

Rusty hurried over, swept me off my feet, and laid me down on the bar. It was still a bit dusty, but at this point I didn't care.

"I can't believe we're really doing this," I said breathlessly.

"I know," Rusty said with a panty-drenching grin. I'd never wanted—*needed*—him as badly as I did right now.

He quickly went to work on relieving me of my jeans and panties, and soon I was half-naked before him. I watched with desperate anticipation as he slid his own jeans and underwear off.

Rusty climbed up on the bar, where I wasted no time grabbing his shirt and practically ripping it off. His muscular chest always got me going like nothing else; I feasted my eyes hungrily on it.

He slid two fingers inside me and found me totally soaked.

"You're ready, aren't you baby?" he asked.

"Yes," I whispered. "Do it. Do it *now*."

He rammed into me. An agonizingly sweet bolt of sheer pleasure shot right between my legs. I screamed, then slapped my hand over my mouth.

Rusty chuckled deep in his throat. That only turned me on more.

"That's it, baby. Scream. I know you want to. Let all of Baltimore know we're having sex in here."

He pounded me over and over again, and I muffled my pleasured cries as much as I could. It just felt ... so ... *good* ... that I could hardly contain myself. I'd never felt so wild and out of control in all my life. And Rusty was living up to his last name.

I certainly felt the full force of his power between my legs. I'd seen him at his worst, and now I got to see and feel him at his absolute best. My patience with him was paying off. It was as if he was channeling all his zest for life into his lovemaking, and I was the lucky recipient of all that renewed vigor.

Rusty panted heavily on top of me, but I wasn't worried. I knew all his facial expressions and sex sounds by now, and his heavy breathing just meant he was having a good time.

I gripped the sides of the bar above my head to help me handle Rusty's pounding of a lifetime. I could already feel an intense climax building when I happened to glance to my left and saw the mirror behind the bar. I saw my legs in the air as my deliciously handsome boyfriend thrust hard *in and out* and *in and out* of me.

It was the most erotic image I'd ever seen.

My orgasm slammed into me, sending my entire being into heights of bliss I'd never known were possible. I screamed, all right, and it was as if Rusty's name was the only word I knew anymore.

Panting wildly, it took me a bit to recover. I could tell by Rusty's face that he'd climaxed too, but I'd been too preoccupied to notice.

"Oh my *God*," was all I could say.

"Yeah," Rusty said breathlessly. Still on top of me, he bent to kiss me. "I love you so damn much, Amanda."

"I love you too, Rusty."

He offered me his hand and helped me to sit up and then to get down from the bar. Rusty handed me my panties and underwear. I struggled to put them on since my legs were still shaking.

Damn, that was some good lovin'.

I was a bit wet and sticky between my legs, but it was very hard to care right now. Not only was I utterly sexually satisfied, I was thrilled at the new memory we'd just made.

"Every time we come in here, we'll remember," I told him, pulling him in for another kiss once he'd gotten dressed.

"Yeah," he said, tenderly caressing my hair. "You know, Brady told me that the secret to a happy relationship is to always have each other's backs and never stop having fun. That's us."

"Yes, it sure is," I said softly.

I leaned over and gently kissed his heart.

32

AMANDA

I saw Wilder about a week after my X-rated encounter with Rusty at Harborplace. She and I met up at one of our usual haunts, but it made me happy to think one day we'd be toasting each other at Power Bar and Grill. Naturally, I told her all about having sex with Rusty at his future restaurant location. I lowered my voice to keep my sex life private from the people sitting nearby. The two of us giggled like schoolgirls as I recounted my saucy tale, drawing attention from several men at the bar.

"Good for you," Wilder told me with a smile. She knew how unlike me it was to do something so crazy, and I could tell she was proud of me.

The bartender approached us with a fresh beer.

"Compliments of the gentleman at the end of the bar," he said.

I resisted the urge to moan as I watched him set the glass down on the bar between us. And yet, that kind of thing didn't bother me all that much anymore. Wilder could have any man in the world she wanted. Rusty was the only one I needed.

I slid the beer mug toward Wilder, but the bartender stopped me.

"No, no." He looked at Wilder and said, "Sorry." Then he slid the glass toward me. "It was meant for you."

"No way," I scoffed, before I figured out what was happening. Giggling, I said, "Rusty. He finally did it."

"You really think it's him?" Wilder asked, looking around the bar for my anonymous benefactor.

"Of course. Who else would it be?"

"Don't say that." She swatted me on the arm. "It could be anybody."

"It's Rusty," I said definitively. But I certainly didn't mind. I loved him, and he was the only one I wanted buying drinks for me anyway.

I turned around, scanning the bar to find my favorite redheaded, blue-eyed lover boy. Finally, he emerged from the crowd and stepped forward with a grin.

Ignoring me, Rusty walked right over to Wilder.

"Sooo," he said in his best bad pick-up-line voice. "Your friend over here's pretty cute."

Wilder laughed. Playing along, she glanced over at me. "Yeah, she's all right."

Still focusing all his attention on Wilder, Rusty asked, "Would it be all right with you if I asked your beautiful friend here to marry me?"

I blinked, unsure if I'd actually heard right.

"What?" I asked.

Wilder and Rusty exchanged a knowing smile. She stepped aside, pulling her barstool with her.

My breath caught in my throat as Rusty turned around and got down on one knee. I gasped. I'd always dreamed we'd get married, but I hadn't expected it so soon.

But Rusty and I knew more than anyone that life was short. Why wait when you knew what your heart wanted?

"Amanda," he began as he held up a lovely, sparkling engagement ring.

"The first day we met, you saved my life," he said, gazing up at me with tenderness. "And every day since then, you've given me something to live for. You've seen me at my worst, and you stood by me. Now I want to ask you to see me at my best."

The image of his stellar lovemaking on the bartop flashed through my mind. Rusty was *incredible* when he was at his best.

"With you by my side, I know the best is yet to come."

My eyes filled with tears. *Hold it together, Amanda.*

"I want to marry you, Amanda, so we can buy a big house and get a dog—"

I held up two fingers.

"*Two* dogs," he amended, making the people who were within earshot chuckle. "And have a bunch of kids and live happily ever after. Amanda Miller, will you marry me?"

"Y—y—yes," I stammered, letting the tears fall.

He slipped the ring on my finger. He stood up and pulled me into his arms.

The bartender rang the "somebody just gave me a tip" bell behind the bar and yelled, "We got a marriage proposal over here!"

The people in the bar cheered and applauded. I felt surrounded by joy and laughter from total strangers, evoking a vision of all the happy days to come at Rusty's bar when people would gather to eat, drink, and cheer on the home team.

I hugged Wilder as we cried together, and Rusty and I accepted lots of congratulatory toasts from the patrons at the bar. I couldn't get over his sweet and thoughtful proposal. Such a beautiful way to show how well he knew me and how much he cared.

"Amanda," Rusty said, pulling me close again.

"Yeah?"

Smiling, he said, "You just made my mother the happiest woman in the world."

Laughing, I wiped fresh tears. "Oh my gosh, you're right."

33

RUSTY

In late September, I returned to Old Bay Stadium for the first time since that fateful day when I'd nearly died and subsequently met my future wife. It had been my idea to go to the game, and Amanda was thrilled that I was willing to go back. We both knew it would be hard on me, but with her by my side, I knew I could get through it. Her love and support meant I could do just about anything.

We were using Amanda's usual season tickets, but she'd asked her friends not to show up too early, to give the two of us a little private time before the game. When we first got to our seats, the sights and sounds of the game threatened to overwhelm me.

Amanda kept quiet, giving me space as she sat beside me. When I'd gotten dressed in my uniform that day so many months ago, I'd had no idea that I would never play again. That suddenness had contributed to my pain, but being here was already helping me get some closure. I needed to take a moment to say goodbye to Rusty Power, professional baseball player.

Time had dulled my grief a bit, and it turned out being here wasn't as painful as I had feared.

I drew in a deep breath, taking in the smell of baseball. We were too far to catch the whiff of the dirt and grass, but I remembered its scent clearly. From my seat, I could smell the fried foods and popcorn, hear the chatter of the crowd, and see the players tossing the ball around the horn. As I sat there, I was struck with a realization.

This is still my home.

"How did I think I could stay away from the ballpark forever?" I whispered.

"You okay?" Amanda asked, her eyes filled with worry.

"Yeah. I am. I really am. I'm glad we came here. It was the right thing to do."

She smiled with relief and squeezed my hand.

Amanda's friends Kellie and Lynn eventually showed up, and we had fun talking about baseball and other stuff. Sadly, this late September game was a meaningless one for the Bay Birds. Having been knocked out of playoff contention by Toronto, they'd have to wait until next year for another shot.

However, we were playing the Boston Rebels, who were huge rivals of the Bay Birds. The Rebels were still in the race, so we had a chance to play spoiler. It would still be a fun game.

At one point during the game, the Jumbotron camera found me. I didn't see it at first— Amanda nudged me to get my attention.

I waved excitedly, and the camera stayed with me. Then the sound system started playing the theme song to *Welcome Back, Kotter.* They frequently did that when a former Bay Bird was in attendance, often as a member of the opposing team. The crowd began to cheer, and I was genuinely touched.

They haven't forgotten me.

Amanda squeezed my arm, and I pulled her toward me. We were both still on camera, so I murmured in her ear, "You know, you could hold up your ring if you want to show we're engaged. Totally up to you."

"I *love* that idea!"

Smiling, she held up her left hand and pointed at the ring. The crowd cheered even louder, and I felt those well-wishes deep down in my soul.

"Best fans in all of baseball," I said, my voice cracking with emotion.

Still. My. Home.

I blew kisses at the camera, then they cut back to showing the players on the field.

A short while later, a Bay Birds representative approached me in my seat.

"So, Mr. Power," the man began. "Julia Frederick tipped us off that your fiancée is Amanda Miller? The woman who saved your life?"

The guy looked curiously at Amanda and then back at me.

Giggling, Amanda said, "Typical Julia."

Amanda had become fast friends with Julia, Lyric, and Sarah. She fit right in with the players' wife-and-girlfriend crowd.

"Yep, she's my old lady all right," I said, and Amanda punched me in the shoulder.

"Would it be okay with you if we said that on the Jumbotron?" the man asked.

I looked at Amanda, and she nodded and said, "Of course. That would be lovely."

"Great, thanks!" The man dashed back up the steps.

Sure enough, after the next half-inning, Amanda and I were front and center on the Jumbotron. Then the words appeared: *Remember the brave fan who saved Rusty Power's life ...?*

The crowd got quiet for a moment, and I was surprised at how many people had noticed the message.

Rusty's gonna marry her!

The crowd went *crazy,* and before we knew it, Amanda and I were getting a standing ovation.

Which made Amanda positively *weep.*

"Best fans in baseball," I said again.

That beautiful, surreal moment really showed how sports can bring a community together.

We stood up together and waved to acknowledge the crowd. For a moment, it felt like we were baseball royalty.

"Oh, Rusty," she said, her eyes still brimming with tears. "I'm so happy that I can share my love of baseball with you now."

I turned to look into her eyes, and I knew this was the first of a lifetime of ballgames we would go to together.

And for that, I was truly grateful.

34

———————

RUSTY

Power Bar and Grill had its grand opening just days before baseball's Opening Day. I'd planned it that way—so many of the Baltimore Bay Birds would be in town to attend before the season got going.

On the day of the opening, Amanda and I arrived super early to make sure everything was ready. I took my time looking over all the framed photographs and signed bats and balls I had on display. I was in awe just gazing at them, overwhelmed by the history of the game and its significance to the country. My emotions were running high: proud to be a part of such history, but sad that I couldn't have stayed longer. I found my eyes getting wet.

"Are those happy tears?" Amanda asked gently from just beside me.

"For the most part," I said quietly.

"I understand."

Turning to face her, I said, "I know you do. Thank you for everything."

Amanda tenderly touched my face. Just looking at her

got me excited about our future all over again. I loved this place already, and I loved *her*.

Life was good.

"Everything looks incredible," Amanda marveled.

She wasn't wrong. All the tabletops were painted like baseballs, the memorabilia on the walls shone like new, and the bar was stocked and ready to go. I absolutely *loved* the neon sign out front, with the huge, glowing baseball for the "O" in Power.

And we both loved the notion of serving drinks and food to customers who'd never know what we'd done on the bar where they sat.

"You know," she said. "I work so close by now that I could even stop in here for lunch sometimes."

"Hey yeah, you're right," I said.

Amanda had landed that hospital HR job, and she kicked ass at it. She loved helping people, and she was truly in her element there. She even got to see Lyric there once in a while. The icing on the cake was that things were a disaster at her former job. Several of her old coworkers had texted Amanda to say Bella had no clue what she was doing and had little motivation to get any better. There had damn near been a mutiny when everyone's paychecks got delayed because the girl didn't learn the new system.

Knowing that Amanda was happy in her new job made the grand opening of my bar an even sweeter victory for me. She and I excitedly greeted everyone as they arrived for the grand opening. Her family came, as did mine. My mother was still positively giddy over my upcoming wedding to Amanda. Brady, Matt, Trace, and a bunch of other players were in attendance, along with Lyric, Julia, Sarah, Wilder, and Amanda's other friends. My old buddy Charlie showed up as well.

"Great to see you, man," I said, shaking his hand.

"You too," Charlie said with a grin. "Glad to see you've landed on your feet. I been to lots of sports bars, but I've never seen one that was devoted just to baseball. I love it! Good on you."

"Thanks," I said, and then slapped him on the back.

Just before the ribbon cutting, Brady said he wanted to make an announcement.

"Oh Lord," Amanda muttered. "Should I be nervous?"

"Not sure," I said. I was definitely nervous. Brady was a great guy, but he could be kind of a loose cannon. You never really knew what he would say.

Standing in front of the bar, Brady clapped his hands to get everyone's attention. "On this historic day of the grand opening of the best damn sports bar in Baltimore *history*," Brady began with a flourish. "I would like to present this gift to Rusty Power on behalf of myself and the Baltimore Bay Birds."

He came forward and presented me with a huge rectangular gift.

"Open it!" he commanded.

I ripped open the wrapping paper to find a glossy photograph of myself catching a ball at first base. It reminded me of the one Amanda had on her bedroom wall, only much, much bigger. Underneath the photograph, there were hundreds of autographs, some of which I recognized from the team.

Above the photograph were the words engraved in big bold letters: *The Greatest Has-Been in All of Baseball.*

Amanda gasped. She knew how much I hated being thought of as a has-been.

I stared at the photograph for a moment. "I love it. I fuckin' *love* it!" Then I added, "Sorry, Mom."

My mother just smiled.

Brady laughed, and everyone applauded.

Under her breath, Amanda asked, "Do you really love it?"

Setting it down to rest against the bar on the floor, I stood back to take another look. Then I turned to her and said, "I do, Amanda. I really do. You wouldn't think it, but ... rather than run from the truth, I like the idea of leaning into it. Accepting it. Embracing it."

I smiled, filled with yet another burst of excitement.

"I'm proud to be the best damn has-been in Bay Birds history!" I said truthfully, and people applauded.

"They can put *that* in your obituary," she said.

"Yes!" I yelled, making her laugh. "But not just that. It should also say loving husband and father to a bunch of dogs and kids."

"Yeah," Amanda said softly. "But no obituary for a long, long time. Right?"

"Right," I said, wishing I could promise but knowing all I could do was hope for the best and live life to the fullest. I gave her a kiss, then went over to thank Brady and the guys for the gift that I genuinely loved. I couldn't wait to display it prominently in my new place. Perhaps right behind the bar where everybody could see it.

Finally, the time came for the official ribbon cutting. We herded everybody outside where, thankfully, the late-March air wasn't terribly cold.

So far, Power Bar and Grill was the only occupant in the Harborplace building. I hoped with all my heart that would change soon, and that the Inner Harbor would realize its full potential. Brady in particular had been thrilled at my idea for the bar, since the city held a special place in his heart.

"Thank you all so much for being here with me today," I said to the crowd comprised of family members, friends, and members of the press.

Amanda handed me the giant novelty scissors that I would use to cut the ribbon.

"I want to dedicate this new business to my amazing family, friends, and my wife-to-be, Amanda Miller."

She smiled and put her hand over her heart as I spoke. "Just a few months ago, I felt like my whole life had fallen apart." I paused for a moment. "And during that difficult time, you guys never left my side."

My mother started to cry, which made it difficult to look at her. The last thing I needed was to break down in front of the cameras.

"It was hard to put those broken pieces of my life back together, but because of your love and support, I began to feel whole again."

I heard my mom let out a sob and I swallowed hard. Hers were tears of pride, but my God, they'd come so close to being tears of grief.

If not for Amanda ...

I knew I had to wrap this up because I couldn't hold it together much longer.

"I'd like to dedicate Power Bar and Grill to my family and friends, to the Baltimore Bay Birds fans who are the best in all of baseball, and to the people of Baltimore. Thank you so much."

With that, I cut the ribbon, officially beginning the next chapter of my life.

The rest of the afternoon was a delightful blur of eating, drinking, laughing, and celebrating. It was much like our wedding would probably be—lots of celebrating with the people we loved.

The "has-been" photograph wasn't the only framed picture I couldn't wait to display. I'd recently received an advanced copy of the cover article *People* magazine had done about me and Amanda. Our love story had become quite the sensation once the news broke on the Jumbotron at Old Bay Stadium. With Amanda's permission, I'd given a lengthy interview on my health, my plans, and everything she had helped me through. I wanted to put the entire article in a large frame and display it here at the bar, so people wouldn't only know me, they'd know my wife.

I could hardly wait for her to see the headline of the article.

First She Restarted His Heart.
Then She Captured it Forever.

THANK you so much for reading the fourth book in The Boys of Baltimore Series. I hope you will continue on with the next book in the series, Fifth Inning Official!

Heartfelt thanks to you for reading!